the space between you and me

Also from Islandport Press

What the Wind Can Tell You
Sarah Marie Aliberti Jette

The Sugar Mountain Snow Ball
Elizabeth Atkinson

Mercy
Sarah L. Thomson

Uncertain Glory
Lea Wait

The Door to January
Gillian French

Billy Boy
Jean Mary Flahive

The Fog of Forgetting
G.A. Morgan

Chantarelle
G.A. Morgan

The Kinfolk
G.A. Morgan

the space between you and me

Julie True Kingsley

ISLANDPORT PRESS

ISLANDPORT PRESS

Islandport Press
P.O. Box 10
Yarmouth, Maine 04096
www.islandportpress.com
info@islandportpress.com

First Edition: May 2024
Printed in the United States of America.

ISBN: 978-1-952143-66-3
Library of Congress Control Number: 2023935050

Dean L. Lunt | Editor-in-Chief, Publisher
Shannon M. Butler | Vice President
Emily Boyer | Cover Designer
Emily A. Lunt | Book Designer

To the resilient souls who come to Maine for a better life.
(May "Vacationland" be as good to you as it has been for me.)

prologue

Every farm girl knows there's a season for everything. You order seeds in winter, plant in spring, cultivate in summer, and put up in fall. What this quasi-bicoastal girl didn't know is that life, too, has its seasons.

When I was little, my roots dug into Maine's rocky soil. And every summer since, I have grown taller, smarter, stronger. It was the summer of 2016 when I finally grew into myself. The problem is I grew too fast that year. A piece of fruit that grows too fast—well, it usually bursts in the sun.

chapter one ♡
Rhubarb Season ~ June

MOM ALWAYS SAID DREAMS are the guideposts of a life well-lived. Aunt Vivi always said dreams were found in a good skinny dip into the Atlantic. *Mémère* always said dreams are illusions guiding you to the *real* goals, the ones you don't even know about but nevertheless need.

I shove the last Flamin' Hot Funyun into my mouth and lick my fingers one after the next, staring at my phone's email icon. Nothing happens. It stays a solid, unwavering 552. It could be considered sad, letting all my hopes and dreams of summer—hell, of life—be centered on a single email. But here we are. The Greyhound bus station is empty. Dad's twenty minutes late. Without the women in his life to keep him centered, he's a man with too many plans and not enough hours in the day. I crumple the Funyuns wrapper and shove it deep into my backpack. Still 552. *Dammit.*

Outside, a bus idles softly. The driver kicks suitcases into the storage underneath, his khaki pants hanging dangerously low. There's a fluttering of Spanish. I perk up. Nobody looks familiar until the group of migrant workers board the bus, leaving behind a girl about my age—seventeen or so—a tell-tale bandana tied to her neck, wearing thick jeans and long sleeves despite the heat. Her hair is parted down the middle, which only accents the perfect slope of her nose. It's Rosa, who came to Laurel Hollow at the end of last season to pick berries. I'm sure of it. I wave. She doesn't notice me. She stiffens, pulls a trucker hat over her eyes, her back still.

The bus driver yells, "One minute till we're outta here."

I twist to get a better view of the bus station, empty except for a bored ticket lady scrolling on her phone. California shifts away from me completely, and I can feel my farm girl rising. He can't leave her. I'm outside in two seconds, blinded momentarily by the late sun.

"Everything okay?"

Rosa's eyes finally focus on me. She pops an eyebrow into the air. "Miss Fountaine, what're you doing here?"

"Clem! Please. What's wrong?"

"My friend, he was here, and now he's gone. We're heading to the strawberry harvest in Camden." She lifts two tickets into the air. "I've got his ticket. I can't lose the job . . ."

"Look for him. I'll stall."

She disappears through the door to the Greyhound station. The smell of the exhaust burns my throat, but I run along the side and up the stairs, not sure of my plan, but diving in anyways.

The bus driver barks, "Need your ticket and we'll get this show on the road."

A lie slips off my tongue easy as a bird song. "I'm looking for my boyfriend. He is six foot two. Handsome like you wouldn't believe. I'm supposed to meet him on *this* bus, but I don't see him. Did you say . . . ?"

"We're on a schedule, little lady. Get in or get out."

I don't like the tone.

"Here's the thing. I don't think you're understanding the situation. I said I was waiting for MY BOYFRIEND. And you said, 'We're on a schedule.' That line doesn't work for me. You see, I'm on a schedule, too. A schedule to see the love of my life. The keeper of my soul, the future father of—"

"If you aren't going to Camden. Get. Out."

The driver pushes the gas, and we bolt forward.

A voice booms directly behind me. "Clementine! What're you doing on that bus? You're not leaving. Get off!"

It's not Dad. Instead, it's Johnny LaMonde, Dad's oldest friend, looking official in his border patrol uniform.

I smile. "Are you here to inspect the bus?"

The bus driver sighs, "And here we go . . . "

"Clem, let's go," Johnny insists.

A tired-looking mother with two little kids snaps. "Honey. We're going to *Disney on Ice* down in Augusta. We can't be late." She wags a finger at me as I lean toward the kid with the gooey Ritz cracker smile. "Oh, I love *Disney on Ice*. With Belle and Cinderella and—"

Johnny puts hands on his thick belt. "For the love of lobster, Clem. Get off the bus."

I pat the kid's head. "And Ariel, and . . . "

"Pocahontas," the kid whispers.

"And Pocahontas."

Out of the corner of my eye, I see a dark-haired guy with a baseball hat dashing out of the bus station. He trips on a loose brick, sending him sprawling to the ground. His toothbrush, a paperback book, and wallet skitter out of his bag and across the pavement. Rosa runs toward him, pulling him from the ground. Johnny leans into the bus and tells the bus driver to stay put.

The driver gives me the hairy eyeball. I don't blink. The bus gets very still; the migrant workers watch Johnny. I want to tell them Johnny's not a police officer. He's just border patrol.

It's all good now. Behind me, I hear footsteps. I scoot over while the missing rider, followed by Rosa, bombs up the stairs toward the back of the bus.

Rosa and I meet eyes.

It's all the *thank you* I need.

I hit my forehead with the back of my hand. "Wait. What was I thinking? This isn't my bus. I've arrived. My bad." I get off the bus and stand for a moment in the perfect Maine sunshine. The bus driver slams the door shut. As the bus drives away, Rosa holds her hand to the window. My heart melts.

Waiting to hear about getting a second-round audition to the Summerset School of Dance reminds me of being a kid at Christmas: the gnawing excitement in the back of my stomach, the nervous flutters moving up my spine. But I must admit, there's a sharp edge to it all. Christmas, at least, is orchestrated by people who love you, while the judges who look over audition film care only about the bottom line. Or, as my dance teacher would say, "They're looking for the epitome of perfection! The lines of an angel! The person who encompasses the spirit of the art!" Madame Ouelette was always a tad dramatic.

Johnny grips the steering wheel, his mammoth hands making it almost look small. He doesn't take his eyes from the road. "You okay?"

"Yup. Couldn't be better."

"But, coming back. It must feel weird after everything that happened last summer . . ."

"And the summer before that." My throat constricts, trying to block the images of my grandmother, her hospital bed lying in the corner of the kitchen, so she could watch the blueberries grow. "I'm getting kind of used to things being different around here."

"Doesn't make it easy."

I brush some dirt off my knee and flex my quads. Out the window, I count American flags flapping in the wind. One. Two. Three. Patriotism runs high in Maine. We roll past the Penobscot River, swollen over its banks, an unpredictable snake pushing over rocks and trees. Johnny says, "If you wanted to talk. I do have the gift of gab . . . "

"Can I hold your gun?" I say flippantly.

"So, you don't want to talk?"

"Nope."

"Okay, I'm here if you need me."

I stare at the phone. 552. Unwavering. We drive past a man in green Dickies pants, slowly piling sandbags around his barn, trying to hold the water at bay. If I could put sandbags around my heart, protecting it from more disappointments that might come, I would.

I climb out of Johnny's border patrol truck, shaking the rest of California from my bones. Gone are the pressures of St. Andrews, where another year of honors classes are in the books. Gone is my face superimposed on the Los Angeles bus system, advertising our string of organic smoothie shops. Gone is my ex-boyfriend, Travis, the dumbass who cheated on me with my lab partner, Trinny Williams. Gone. Gone. Gone.

The farmhouse never changes. It's an old-fashioned Cape, built in 1953. It sits on the highest point of the blueberry barrens, next to the huge red barn that holds all the gear.

Geraniums sit in clay pots all along the wraparound porch. Bright orange pillows rest on Adirondack chairs around the fire pit. Dad—five feet, five inches of pure French energy—opens his arms wide from the back porch. I close my eyes for a second and try to imagine three years ago when I'd arrived for the summer. Mémère plucking weeds from her cutting garden. Mom smiling like crazy, her finger pointing to a huge bow on the barn door. She was excited for me to see the studio she built for me.

"Mon chou!" Dad's at me in a flash, grabbing me into a bear hug. I lean my head on his chest, taking in musky dad smell—part sweat, part Old Spice.

Johnny coos from the driver's seat. "You're still his cabbage."

"Such a cute little cruciferous," Dad teases before letting me go.

"Dad, we've got so much to talk about."

Johnny points a thumb at me. "Dev, I pretty much caught her holding up the entire bus at the Greyhound station." Johnny's scanner blares: *Officer LaMonde, we need your assistance with a suspicious lobster boat off Cousin's Beach. 10-4.* I don't even have time to say "Thank you" before he's gone, barreling toward trouble.

In the old, sloped mud room, Roscoe, our black Labrador retriever, dive-bombs me. He shoves his nose into my crotch, practically knocking me over in the process.

"How's my canine pervy-perv?"

He pulls his wet tongue across my ankles. I yank my ratty Converse high-tops off my feet and drop them on the floor. Roscoe eyes the left sneaker with interest, so I open the closet door and kick it into the darkness. I stop, surprised to see Mom's vintage red raincoat still there.

"You still have her raincoat? Should we mail it to her?"

Dad mumbles something about processing rhubarb before disappearing into the kitchen.

He doesn't like talking about my mom any more than I do. I reach for the necklace Mom gave me with a ruby at the clasp and three diamonds across the front, representing the "girls in our family," for when we thought there'd be three of us, if you included Amalie. I should call Mom. I reach for my phone and stop. Since she left, things have been different. I'm not sure where the conversation starts or finishes. It's too much.

My phone finally pings.

553.

The Summerset School of Dance.

I sit on the bench. I brace myself. It's okay if I'm not selected. My life won't end if it's a "No." In reality, these thoughts are lies; if I don't get in, I'll go to a little blueberry hollow, curl up in the fetal position, and die.

My thumb hits the screen, and the email springs to life:

Congratulations! Summerset School of Dance invites you to the final evaluation in New York City on September 15, 2016. The winners of this competition will participate in the semester abroad program at our prestigious school in London, England.

Please confirm receipt and attendance.

Fondly,
Sonia Mathers, VP, Summerset School of Dance

I did it. I actually did it! I do a celebratory dance around the mudroom. Roscoe howls in excitement. "That's right, Roscoe. I did it."

"Clem, come on in here."

I text my best friend, Trace:

I'm in! Auditions. NYC. September.

She replies immediately:

Kill it, girl!

"Clem!" Dad calls again. The man has the patience of a toddler. I rush into the kitchen to tell him my news but stop.

Dad's whistling the old nursery song *Frère Jacques* and spreading rhubarb out on the wooden table. The new addition, renovated two years ago and a finalist for Country Home's Kitchen of 2014, is trashed. Magazines are piled on the floor near the fieldstone fireplace. Books on social media lay open on the sectional couch. There are books on branding, books on living well, books on backyard chicken farms. The wide marble counters are covered in papers and half-eaten bowls of nuts, like he's needed endless amounts of protein to keep him going. I scan the piles cascading across every flat surface. *The Loss of Bees in America. How to Keep the Queen Alive. The Medicinal Effects of Blueberry Honey.*

I pluck a Post-it Note from the cupboard. "Homeland Security Audit. July 15th."

"Yeah, that too. Gotta make sure my paperwork is up-to-date. No worries. I'm on it all."

"But—"

"I said I'm on it." He gives me a wild grin and points to a whiteboard over the table.

"Go look. I have a plan for everything."

At first, I'm impressed by his ability to color code, then it dawns on me; *I* am purple and purple's *everywhere*. In his tight cursive, he mapped out the entire summer: first commercial, stock photos, Blueberries for America 100th Anniversary Special, Facebook Live chats.

"What in the hell is this? I might as well be Barney the fucking Purple Dinosaur."

"Language."

"It's like a grape slushy of chores."

"Purple is the color of royalty." He plucks a cherry from a bowl, pops it in his mouth, and spits the pit into the trash. "Since we put you on the last print ad, our hits have gone up 22 percent. Plus, what do you want me to do? All I hear on the news is people trying to keep my workers out of the country. We're going to need a plan to survive."

"Dad, I said I'd help, but this looks like a full-time job."

"What do you think farming is?"

"Dad, you know I'm a dancer."

"Oh, I know . . . that's why I used your old shots for the promos while you were in school. Use the studio whenever you want. But we need this farm to be a success, and *you're* part of the farm. Dancing *takes* the money. It doesn't *pay* money. Things are tougher now your mom's gone and I have the whole kit and caboodle on my plate."

Panic rises—starting at the back of my thighs, moving into my spinal column—and lodges itself in the back of my throat.

"No dance?"

"Not this summer, hon."

"When?"

"Well, you're still in that fancy school. If it's a banner harvest, you're back in. If not, well, we just gotta work harder." He shakes a rhubarb stalk at me, picks up a knife, and chops it to pieces. "Remember when Laura Ingalls Wilder was a girl? A little 'half-pint?' She was dealing with the same problems. Locusts descended upon the harvest and ate everything, just everything. You have no idea what will happen when you farm. Remember the year we had hail? In August. Ruined everything."

"2011," I say.

"2011 sucked." Dad whacks the rhubarb like an executioner. "Hated that year. This year's going to be different, especially with you running the social brand."

When Dad came up with the winner idea of me being the face of the family business, I squealed, "Okay, jokester! Give me another." But it was all too real.

I push a pile of *Blueberry Today* magazines onto the floor and sink into the couch. Dad hands me one of Mémère's dainty dessert plates with a piece of rhubarb pie placed perfectly in the middle.

"Plus, we gotta make enough money to buy a new roof."

"I dunno about all this, Dad."

"It's all going to be fine. I promise."

"You promised me a pony in fifth grade."

"I got you Roscoe."

Hearing his name, Roscoe lumbers in and falls at my feet, proof sometimes you don't get what you want, but you do get what you need. Dad flings an arm over my shoulder, and I give him a chunk of pie. He raises both eyebrows, chews thoughtfully. "It's you and me, kid. The Fountaine dreamers, together again!"

"To dreamers!" I echo. "Making things happens from 1953 to today!" And I *will* make it happen. My audition, the berries, all of it.

Renée, my oldest Maine friend, pulls up. I'm impressed to see her 1995 Volkswagen still chugging. We hug. It's like putting on a pair of well-worn L.L. Bean slippers, easy and comfortable. Not that I'd say that to her. She would hate being compared to slippers. It's way too pedestrian for Renée Robichaud. We break away. She's grown in the last year, now standing a good four inches taller than my five-foot-three. The apples of her cheeks have thinned out, making almond-shaped eyes seem larger on her angular face, but her wide smile's the same, crooked front tooth and all.

"Let me admire."

"Please do." As we walk into the house, Renée twists for me to get a look at her newest fashion statement: simple skintight black leggings and a cut-off T-shirt, offset by a delicate sculpture hanging from a silver chain. I poke it, expecting it to be plastic, but instead, it's a cool white bone. "It's a chicken vertebra!"

"*Okay . . .*"

"Stop. It's original."

We met the summer before first grade, back when Renée was still a demon child. I got too close to her ratty stuffed bunny named Duke, so she belted me. I fell, broke my arm. Besties ever since.

Dad smiles, happy to see Renée. "I've got some new smoothie ideas." He points to the kitchen, "If you're feeling motivated?"

"Sounds delicious." Renée grins. Her older and younger brothers devour all the food in her house as soon as her mom buys it so, when somebody offers her food, she usually takes it.

"But I'm actually good."

We race up the stairs to my room. It, at least, is the same as I left it last August: white walls, a forest-green bed from the 1930s with a massive steamer trunk at the foot. Dad puffed up my thick down pillows and left a pint-size Ball jar of hollyhocks on my bedside table. I walk across the wide pumpkin-pine floors to push the window open. Renée opens up my bag and starts unpacking my stuff.

"How was your trip?"

"Hellish. I took the red-eye to New York, boarded a puddle jumper to Portland. My Uber driver to the bus station was hella creepy, but I slept all the way to Bangor on the bus. Then, total drama at the station."

She holds out the vintage Rolling Stones shirt I bought at a boutique on Western Avenue last fall. "I love the tongue. Iconic."

"You can borrow it."

"I will." She puts it on a hanger and shoves it in my shoebox-sized closet. "You've got that pinched look around your eyes."

"Dude, is it obvious?" I inspect myself in the reflection of my grandmother's old vanity mirror from the 1940s. It's kind of like a fun house mirror, morphed by age and heat. To use it effectively, you need to have faith that your face does line up in real life. My heart-shaped face is a normal milky-pale nothing-burger with big ol' eyes poking out.

"Tell me. You know you want to."

"I finally got a slot to audition for the Summerset School of Dance. For a chance at a semester abroad in London."

"Brits can be smoking hot."

I nod knowingly. "My father has turned into a social media madman, saying I can dance only if the harvest comes in. Like I'm some sort of Goddess of the Land. Controlling the sun, the stars, and moon. Dictating the flow of the rainfall and the sunshine."

"Is this the dance program you talked about all last summer? The direct shot into Juilliard?" Renée rubs her necklace in thought. "I know what I'd do."

"Tell me, please."

"Nothing. My parents would be like, 'Hell, no, you're not going to New York City because it's dangerous. And you'd get lost. And there're criminals ready to steal your things.' So, I'd probably bail and complain about it for my entire life, like my Aunt Lila who missed her one opportunity to try out for *Cats*."

"Mainers can be so weird." I reach for my phone. "I think I need to RSVP and worry about everything else later." My thumb hovers over the RSVP button. I'm not worrying where I'll get the money or, for that matter, the flight to New York—without my dad knowing. I don't worry about anything. I hit YES. The confirmation comes in with a satisfying *ping*.

"Oh, that felt real good." I roll my shoulders forward and backward. "What a relief."

Renée folds my clothes and puts them in my drawer. "You're a better girl than I am."

"Stop it. You can't help it if your parents like to stay in Maine. You're not alone. Once my grandparents came here from Quebec, they never left. Mémère flat-out refused to come to visit me in California. It's kind of part of life here."

I peer out at the blueberry barrens and recall my Aunt Vivi comparing it to a desert. I can see her comparison when you go to the big blueberry operations, where each direction is rolling fields of low bushes, but here at Laurel Hollow, the ocean breaks the eastern side and thick pine is a half-mile to the west.

"It's quiet here without the blueberry rakers."

"It is," Renée agrees, "like a chocolate factory without its Oompa Loompas."

"Jaysus, don't compare our workers to Oompa Loompas!"

"Sensitive . . . "

I think of the migrant workers at the bus station. "They're not Oompa Loompas, okay?" She starts humming the tune from the movie. *Oompa Loompa, doopitty—*"

"I'll do anything as long as you stop singing. It's awful."

"I'm in chorus, so no complaining about my essential talents!" She sifts through my bag, inspecting a pair of tights and my Doc Martens. "May I?"

"Sure."

Renée slips off her flip-flops and pulls on thick socks before lacing up the boots. She clomps around my room. "They fit perfectly."

At the far end of the barrens, the small village of cabins is lined up neatly at the side of the farm, eager for it to come to life.

Dad always calls Maine his True North. He needs to be here. For me, it's always the people I meet who help me feel like I'm home.

chapter two ♡

WITH DAD BUSY TWEAKING a schedule conflict, I escape out the back door to my dance studio in the barn. The peepers scream *Summer! Summer!* I maneuver around Grampa's John Deere lawn mower, the four-wheelers, a snow blower. I go past the moose antlers hooked prominently to the wall, down the short hallway papered by years of tide charts where the red door leads to my dance studio. I try to push it open. The door catches. *Screech.* The door opens a foot. I kick it and get another six inches. I shove my hand around the corner, fumbling for the light switch. My knuckles scrape something. The entire room is filled with blueberry crates piled from floor to ceiling. Like a Jenga game. My frontal lobe throbs, pain pulsates behind my right eye. I pluck a crate from the middle of the stack. Crates fall around me. I kick one on the way out the door, hurting my big toe in the process. I shake off the pain and stomp into the house to where Dad's humming in the kitchen, surrounded by paperwork.

My fists alternate between rock, paper, and scissors. "What's up with the studio?"

He doesn't even look up. "Temporary. Needed a spot for the gear. You hardly used it last summer."

"Consider me Virginia Woolf, because I need a room of my own, and I need that one."

Dad pulls his glasses off his head. "Listen, can't you see I'm busy getting the paperwork ready for the ICE audit? Can't screw it up."

"But my studio . . . " My voice sounds weak. And then I remember. "Is Rosa coming again?"

He licks his finger and moves through the paperwork. "Rosa Marquez . . . yes, she's applied to come for a second year. Nice girl . . . hard worker." Rosa's worried about a job. I'm worried about my private dance studio. Perspective.

Dad leans back in his chair, "How about I make you a deal? You help with the Maine Migrant Fundraiser. I'll help clean out the studio."

"You already signed me up, didn't you?"

He scratches his chin, buying time. "It's for charity."

"Deal." .

We shake on it. He organizes the raker applications in alphabetical order, one falls from the pile. I reach for it: *Rico Santiago*. Seventeen.

"Here's an S . . ."

Dad slips Rico into the pile and gives me a cheeky grin. "We're all buttoned-up and ready for summer. All the rakers need to do is show up! All the blueberries need to do is grow!"

One week later, I'm a soaked rat, gasping for air, shivering on a bench at the Sagadahoc Rhubarb Festival. "It's for charity," I say to myself, teeth chattering. I close my eyes, think of the money funneling into the Maine Migrant Fund to help when *BOOM!* I hit the water.

"Hey! Hey!" A lanky guy pumping his fist into the air yells, "Wet T-shirt contest!"

I flip him the bird. Dad reaches over the tank to stop me. "Not good for the organic brand."

"Stereo system . . . " I push my sopping hair from my face. "I need a new stereo system."

His eyebrows shoot up. "Excuse me?"

"I'll take new speakers for the studio. That's what I want to stay in this frozen hellish tank."

"Why?"

I push my hair away from my eyes. "Because life's a negotiation, Dad. You taught me that."

"You make two hundred dollars for charity?"

"Deal."

I haul myself up on the dunk tank's platform and start gyrating around. Dad's eyes get kind of wide as I swivel. "I'm looking for a strong arm with good aim to take me down! All proceeds go to the Maine Migrant Fund. They help with education, legal issues, and more. Twenty dollars for three shots! Let's do this!"

Pearson Smith saunters to the booth and hands Dad a twenty. I consider him. He's changed a lot from the boy who used to jog around with his lacrosse stick, beaming the ball on every flat surface, an odd little gremlin. Now, he looks like what you'd expect from the Boston private-school sort. Boxy shoulders over a lanky body, wavy hair pushed away from a high forehead, accenting his slightly crooked nose. If Trace's mom saw him, she'd slide him a card for Platinum Models and immediately cast him as the perfect frat boy or the captain of the football team in one of her comedies. We're not friends, but we're not true enemies. We both spend every summer in Mount Blanc. We're both competitors.

"Pearson!" I yell. "Heard you don't have much of an aim. Give a fifty. You're going to need it to take me down."

"A little pricey for a dunking booth, don't you think?"

"Charity is charity," I croak again, peeling my wet shirt away from my chest. "I understand though. This is a rough game. Everyone looking at you. Wouldn't want to, I dunno, miss."

Pearson flashes ultra-white teeth. "You have no idea of my aim."

"What're you doing?" Dad hisses at me, before turning and smiling wide at Pearson.

Pearson hands Dad another crumpled bill. He makes a big show of stretching out his arm. My teeth chatter, but I grab the edge of the seat and lean forward. If I make him mad enough, he'll keep throwing the ball and spending money. Two hundred dollars, here I come.

I goad him on. "Third grade. Day camp. Kickball. Grand slam."

"I recall you getting picked last. That's embarrassing."

He beams it at the buzzer. I plummet into the cold water. When I reach the surface, I twist my dark hair out of my eyes so I can see.

I climb out of the tub. "I was small for my age, but that doesn't mean I didn't have a kicking leg of steel. Nobody even expected it. I was their ace."

Pearson tossed the balls into the air. "Nah. You were such a runt, when I tried getting you out, I kept missing."

He beams another ball at me.

And another. I fall. Get up. And another. I fall. Every time, I climb out and smile. "That's the spirit."

When he's finally out of balls, there's something in his eyes I've never seen before. I don't know what to do with it when he comes close, so I whisper. "Make your friends pay, too."

"You've changed since last summer."

"Please, I'm just colder."

"Okay, Fountaine. I got you."

Twenty minutes later, I'm at two hundred and out of the water. I hope Pearson isn't going to come calling for some reward. This summer is about me. Single me. Girl-flying-solo me. I pull a towel over my hair; it's time to explore the fair.

Renée and I stop in the crossroads and stare at the fair map, trying to decide which way to go. My hair is pulled away from my face in a sloppy bun, still faintly wet underneath, but my skin has finally dried out from its prune-like state.

Renée points to the fair map. "Because you're a pseudo farm girl, maybe you'd like to go check out the canned fruit section and the homemade pies exhibit to see who got the blue ribbon. After, if we turn right, we can see the baby goats. I heard the ladies at the Old Pines Nursing Home made them sweaters this year."

"That's so cute." I go in the opposite direction toward the carnival games, because going to the agricultural expo reminded me of Mémère, who took great pride in her pickles and pies and dilly beans . . . I shake it off. It hurts too much.

"What's wrong with you? Nobody passes up baby goats." But she follows me through the tunnel of games: basketball, whack-a-mole, fling a penny in a bottle, and balloon darts.

"These are all money grabbers."

"I know, I raised two hundred for charity."

I stop at a shooting game. It's festive, with lights blinking and AC/DC blaring from a speaker. A carnival worker rocks out, really getting into it. I join him, beat for beat. I grab Renée's arm.

"This one!" I drop my money on the shelf, bring the rifle to my shoulder, and peer at rows of colored stars.

She taps my Doc Martens at me. "I've gotta pee."

"I'll be here."

"Don't lose me. You're my ride home."

I wait for her to disappear into the crowd and pick my next spot on the board, flipping the end like a pool player motioning to a pocket, about to pull the trigger when a sharp whistle buzzes my ear. My star disappears, replaced by a little hole in the board. Three feet away, I see the culprit. He's staring at the board with the intensity of a sniper.

"Hey dude, you stole my star. I was pointing right at it."

I notice this guy. Like, notice. His chin is all character, square with a hint of scruff, like he's not trying too hard. High, tan forehead, with a tumble of shiny dark hair tucked neatly behind his ears. Eyes capture me. They move slowly as he takes in one star after the next, like those stars are the most important things in the universe. I want to be looked at like that, like I'm precious and important. He's athletic, too. I can tell by the way he's side-stepping away from me, smooth like butter on a hot skillet. He points his thumb toward the crowd, hitchhiker style and, as his longish hair falls over his left eye, turns to go.

All of my thoughts of being single disappear.

He's the most beautiful boy I've ever seen.

"Wait!" I grab a crumpled twenty from my pocket and slam it down on the counter. "Five for me and five for the star stealer!"

"You're not paying for me." There's something about his voice that reminds me of California, where people's voices have a questioning quality and their speech is smoother than in Maine, where they drop the "r" and make "car" into "cah."

I raise money into the air. "Pony up the cash or I'm paying." I tilt my hip to elongate my short torso and pull my hair out from behind my ear to make my nose look cuter. I've never thrown myself at anybody like I am throwing myself at this guy. The thing is, I can't seem to help myself. There's something about him.

The corners of his mouth tip upward in response to my smile, and I notice the slight cleft in the middle of his chin. He pulls a wallet out from his back pocket—tight leather or pleather, both weird for a kid our age—and retrieves a crisp tenner from the inner compartment.

"What should we play for?" My question sounds like a proposition. Not intended. But it works.

"I was playing for my sister. She's got a thing for berries." He points to an obese stuffed strawberry hanging from a hook. He's not only hot, but he cares about his sister. And I get that.

The carnival worker rubs a few wiry hairs fighting to escape his ribbed tank top and leans against the counter. "You two working together?"

"Yes!" I say.

"Okay, let's shoot some stars!"

Starstealer stands his ground like he knows who he is. I raise the gun. Get ready. He's distracting me, muttering as if he needs to talk himself through each and every step. I take aim at the star in the far corner of the board, pull the trigger, and miss. Starstealer hits one. And then another. Then another.

The carnival worker shakes his head like he's honestly disappointed. "Close, but no cigar. Sorry kids, you've gotta hit the whole thing."

"Wait a second. He's got three stars. There's only a dot of yellow left."

The carnival worker casually reaches under the table and pulls out a yellowing copy of *Shooting Range Rules & Regulations* stuffed into plastic so old it's cracked like a spider web. He juts out a nicotine-stained thumb, "Right here. Rule #10. No point sharing. It's a whoopee cushion or an alien. Final offer." When we don't respond, he flings the fart noise maker and the tired alien into a box in the corner. "You had your chance. Now it's nothing."

"Come on, dude. You know we won. It's for my sister . . . "

I nudge my knee between the rifles bolted onto the top of the counter, stretching my arms until the tips of my fingers tickle the giant stuffed strawberry.

"You can't do that!" The worker's burning cigarette falls out of his mouth and onto his leg. He curses loudly. Sensing trouble, a young mother slowly scoops up her snotty toddler who arches her back and screams, "Me want strawberry!" The carnival guy reaches under his large hanging belly and produces a walkie-talkie, "I've got a wild one over here at the shooting range. Need security. ASAP."

Starstealer steps backwards. He's still. There's a wary look in his eyes.

I grab the giant stuffed strawberry and yell, "It's for his sister! For her birthday!"

"The fuzz don't care," the carnival worker responds.

Starstealer points to the rent-a-cop sprinting toward us. I'm surprised when he grabs my hand, pulling me into the crowd with him.

"Stop!" the rent-a-cop screams. "Oh, shit, I have to chase the blueberry girl?!"

We race together past food trucks, take a sharp left at the apple-shaped crisp stand, and dash through the line of people waiting for a fried sausage. I think for a moment I see a flash of Renée walking through the crowd looking for me. Adrenaline surges as his hand holds on tighter. At the edge of the fairgrounds, we walk across the old horse track and slow down. Enough. We collapse together underneath a tree, secure in the safety of darkness. I'm not sure what I thought would come next, so when he starts laughing, I do, too.

The sheer release of it all is the best I've felt all day.

He turns to me. "The look on that guy's face when you climbed up on his booth. He almost choked on his cigarette."

"Seriously! Maybe not the best move. He could've strung me from the rafters and given me away with the whoopee cushions."

"Nina will love it. Thank you. It was kind."

I pause. He's so earnest I almost don't even know how to respond; he's not like other guys, and my game is off. Finally, I croak, "I'm glad."

We sit side by side, not saying anything. The energy coming from him is like a force field, drawing me closer instead of blocking me away. He plucks a piece of grass from the ground and drags his thumbs along its seam until it splits into two.

"I'm Clementine, by the way."

"Like the fruit?"

"Yeah, I'm named after my great-grandmother. Everyone calls me Clem. And *you* are . . . ?"

He raises a single finger toward my mouth. "No names. I like to keep it simple."

"Can I find you online?"

"No."

This dude is not a specimen of this generation. "Seriously, no social media? Because, let me tell you, I'm social."

"It's a time suck."

"True, but . . . " I try to articulate what I'm thinking, which is "Let's stay in touch, even if it's just a friend following a friend." Instead, I say nothing.

He picks up an acorn top, holds it between his fingers, and pulls it to his mouth, letting out a long whistle. I reach out my hand. He plops the acorn cap into my palm. I try to make it whistle, too, but only hot air blows out.

"What else can you do? Write poetry? Code my computer? Execute the perfect back flip?"

Starstealer pauses. I wonder if he's going to boast about how amazing he is. That's what guys often do, blow up their chest and show you their greatness, but instead, he says, "No poetry unless I'm forced to. I had to do a villanelle last year. Nineteen lines. ABA. I might have cried trying to get it right."

"What did you write about?"

His longish hair falls over an eye. "Boundaries."

"We all cross them."

"Kind of like tonight," he motions toward the stuffed strawberry, still smiling, and rolls back onto his forearms.

"We earned it fair and square. I'm only here for the summer. I spend most of the year in California, where I go to school. But for me, every single summer, Maine it is. My dad grew up here. You know—the whole 'once a Mainer, always a Mainer' thing? He calls coming here his yearly pilgrimage."

"Migration happens," he jokes.

"My mom. She's from Jersey. She says it's what makes her brash. She's writing a book in Mexico with her new boyfriend. So, I'm a girl from here but also from away."

He leans against the tree. I can't tell what he's thinking.

"Am I talking too much?"

He nods—in a nice way, not an awkward way. "You *are* talkative."

"You're making me nervous."

"Nobody has ever said that about me before. I'll take it as a compliment."

My phone buzzes. I make Renée wait. I'm not ready to leave. I tip my head, taking in the mass of tree limbs reaching for the moon. I enjoy the radiating warmth coming from Starstealer's body.

He holds the stuffed strawberry up to the light, looking at it like a rare jewel. "Thank you for giving it such a, should we say, *intense* story around it."

"Intensity is my specialty."

"It's a good quality. Being yourself. Not hiding it. Clementine, I'm a fan."

Darkness hides the warm flush creeping up my neck. So many people in my life have told me to sit down, be quiet, and do what's expected of me. But not this guy. He gets it.

"Are you always this honest?"

He leans toward me, raises an eyebrow, pausing long enough for me to contemplate briefly if he's going to kiss me. Instead, he gets off the ground and walks back to the fair. The stuffed strawberry hangs from his hand. A gift to his sister.

I'm going to think of him for a long time.

I know it.

A tiny plastic heart lives wedged between the cracks in the sole of my Birkenstock. It's an odd little hitchhiker, a little ruby red parasitic reminder of my night with Starstealer. My phone is my best friend. I'm a sad obsessive stalker. But I never find him. I decide to practice, to work on an attainable goal: my audition.

Protein shake in hand, I've made it almost all the way down the hallway when Dad opens the bathroom door a crack.

"What're you doing?"

"Heading to town to practice at Greater Zumba since you reneged on the deal to clean out my studio."

He sniffed. "UMaine has an excellent eco-farming degree. I noticed there's an online class you could take. I could sign you up?"

I feel a break in our relationship. Dance is everything. I'd worked on the quality of my Summerset School of Dance audition, obsessing over the angle of my video, the color of my leotard, my makeup. Everything.

"You want me to get a farm degree? I always talked about . . . Mom loved art. And dance . . . "

Dad takes a step toward me, hair combed back, bright blue eyes sharp.

"Have you talked to her?" His tan, smooth face crinkles into a frown. "Only very few actually make it in publishing. Most writers starve or put their heads in ovens. You've heard of Sylvia Plath? You know why, Clem. They're drunk. Writers are always drunks with trust funds."

"Seriously, Dad?"

He's gone too far, and he knows it. I see my opportunity to leave, so I take it. I'm out the door and into the Jeep within five minutes. My body itches to move, to dive into the rhythm of something beyond me. Up ahead, cars are stopped in the road. I move forward five feet and bake in the sun. Five minutes go by. The person in front of me turns off their engine. I do, too. I strain to see what's happening ten cars up but can't see anything.

I grab my phone and type "Sandrine Fountaine" into Google. Mom's profile springs to life. Nothing has changed on the World Wide Web. There's still the same old picture of her at California Art's gala, head tipped back, crazy hair cascading, and teeth exposed in happiness. On her thin neck, a necklace matching mine, glittering in the flash of the camera. The next picture is a miniature black-and-white, back when she was thirteen and saved two kids from falling through thin ice. She practically drowned in the process.

Honk!

Honk!

The car in front of me moves forward five feet.

I start the Jeep and move forward five feet. I glance at the clock; the class starts in ten minutes.

"For the love of Christmas, I've got to get my dance on. I'm going to miss my class." I throw the car in park, hop out, and stomp past the rows of cars until I get to the front of the line, where Johnny's truck blocks the road. He's staring into the trunk of a light-blue Lincoln Continental, poking around in the wheel well.

"*Pssstttt* . . . Johnny."

He does a double-take when he sees me. "Clem. What the hell? I'm working."

"I'm going to Zumba. Need to get around."

He smooths his beard in thought. "Clem, we're doing a routine checkpoint. I can't just let you through."

I throw my hands into the air. "Johnny, I promise. I don't have any drugs. Just high on life. Plus, we're buttoned-up at the farm. Dad said we were. Can I squeeze around? Gotta get this body moving."

"Fine. This one time." He yells to the other officers, "She's good."

"You're the best."

Back in the Jeep, I zip around the other cars, ignoring the nasty looks of waiting drivers. I beep at the checkpoint, loop around, waving to Johnny as I move past. I make it in time for class. Zumba is housed in the basement of the Order of the Odd Fellows hall. I grab my water bottle and towel, get out of the Jeep, and walk into the musty building. It has a wide red carpet heading down the stairs, but I can hear the flutter of the girls—my dance peeps—as they get ready for the class. I paste a smile on my face, turn the corner, and stop.

The "girls" are nana-types, in their fifties, sixties, and seventies. Most of them have perms and thick sweatpants on, despite the offensive heat being pushed around by the overhead ceiling fans.

I put my fiver in the donations bucket just as the music gets going. AC/DC's "You Shook Me All Night Long." AC/DC reminds me of the Starstealer. My thoughts go to the plastic heart nestled in my shoe. Then I push hard into what I can control and think of nothing else.

chapter three ♡
Strawberry Season ~ July

I STAND IN FRONT of my bedroom mirror in my dance clothes, flexing my legs until I'm high on my toes, pulling my arms back until they're hovering over my head. Zumba isn't doing it, and I think I might be losing definition. I suck in my cheeks, shimmying a bit, and fold down into a forward bend, stretching my vertebrae as far as they can go before pulling into a plank. Music pulsates through the room. Practicing dance slides on my wood floor, I curl my body forward, flowing to the left as the music lowers, pushing into the air as the beat lightens. I keep missing. I close my eyes, let the song invade my nervous system and pulsate there. I think of the last time I was on stage, that feeling of freedom you only get when you totally release into it.

My neck snaps forward. My timing is still off.

If Mémère was here, she'd pull me to her side and whisper, *"What're you scared of?"*

If Aunt Vivi was here, she'd say, *"Fuck it, try . . . "*

If Mom was here, she'd say, *"It's like breathing . . . just breathe."*

I flip to my back and pull my knees to my chest, stretching my quads in the process. Fear isn't something you can quantify like a math problem. If I'm one-fourth afraid of not making it to London and one-eighth horrified of leaving my dad—because I left him alone and he totally lost his shit—and I'm one-third afraid I'll never find a boyfriend who isn't a total and complete ass-hat . . . Shit. I lost my math. What's the equation?

My door opens; Roscoe bombs in and licks my face with his slobbery tongue. Dad is wearing a sport coat and button-up shirt. His salt-and-pepper hair is pushed artfully away from his face, like he's grooming to impress. I'm not going to like this. I know it. "It's the Fourth of July! We could get some firecrackers . . . or go to the Smiths."

"The way you're dressed, it doesn't look like a choice."

He grins. "Imagine who we might meet there? Maybe the head of Whole Foods? I met the producers of *California Today* while eating vegan dogs in Silver Lake. You never know. Think of how proud your Mémère would be, going to the Smiths' house for dinner. It has come full circle for us."

This makes me want to laugh aloud, but I don't. Instead, I squeak, "She thought they paid too *little* for rich people and expected too *much.*"

"But she's *not* working there? *Are we?*"

"No. Not unless you want me to do a shoot there, too. Maybe sipping a blueberry spritzer with a chunk of lime on the back deck? We could have the ocean in the background, maybe with a nice schooner with sails blowing starboard."

"Get dressed."

He closes the door.

Roscoe saunters over to my bedside table and gobbles down my sandwich.

I put on a light billowy dress for the party. I pile my hair into a high bun before coating my lips with Rising Ruby Red lipstick, achieving the line between good girl and defiance—a look I could easily take to lunch at Perefield Country Club or use to score access to the underground party scene in L.A.

This summer, nothing feels right. I'm too California. I'm too farm girl. I'm not Maine enough to be a real Mainer. I'm a dancer who practices at Zumba with old ladies. Shit, I can't find "the one guy" that might have changed this whole summer.

I'd like to say I'm past the point of caring, but there's a small piece of me who always cares about it all.

The Smiths' house sits on a hunk of granite overlooking Perry's Bay. Classic understated elite: weathered natural shingles, beveled glass, and green multi-pitched roof. An old swing hangs from a giant maple, potted blue pansies line the path to a faded screen door, which, unfortunately for us, is guarded by a giant rooster.

"Oh no, Dad. It's like a test for an epic quest. Can you get past the rooster to eat the Smiths' shrimp?" I sputter lines from Monty Python's *Holy Grail*. Dad ignores me with a singular shake to his head.

"The *coq au vin* looks delicious."

"Funny!" I know full well he's only half-kidding. "Shoo! Go on. Shoo!" I wave my hands in the air, as though gyrating like an ass is going to prove my dominance. The rooster puffs its feathers. He stakes his claim as King of the Walkway. I dive into the flower bed, trampling pansies as I race from the bird.

The rooster takes in my father with beady eyes and feathers puffed. It weaves back, kind of like a bull getting ready to charge, and dives for Dad's ankle. Dad screams something that sounds like, "Mother fucking fowl!" his crisp blue shirt dotted with sweat. I yank off my wedge and nail the bird on the side of the head. Feathers fly. The rooster hightails it around the corner, finally leaving us in peace.

Christine Brommage Smith, Pearson's mother, stands in the middle of the door. Holding a frosty gin and tonic in a well-manicured hand, her mouth hangs open in a round little O.

I raise my hands in the air. "Reporting safe from the Great Rooster Disaster of 2016!"

Pearson steps into the sun and calls to me, his voice Beacon Hill deep. "Clementine, did you fend off the guard rooster?"

Christine shoves her gin and tonic onto a corner table and motions for Dad to follow. The edges of Dad's blue eyes crinkle into a smile. He slips into his posh party veneer by relaxing his face while, at the same time, digging a piece of Laurel Hollow's organic dirt from underneath his fingernail. Pearson helps himself to the drink his mother left behind. He touches the small of my back and leads me into the house, which I'm sure isn't him being polite.

He grins. "Haven't seen you since the fair."

"Yeah, I guess I should say thank you for dunking me for charity."

"I like a good cause, Clementine. Can't help it. I would've hung out with you more that night. You know, bought you some cotton candy, maybe asked you to ride the tilt-a-whirl. But, the next thing I knew, you were running through the fair with some guy, being chased by the police."

"You don't happen to know that guy, do you?"

He makes a small noise in the back of his throat. "You almost got arrested because of somebody you didn't know?"

"Yeah."

"You're sure different." He pushes through a double swinging door into the cavernous main portion of the house.

My mouth is sandpaper dry. Being here feels wrong. All of it feels wrong. "Do you think I could grab a glass of water? The rooster episode was dehydrating."

Pearson looks at me out of the corner of his eyes, and his mouth drops open provocatively. I know there is a smart-ass comment in there, but I appreciate him holding it in as he nods to a door down a long hall. While we walk, I wonder what else he holds in, what else goes unsaid. In the main room, the kitchen door blends into the mahogany wall, like the family doesn't want to be reminded that people cooked there. I enter, and the door closes behind me in a silent *swoosh*. I half-expect a popsicle-inspired relic out of the fifties with lime-green cabinets and peach countertops; instead, I find a huge slab of marble, a Wolf stove, and a Sub-Zero built into the wall, flush with the beachy white cupboards, all sparkling clean.

Pearson fills a glass with filtered tap water.

In the corner, there's a breakfast nook overlooking the ocean, with a group of black and white pictures all over the wall. I clearly recognize my grandmother, my Mémère, with Christine when she was little. Despite all of her complaining, she looks, well, happy.

Pearson hands me the water. I take it. He stands too close to me, and I don't like it.

I show him my dimple; it's my fake way of looking innocent while I make my escape.

"I'm going to use the bathroom. Okay?"

"Sure, meet me at the dock."

In the bathroom, I lock the door tight. A weird painting is on the bathroom wall. It's a Victorian girl sitting on a pink ottoman, her boobs puffing out of her honey-colored dress and fingers clawing at the air like she's trying to grab a ghost. Out the bathroom window, a khaki jungle of guests mingles in the long evening light. Dad holds court, charm dripping from his pores, a glass of chardonnay in hand. Christine joins the crowd and hands him what only can be a Band-Aid by the way he throws back his head in laughter.

"Traitor."

I bust back into the kitchen. My stomach grumbles, and I open the fridge to find Tupperware containers full of nibbles: potato salad congealed around the edge, black olives floating in brine, baby-sized bites of steak. I fish out a hunk of crumbled blue cheese and grab a chunk of fresh lobster meat from its bowl. A door slams. I choke, cough. The lobster dislodges and lands on the floor. I quickly kick it under the cabinet.

Voices, light and teasing, float in from the other room. "Can you believe Dev Fountaine got attacked by my neighbor's rooster? You can take someone off the farm . . . "

Hot blood rises into my skull, a slow consistent boil. A short burst of laughter echoes through the great room. A clink of ice and high heels on the wood floor get louder by the second. "Remember the raging infatuation you had with him all those summers ago?"

Oh, Jaysus!

I scan the breakfast nook for a place to hide, consider pushing out one of the old screens, but for some reason, I can't walk away from this conversation.

"Connie. He's still good-looking now. Maybe even better now Sandrine is gone. Did you ever hear the story about what happened with those two?"

My fists clench.

Don't.

You.

Dare.

She *dares,* her voice breathy. "I heard the scoop from Samantha Lavadere. She owns the little boutique pet store that opened up in Bensonville. I know, right? How're they ever going to stay in business through the winter? Anyways, she's good friends with Johnny LaMonde, who filled her in. The story is Dev was all by himself dealing with every single aspect of Laurel Hollow. Clementine was off dancing at Bates College. Sandrine decided—mid-harvest, mind you—to go to a writing retreat in Costa Rica. There, she met the famed poet, Wilber Montrose."

"The sexiest poet alive?"

"Exactly."

"You would have done the same thing."

"Maybe, you never know."

I touch the necklace Mom gave me with one hand, squeezing a grape with the other. It splats all over the counter. I whisper through clenched teeth, *"Ferme la bouche,* Madame Smith," a nicer French translation of "Shut your *damn* mouth, Christine."

Christine says, "I really miss her, though. She always made parties better."

"She sure did."

I pluck lipstick from my bag. I add another layer and rub thick kohl under my eyes. I might have my own issues with my mother, but I'll be damned if I'm going to let Christine gossip about my family. The only revenge is to go out there looking like a child of Hollywood without a care in the world.

I saunter through the double doors. Despite my annoyance with Christine, I appreciate the view of the side yard extending into a peninsula between the Atlantic Ocean and a spit created by a little pebble beach. A group of younger kids are taking turns cannonballing into the ocean. I weave through the crowd, giving Christine a sly smile.

She plops sunglasses over her eyes.

It feels like a small victory.

On the dock where Pearson hangs with his homeboys, he slides over on the wide wicker couch. "There she is. Everyone, this is Clementine."

"Clem. Please."

Pearson brings out a little shiny flask. I let him tip some clear liquid into my Diet Coke and settle into an Adirondack chair and listen as Pearson's boys talk about their team.

"Remember when you faked right and beamed it between Andover's legs?"

Pearson's handsome face is rosy from vodka, but I can't help but notice he's trying. He makes sure I'm included in the conversation. When the group moves to Frisbee, he always passes dead on center so I can easily catch it. He does the same during a game of bocce ball and even finds me hot sauce for my grilled chicken. Pearson spreads out on a lounge chair with country-club ease, and for the first time, I notice the dude could be an ear model because those are not only good-looking lobes but also perfectly placed on the head.

A mosquito sucks on my ankle bone. I smack it hard. Both Pearson and I watch it fall dead to the ground. We sit in awkward silence for a moment before he asks, "Is it weird for you?"

"I don't know."

His teeth are perfectly straight and perfectly white, a true testament to the benefits of orthodonture. A breeze picks up, sending the corner of my dress up around my thighs, so I frantically hold it down. Pearson motions toward an old maple tree over by the corner of the house. "I have a picture of the two of us. Did you know your grandmother brought you once? We were snoozing on little blankets under the tree."

"I don't remember."

"Come up to my room, I'll show you the picture."

"I'm not going up to your room."

"Why? I'm not a creeper."

"I have no proof you're not a creeper."

"We could make a bet." It's like he sees right through me. I am a gambler at heart. "If it's you in the picture, I take you out for dinner."

I pause, rifling through ideas, before coming up with the perfect one. "Fine. If it's not me, you come to exercise class."

"Win-win."

I take another sip of my drink before following Pearson through the pampered people gorging on sliders, miniature crab rolls, and scallops wrapped in bacon. Dad raises a glass, seemingly pleased to be off the farm. Pearson holds the door open for me. He points left toward a dark, steep stairway. I slip off my wedges and climb the stairs, turn to a long hall, surprised by the amount of doors.

"How many bedrooms do you have up here?"

"I dunno. Eight? My great-grandparents had lots of kids."

"And servants."

"Come on, Clementine," he bristles, "it was a long time ago. You know we loved your grandmother." A layer of ice around my heart melts for Pearson. I ignore it.

Pearson pops open the door at the end of the hall and says, "Ladies first."

My nose tickles, the smell of old house baking in the hot summer sun. He follows me in, a peacock proud of his lair. Yale banners are tacked artfully on the walls, with an honest-to-goodness collection of deer antlers and almost an entire wall of black and white photos of all the Smiths who had this room before him. The only mar in its perfection is a pair of tighty-whities in the corner by the closet.

I suppress a grin.

Pearson points to a picture of a bunch of kids racing sailboats in the harbor, collective blonds in the wind. "My dad back in the seventies . . ." He drags a long finger toward another picture over in the corner. It's of a group of women, long skirts barely covering skinny ankles.

They're sitting under a maple tree, sipping from dainty teacups, sandwiches piled on a plate. Pearson opens up his bureau and rifles around in a drawer. I meander over to the window. "Got it," he says, holding the picture in the air and bridging the three feet between us.

"Look, it's us. It's totally you and me."

I grab the picture. Pearson is a chubba, all watery eyes and puffy baby cheeks. He's in the process of flinging off his blanket, and it's cracking him up. I take in the other baby he *says* is me, sitting on the ground with a scowl on its little face. Yes, this baby is a little blue-eyed, dark-haired pipsqueak, but it's too curly-haired to be me. I flip over the picture, and in perfect penmanship, it says, "Pearson and Lillian."

I beam my fist into his shoulder, surprised how much muscle he has. "This isn't me!"

He protects his chest. "Ouch." His voice becomes playful, and I wonder if this shit ever works for him. "I thought you and I could get to know each other better. It makes sense. You're here every summer. I'm here every summer. Why don't we make the best of it?"

I set the picture of the *not me* baby on the table and peer out the window at the people still milling about the lawn. Uncomfortable silence. Pearson grabs his lacrosse stick and ball and pops the ball lightly in the air with the side of the lacrosse shaft, tongue hanging out of his mouth like he's trying to thread a needle.

"Fountaine . . . I'm your dream boyfriend. You just don't know it yet."

"I'm not dating anyone this summer. I'm taking a break. Plus, I have a tryout in New York for a dance school. It'll need my focus. All of it."

He laughs at me, twists his stick, and catches the lacrosse ball neatly in the mesh. "That's what they all say."

It's nearly 9 p.m., and the sun has finally set. The Mount Blanc dock, where the entire town gathers to watch the fireworks, is packed. Renée and I dodge little devils with sparklers and jump when somebody drops a firecracker near our feet. It's a scene from an old movie, small-town goodness, make-your-own-fun type scenario. A group of old guys dressed in red, white, and blue vests, white pants, and weird top hats play "The Star Spangled Banner" in a crooked gazebo. Booths sell kettle corn and lime rickeys and Mount Blanc's French twist of the day: homemade strawberry crepes. Being with Pearson reminded me of *that* feeling, the feeling of being under the tree with the Starstealer. I search the sea of people for him but, like every other time I look, he's simply not there.

The look on Pearson's face when he sauntered into Zumba at the Odd Fellows Hall is pure gold. He does a stutter step backwards; his eyes dart from me to Miss Evangaline DuMonde—famous for teaching kindergarten for 42 years at Mount Blanc Elementary School—and back to the over-70 crew: Sonja, Tammy, Ruthie, and Beatrice.

I pull off my sweatshirt and motion for him to come over. "What's up, Buttercup? Come on over and get stretching."

"What're we doing?"

"Zumba."

"Which is . . . "

"It's all kinds of fabulous, Pearson. You're going to be sore in places you never even thought about."

Ruthie's face wrinkles into a thousand folds as she grins at me. "What would your mother think of him?"

"Excuse me?"

"Adorable," she practically coos. She shoves her hands into her too-thick sweatpants and gives her hips a swivel.

My God, she's hitting on him.

"Clem, do I need to do this?"

"A bet's a bet," I hiss, then turn back to Ruthie. "I'm not talking to . . . wait, how do you know my mother?"

"Breakfast at the soup kitchen. I miss her. She always gave me extra bacon. Protein is key to get through these workouts." She pulls a matchstick thin arm across deflated breasts. "I'm ninety-two, you know."

Pearson sizes up Ruthie. "Don't look a day over eighty."

"Right?" she beams.

Oh. My. Good. Gravy. They. Are. Flirting.

"Yeah, I've helped at the soup kitchen, too."

"With my mother?"

"I don't know. It's early. I'm always bleary-eyed when I'm there. My school forces goodness. Like I'm not already good or something."

"You look like an angel to me," Ruthie coos.

The teacher, a sixty-something spitball named Clarice calls out. "Let's do this! Yeehaw!"

Pearson goes directly to the front of the class next to Ruthie and spends the entire time directly in step with the music. I'm surprised; he surprises me. And I kind of like it.

❀

Pearson gnaws a protein bar after class, waves goodbye to all the ladies, and even gives Ruthie a hug. His cheeks are lobster-red, his breath shallow as he grins. "I like how those ladies stay active. Did you see Clarice's tattoo?"

I cock my head. He stands tall like he's proud of himself for getting my attention.

"Clem, it was on her back shoulder. She's got the whole damn thing covered in monarch butterflies with the words *Rise Above* dead center. During Zumba, I was thinking about what it means to be different, how if you have a big audition, that's exactly what it is about to get to the next level—rising above. Though, she also had an evil eye down near her elbow. It kind of freaked me out . . . "

"You're really observant."

"Do you know the difference between good athletes and great ones?"

"Talent?"

He pulls a towel out of his bag and wipes sweat from his forehead. He's about to head into epic coach mode. I'm not disappointed. "Raw talent's something many people have. It's the devotion to the sport; it's being a true student of the game. Seriously, Clem. What have you done to set yourself apart? What have you done to make yourself different?"

I try to defend myself, but he keeps on talking.

"Tell me, what's your signature move?"

I push off the wood floor. "Oh, you want to see it?"

He gives me an impish grin, which must've worked on plenty of the girls he's met before. I feel self-conscious, not sure where to put my body with him looking. I center myself, tilting my hips from left to right. I pop my head to the right and left, not finding my favorite move. Dance is about staying in the rules, not making your own.

"That's what I thought." Pearson pushes off the ground. "You stand here. You are defense." Pearson leans in so close I could count the gray flecks in his deep blue eyes. "On the lacrosse field, it's all about executing the perfect essentials with your own dose of style. I'm not sure you've found yours. Your girl Renée has it. She knows who she is. You, I'm not sure you know."

"Bullshit. I know who I am."

"Prove it."

"What do you have in mind to help me find my *personal style*?"

"For me, it's all about cross-training. It puts you into situations you might find uncomfortable. You'll utilize muscles you've never even thought about, sinking into rotations. Maybe you'll surprise the judges."

"And where do I get started in the middle of nowhere? There are no cross-training centers here. Plus, I need to keep it a secret from my father, who's all about social right now, and my practice studio is full of the crap my dad shoved in it last fall."

An idea dawns on me. The Smiths were wild about volunteering, forcing their kids to do community service every summer instead of working, because they obviously don't need the money.

"How many hours do you need for your community service?"

"I dunno. Thirty every summer."

"I'll be your community service project."

"It's supposed to be helping out somebody who's underprivileged. So, it'll be sort of a lie. You seem to be doing fine."

"I'm lying to my dad every day about a dance audition I want to go to. It . . . " Oh, damn, my voice cracks, but I smile brightly. "Dance is secondary now I'm the . . . " I shake my hands in the air. "Face of the brand."

"Fine . . . I'll do it, but what will you do for me?"

"You want me to curate your Instagram account? It could be an advertisement for not only your lacrosse skills but for your future life coaching brand."

Pearson laughs and pulls a sweatshirt on. "Question though. You with the guy I saw you at the fair with?"

I take a sip of water, disappointment cruising in my veins. "No, I haven't seen him again. He was real nice, though . . . "

"Cool."

We high-five, and, at the end, he clasps my hand.

What would Mémère think of this? I have no idea.

When I arrive home, the guys from ICE are heading toward their vehicles. They're serious sorts, not at all like Johnny, in dark blue uniforms with big white letters on the back.

There's nothing about the shape of their mouths that inspires one to strike up a conversation. Even Roscoe stays in the shade, tail still and obstinate, looking at them suspiciously. The smallest guy seems to be the leader of the group of three; he's got straw-colored hair and fish-scaly looking skin. He pauses and peers out over our fields where blueberries are baking in the sun.

"It's going to be a banner year."

I bite my tongue, because what I want to say is "*Sure, if we get to have our workers.*" Without the workers, those berries are bird food, and the roof isn't done, and dance . . . well, *I can't even.*

Dad meets me at the door with a cheesy thumbs up, like he's won the lottery. "For the most part, we're good! Bring on the season!"

"For the most part?"

"Nothing's perfect. So I'll take the B+."

"What'd you lose points for?"

He unwraps a stick of gum. "Nothing's perfect, Clem. Nothing."

chapter four ♡
Blueberry Season ~ August

A FORD PICK-UP TRUCK leads the way, followed by Subarus and Broncos packed full of people. Rap music pumps, and my body moves effortlessly with the beat. Rambunctious cheers. More honking. The migrants have arrived for harvest. The rakers are here. Workers pile out, flinging backpacks and duffle bags over shoulders, looking expectantly over the fields. José Luis García, our farm manager, greets my father with a big hug. Another truck comes to a stop, and a dog dives out of a Subaru station wagon window and runs an excited lap. Roscoe howls in delight and books it toward the camp. The air feels alive with the sudden change.

I search the crowd for Rosa but don't see any sign of her. Did she miss the bus? I hope not. A soccer ball pops high toward the rec hall. A raker follows. He moves like a natural athlete, effortlessly, with power in each step. He gets the ball into the air via the corner of his foot, changing directions. I can't stop watching. The way the sun shines on his hair, the ripple of muscle, the speed. From this point on, we're all in it together. We're a group of farming warriors.

A farming family. A team.

The soccer ball goes high into the air and lands on a roof, and the raker pops it off his forehead directly onto a cabin's door.

Score!

Pearson picks me up in a campy, vintage Wagoneer from the sixties, complete with faux wooden panels on the side. The windows stay open since this beast spends most of the year in the Smiths' garage; it's musty, and I'm pretty sure a mouse family lives in the passenger door. Pearson sings along to the old cassette tape in the player, a mixed bag from the eighties, his voice surprisingly good. These songs are depressing: "Tainted Love" by Soft Cell, "Don't You Want Me Baby" by The Human League, and "Hard Habit to Break" by Chicago.

I finally ask, "What exactly are we listening to?"

"It's a break-up tape. It was a thing back in the day. Somebody would do you wrong. You slam back with a mixed-tape so they know exactly what they're missing."

"Pointed."

He taps the eject button and hands the cassette tape to me. The writing across the top is faded, but it clearly says: EAT SHIT, CRAIG!

"Craig's my cousin. He's currently a coach for professional surfers in Maui. The guy rips. You wouldn't believe it."

"Nothing shocks me about you and your family."

"We're a motley crew."

I think of his mother and nod. "Sure are . . . "

Pearson parks in a cow pasture. I step carefully through the tall grass, farm girl proud, and say, "Be careful of the patties."

"The what?"

"Cow poop, Pearson!"

"Everyone poops," he says like a toddler. "Except my mother."

This cracks me up. Maybe Pearson could be somebody I'd go out with. I'm not sure why I didn't see it before. Music pulsates into the fog. We walk past the tall rows of corn and through the wide barn doors. My nose tickles with the delicate perfume of keg beer, sweat, and horse manure. Every kid within a forty-mile radius is here because when it comes to entertainment:

This. Is. It.

"Okay, so we're going to stay healthy here tonight. One beer."

"This coming from you. I seem to recall—"

"Listen, that was before we were in training."

"Pearson, have you ever differentiated on summer kid or local-yokel via people's hands?"

"What the hell are you talking about, Clem?"

I tip my head back to meet his eyes and gesture across the room. "Beau Routhier's over by the keg, small hands moving as quickly with the tap as they do when he hauls lobster traps with Paddy O'Malley. Paddy's a basketball player, and his hands are so big he could palm your head if he decided to. And look, Pearson. My own fingers were painted perfect blueberry blue hours ago in preparation for tomorrow's commercial shoot, but I've already chipped my middle finger." I flip him the bird. "I'm not meant for commercial greatness."

"You are one of the weirdest girls I ever met."

"I'm going to go find Renée. She's supposed to be here. I'll see you in a bit."

"One beer."

"Got it. One beer."

I scan the room for Renée.

But someone else catches my eye.

In the shadow toward the back of the barn, a guy runs his hands through shiny dark hair. His shoulders are the same as the Starstealer's, wide and impressive. I rush forward and grab his arm. Even though it's been over a month, I haven't forgotten him. I forced Renée to go to the Clam Festival in Yarmouth and to the Lobster Festival in Rockland. It seems the dude doesn't like crustaceans because he wasn't there. The good news is I've spent so much time at shooting ranges, I've got a closet full of carnival toys: a giant green alien, a big yellow duck, and an obscene-looking banana.

"I found you!"

My mistake is obvious, because this guy not only has googly eyes but a full-blown goatee. The dude holds out an icy cold keg beer for me. I blink, not sure how I made the mistake. "Just one," I raise the cup into the air. "Gotta work tomorrow."

"Right," The Starstealer wannabe and I toast, "Summah."

The beer floats down my gullet with such easy abandon I find myself having a good time. It's like the ghost of the Starstealer *is here*, making the entire night better. Inspired, I join the games. I play some pong, kicking both Paddy's and the local queen bee Sierra's butts. I've got a mean toss! I join Beau for ring on a string, a ridiculous game that involves shooting a brass ring tied to a long string to a hook on the barn wall. Success is all about the arc. It's true: physics can be your friend.

At the keg, I decide to have one more beer. I listen as two girls gossip about Pearson.

"Did you see that Pearson Smith is here?"

"He's a man whore."

"Right . . . because he lives in . . . "

I strain to hear more, but they're gone.

I take a few tentative sips of beer, looking for the girls, maybe looking for Pearson, when it happens. *My* summer song comes on.

Justin Timberlake's "Can't Stop the Feeling."

I set my beer down next to a wrench set on a paint-spotted workbench. My hips start moving, my head bobs, and my arms get into it. Happiness. Just thinking about the festival and dancing pulls up my spirit. Everything this summer is going to work out exactly like it's supposed to. I know this. Other people feel it too, and, before I know it, shoulders are against mine, hip meet hips, and we're all dancing together.

Out of the dancing crowd comes Seb Michaud, swimming in an oversized sweatshirt. I find myself analyzing the way his knobby knees seem to smile and wink at me as he dances forward. Sebastian, Sebby, Michaud Pishoo. He's a fixture in Mount Blanc. He's skinnier than the last time I saw him. Taller, too.

The crowd clears for him. He owns his space, making all of these horrible dance moves. Never one to let a dance circle leave me behind, I groove out to him. He points to me, and I unleash my dance beast. He surprisingly matches my steps, but the top of his body is so loose, it looks totally different when he attempts my moves.

"Stop! You're killing me."

He pulls me into a quick hug. "Clammy-Clemmy, good to see you." I groan when he uses my stupid old nickname that made me cry back in sixth grade. A year no girl wants to be compared to a mollusk.

Pearson points to his watch, "Fifteen more minutes, Fountaine!"

"Yes, sir!" I salute him, pulling Seb from the dance floor.

Seb whistles. "You and Smith? I can't see it but, whatever . . . Rich boys rule the world."

"Stop it. If you need to know, he's my new trainer."

"Well, okay," Seb laughs. "I'll try not to envision . . . " He picks up a red Solo cup, pumps the keg, twisting with a quick flip of his wrist to reduce the foam. It's pretty much party perfect.

He offers it to me.

"Why not?" My words slur so it sounds more like, "Wear shot."

Seb rubs at the few whiskers poking their way through his chin, little barbs on a sad cactus plant. His ash blond curls have turned darker, making his face seem paler. But he still has adorable freckles speckling his nose, and his eyes are the same shade as a granite pebble Trace once found at La Jolla Beach. Fondness for him overtakes my thoughts. I remember the storm last summer and how he'd pulled over to the side of the road to pick me up. The cab of his truck was Templeton's hidey hole with empty chips bags and dried apple cores rolling around the floor, but I appreciated the warm air pumping through the vent and the assured way he held the wheel.

"I'm glad to see you. Is your dad hiring?"

"The rakers arrived. Why don't you swing by and talk to José Luis?"

"Doesn't seem fair. We've got a bunch of guys who'd like the work right here in Mount Blanc, but instead you guys import the Mexicans, like we import the avocados."

My eyebrows shoot up my forehead. "My God. Did you really just say that? Walk away from me right now. That's not okay."

"Listen, I'm sorry. It came out wrong . . . "

My shirt sticks to my back, and the room feels like it's closing in on me. I give Seb's arm a squeeze. "No worries, swing by tomorrow or the next day. We'll see what we can do. Okay?"

"Sure, I appreciate that."

I twist backwards, spilling some kid's beer all over his sneakers. Somebody yells, "Party foul, blueberry girl!" The room tilts; my stomach lurches. I'm going to throw up. I dive across the dance floor, pulsating under the weight of kids jumping in unison. Paddy has ripped off his shirt and is whipping it through the air. I search for Pearson, but it's gotten so crowded I can't find him anywhere.

Somebody lifts a beer bong in front of me. I shake my head and dive for the back door.

Outside, the air is cool. I tilt my head up and take in the Milky Way. The stars are bigger in Maine. They pepper the sky, dazzling tea lights, little pockets of wonder. It feels good to be with the stars. I grab the door handle to go back in, but somebody must have locked it. I slam my fist on the door, but the music is too loud for anybody to hear me. I try to bushwhack through the thicket, but I'm stopped by prickle burrs tangling in my long hair. When I finally get around the corner of the barn, I walk over to where we parked and can't find the Wagoneer anywhere.

He *left* me. People are always freaking leaving me.

I should have known never to trust a Smith. Tilting my head to the universe, I yell, "Mémère, I know. Pay too little. Expect too much."

I fumble with my phone. It goes straight to Renée's voicemail. Where is she?

I start the long trek, away from the pulsating barn, around the cow patties, down the long dirt road toward home. My stomach clenches. I lean on both my knees as the beer steadies itself at the back of my throat. A truck's headlight blinds me. I throw up for real. The truck pulls to a stop. A door slams. Footsteps come closer.

"I'm okay. Nothing to see here," I wipe my mouth with the back of my hand.

"Clementine?"

I recognize that voice.

"Oh, Jaysus . . . "

I moan, stepping closer to the light to see José Luis standing there with both hands on his hips. "You came? Like every year. The rakers. Like clockwork . . . " I'm spewing garbage. "Oh, did Rosa make it? I've been worried. Did you know I saw her, I helped. It was a long time ago, at the start of summer. When I had California on my mind. José Luis, did you know I'm auditioning for a dance intensive. Shhh . . . it's a secret."

José Luis clicks his tongue and motions me away from the ditch with his nimble fingers.

"Come! Time for rest."

I lean over and puke again. It splats on a rock, reverberating back at me and hitting my bare legs. *Gross! Gross! Gross!*

"She's having a hard time," José Luis yells to a figure standing in the shadows and gives me a hand out of the ditch. I take it. It's rough and dry, full of calluses. José Luis pats me on the back. "The morning isn't going to be your friend."

I climb into the passenger side of the truck and rest my head against the cool glass window. The person in the truck cab stays very still, doesn't say a word.

A text pops in.

> Pearson: *I thought you left. You okay? I'm worried about you. Should I come back?*

"Look, it's my boyfriend." I hold up the camera in the perfect selfie position. I give my lips a little L.A. pout and *click*. I inspect the picture and hit send.

"He's slick. Like a racehorse. And his socks match. Always. But there is another boy . . . "

José Luis shakes his head. "Oh, Miss Fountaine."

"Oh, José Luis. How did you know?"

I look down. Seven missed calls from Pearson. "*Shoooot.* Pearson called my dad, right?"

José Luis purses his lips. "Technology is useful."

My head spins. My mouth's sour. I lean it against the car window.

The voice from the backseat whispers, "I thought you were a nice girl, Clementine Fountaine."

"Hah!" I say, mostly to myself. "You thought wrong."

Later that night, I get up for water. I pad down the long hallway to the little nook overlooking the raker village. It's dark, except for a single cabin, its window glowing gold. Somebody's awake like me. It's tough to sleep in a new bed for the first time, to adjust to the shadows of the moonlight. I send the person good energy and a nice puff of blueberry magic, turn, and get back in bed.

chapter five ♡

DESPITE THE RIDICULOUS HOUR of 6 a.m., the farm's buzzing with the rumble of four-wheelers and trucks getting ready. The barn door slams. Roscoe howls. Laurel Hollow Farm is ready to harvest the berries, even if I'm not ready to sell them. My bed is an island. I don't want to leave. I've slept in my clothes. My tongue is furry and thick. My necklace is caught in my hair. I yank it free carefully, making sure not to break it, rubbing my fingers along the three stones but finding no comfort in it.

Last night was a systematic shit show . . .

I recall José Luis dropping me off at the house last night, telling me he had to get to bed to be up early tomorrow morning. The quiet raker in the back seat: *judgy, judgy.* The way I hung my head out the window, in case I had to vomit *again.*

When I came home, Dad acted like it was no biggie. He didn't even get up from watching Canadian television. He called out to me, "Hope it's okay I had José Luis pick you up. We were having a cup of coffee when the call came and Pearson said his car broke down. José Luis wanted to grab some snacks at Cumby's. I wanted to watch this documentary about the Micmac tribe, so it all worked out."

"Sure did!" I tip-toe out of the room.

"How was the movie?"

"Great," I lied from the hallway.

"Really like that Smith kid!"

"Don't I know it . . ." I slurred.

My phone is charged and ready to go. The calendar mocks me: thirty-two days until the audition. Thirty-two days until I find out whether the path to the rest of my life starts with a single dance or crashes and burns into a pit filled with other farming students at the University of Maine. And all I'm doing is screwing it all up.

Pearson texted me four times throughout last night:

P: *You okay?*

P: *I'm worried about you.*

P: *He launched* Find Your Friends. *He's going to get you. I'm sorry. Need to have the Wagoneer back by eleven or my mom takes it for a week.*

P: *Your dancing last night, Clem… You're amazing.*

I reread Pearson's last line. Yes, my dancing is amazing. *Why wouldn't it be?* I've done it for my entire life. Or did he mean: I'm amazing. *Shit,* I can't think now. I force my aching body out of bed and pad down the floor to the bathroom. The reflection that greets me in the mirror is nothing a seventeen-year-old girl about to shoot her first commercial wants to see. Black mascara raccoon eyes make me look ready for a football game. My pale skin is pee-green yellow in the light, like I'd somehow evolved into more lizard than human teen. My prickle burr event is evident via an angry welt on my right cheek, a red, slightly bloody half-moon.

Dammit, dammit. Pearson was right. Only one drink. Not two. Not three. Only one.

I rotate my torso in front of the mirror, trying to get blood moving into my head. Blood pumping feels better, so I get my head into it. My neck cracks and pops as my brain engages. There's a solution to every situation. I lie down on the floor and put my legs up the wall so I can think. It's calming.

I add a yogic *"Ommmm . . ."*

Dad pounds on the door.

"Mon chou! It's game time! Joanie will be here in 50 minutes. Go get breakfast and be ready to impress."

"I'm showering!"

"I don't hear the water."

"Dad, please." He doesn't walk away. "Leave me be, I'm making myself fabulous."

"Fine. Fine. I'll see you in a bit."

I rifle through my makeup for concealer or old Halloween face paint. I stop. Can you even put concealer on an open wound? I paw around the drawer with the tiny hotel shampoos, conditioners, and lotions. A gross old piece of dental floss is stuck on Mémère's old class ring. My stomach clenches, and bile pushes into my molars. I'm going to throw up again. I hover above the bowl; nothing happens.

There, I see my answer.

On top of the dented cupboard, next to a jar of questionable-looking blue bath salts, is a box of Hair Glow Blue #4 Dye. It's the color of my eyes and the blueberries. I dump the contents of the box into the sink. I pour the dried dye into a little bowl and stir with the plastic brush. I suck in my cheeks. A blue streak is what I need to divert attention away from, well, everything else. The comb runs first through my hair, getting out all of the snarls, plus a few stray burrs, which I toss in the toilet. They float around, little ducks of shame, reminding me of getting stuck outside, drunk and alone. It's true, "obnoxious" can be a noun. And I'm it.

Mémère's voice whispers in the hum of the overhead fan: *"You do know how to get yourself in a good predicament!"* She falls into a chuckle and disappears in the hum. Mom would say: *"Clementine*

Theresa Fountaine, what have you done now?" Aunt Vivi would say: *"Fuck it, you only live once."*

I sit on the toilet and set the phone timer for twenty-five minutes. I wait while the ghosts of my mistakes swirl around me, a micro tornado of devilish impulses, as my hair turns from black to blue.

Roscoe lays in the middle of the floor blissfully gnawing a rawhide bone. Johnny's drinking coffee at the kitchen island. He's unbuttoned his border patrol uniform, showing off his surprisingly hairy chest and a gold necklace of Saint Thomas More, the patron saint of civil servants. Dad spies my new hair and spits his coffee across the countertop. He's at me in a split second, a seagull stalking an open bag of chips. He walks around me, beady eyes squinting, head bobbing, his lips looking like he was ready to give me a good peck.

"What in the hell were you thinking, Clem? Blue hair? Come on! It's not what somebody from Maine does."

"It was a surprise for you. I thought you'd like it. It matches the blueberries and my eyes." I lift the blue streak up over my head. "I think it'll be a nice touch for today. You know, a little pizazz, that something something . . ."

"Don't you think we should've discussed something as significant as this? I take it very seriously, you know, for the brand."

"You're not the CEO of my hair." My voice sounds petulant and spoiled. I gnaw on a hangnail, about to say something about being seven months and four days from eighteen and a legal adult in the eyes of the world. Instead, I show my dimple. "Next time, I'll ask. Okay? Go . . . Go . . ." I hold my fist in the air and give a full St. Andrew's battle cry. "Team!"

Dad pushes his glasses up his straight nose and tries not to smile.

Johnny LaMonde points a Ski the East mug at us. "For what it's worth, I like it. It works for you, Clem."

"John, come on. You always take her side." Dad grabs an apple from our fruit bowl and polishes it on his Laurel Hollow T-shirt. Johnny snatches the apple from Dad and takes a huge bite. I grab it and bite the other side. We fist bump.

"I hate when you two do this. It's like you have the same brain." Dad pours more coffee, walks to the window to inspect the hot haze trapped in the hollows. José Luis walks onto the back patio holding a clipboard and a bottle of water. Dad meets him near the fire pit, leaving me and Johnny alone in the kitchen.

I wrap my arms around his wide chest. "Thank you."

"Don't pay him any mind . . . the papers came yesterday. He's sad and kind of mad and missing your mother."

Divorce papers? All so official. She's gone. He's here. I rub the worry bone on my sternum and arrange my necklace back into its spot. I can almost see the room like Mom would have had it if she were still here. Instead of three-day-old *Bangor Daily News* papers all over the counter, it'd be scrubbed clean with her homemade lemon cleaner. There'd be Mason jars filled with flowers from the cutting garden—black-eyed Susans, bachelor's buttons, or whatever was in season. Homemade muffins would be waiting for me in Mémère's old wooden basket, and the butter would be in the butter bell, not melting on a plate next to the toaster.

Johnny pats my back. "It'll all work out like it's supposed to."

Across the field, rakers head to the south side for harvest. José Luis rides across the barrens in the four-wheeler. Johnny joins Dad out on the patio, leaving me one more moment to think about my mom and wonder if she ever thinks of me.

After Renée and her mother, Joanie, work magic on my hair and makeup, and the scratch is hidden beneath a layer of I-don't-know-what, I'm ready. My hair is in perfect blue/black formation down my back. I'm wearing a romper, the unfortunate combination of a dress and shorts, and my entire body has been powdered to perfection, so I will look silky white next to the deep green of the blueberry bushes for today's shoot.

Renée's wearing an oversized white men's shirt and short tan shorts. Her long hair is pulled up in a ponytail, bangs smoothed over her brows. No funky vintage. No bone jewelry. She's not wearing anything that's mine. She looks like a J.Crew model. She's normal. I'm kind of weird.

Joanie snaps her makeup case shut. "Clementine, don't you dare touch your face. Makeup isn't super glue. It won't last forever. Especially in this heat." She rubs her forehead with the back of her hand, looking so much like Renée, they could be sisters. "This summer, I tell you, it's raining or it's hot. Just won't give up."

"Mom. Seriously, it's the third time you told her about the makeup."

I grab my keys and pad across the floor, sticky with humidity, toward the door. "Joanie, you're a miracle worker. I got it."

"Like you two birds ever listen to anything I've ever told you."

Joanie is nothing like Mom, but she's so much like Mémère: a Jackie-of-all-trades, a no-nonsense, straight-talking badass. All the women in my family being gone makes me feel unmoored in the bay. I run back and hug her tight.

"What is this, honey?" Joanie pats my back like Johnny did.

"A 'thank you' for fixing me."

"You didn't need fixing, just polishing."

Renée whispers in my ear, "Maybe you need some intravenous hydration therapy. My cousin is an EMT. He might be able to come before you start?"

"I'm fine."

"I saw Beau this morning; he said you were *on fire* last night."

I touch my forearm and make a sizzling noise.

"Weirdo."

I toss keys at Renée, who is going to drive me the half-mile from the farmhouse to the shoot down by the ocean. I almost feel as if somebody's eyes are on me, watching me. Doesn't make sense. The only thing is the dirt road ahead of us and the blueberry plants surrounding us. Renée reads my mind. "You'll be fine. Every kid at that party last night is working."

Maine kids get it done, except Pearson.

I'll get it done.

She drives past the rakers scooping berries into the buckets with their Bouchard rakes—which isn't like a lawn rake, but more like a contraption you pull through bushes. Some rakers use an electric version, powered by a small engine, like a snowblower for blueberries. I search to see if there is anybody from the bus station, but nobody looks familiar. I'm lonely, but I don't know what for. I turn up the stereo loud, as though Jay-Z will fill the empty place in my heart. We pull in and park near an old stone well Dad covered up years ago. The camera is set to capture the sunlight as it crosses the tree line and a thin line of the bay.

Renée pulls to a stop, tapping her thumbs on the steering wheel. "Get outta here! Go commercial. The Muffin's catering the cookout, so I'll be back 'round three."

I settle into the scene.

Dad's missing.

Lou, our director here and in L.A., chews at the end of a pencil, muttering about off-location shoots, the elements, and the importance of finding good people in a world of bad. "Clementine, let me look at you. First, love the hair. It's fresh and interesting. Somehow, perfectly organic. Do you have your lines set?"

I nod.

"Perfect. It'll just be a few minutes. It's so bright that we needed more guys to hold the sun reflectors. I'm not sure what's up with this bloody heat. Awful. Isn't Maine supposed to be Vacationland? Did you know our motel didn't even have air conditioning? The lady told us to open our windows."

"Sorry," I croak.

"Get in position," Lou motions toward the large X spray-painted on the hay directly between the low bush blueberry bushes. The last remaining cloud seems to dissipate into the atmosphere. I blow air between my boobs to dry the building sweat. The smell of blueberries baking in the sun is heady and sweet—and slightly nauseating. The old Ford hauls at 40 mph around the perimeter of the field, which means my father is behind the wheel. He and Renée drive alike. Lawless lunatics.

The makeup is melting off my face.

I yell, "Let's go, Dad. It's hot!"

Dad tucks an $80 Brooks Brothers shirt into torn khaki shorts. I half-expect to see a couple kids from town, or maybe one of the guys from third shift at The Gullop (the fish processing plant in Bensonville) holding up reflectors. Instead, Dad points to two blueberry rakers about my age standing awkwardly at the edge of the photoshoot. I can't believe it, because once harvest starts, Dev Fountaine is all about harvest finishing. They don't say anything, so I don't either. He points to one after the next. "This is Felipe and Rico."

Felipe is stocky, with one of those grins that makes you want to smile back at him. He's rocking back and forth like he's won the raker lottery, but I see the earbuds in his ears and come to the conclusion he's dancing to a beat only he can hear. I wave to him. He waves back.

"Rico Santiago. S . . . Dad . . . It's our S!"

He's tough to see from this angle. I shift, embarrassed by my stupid outfit.

Lou calls, "Rico, stand over there, about five feet from Clementine."

Rico moves. Our eyes meet. I see something there, a flash of recognition, before he looks away. It looks like the guy from the fair . . . holy balls, it's my *Starstealer!*

Or is it?

His mouth is a firm hard line, and he doesn't even look my way.

Maybe he's a mirage.

Those dark eyes.

A little figment of my imagination.

The line of his shoulders. The fantasy I've been waiting for.

Dad clears his throat. "You okay, Clem?"

"Yeah," I lie, pulling my eyes from Rico and finally focusing on Lou, who is looking at me like I've grown a third arm.

Dad fumbles with his backpack and pulls out a bottle of water. "Take a sip."

I can barely feel the liquid slipping down my throat. Rico seems to hide behind the reflector screen directly in front of his body, leaving me with only a view of his magnificent lower quads. I resist the urge to squeeze them like I'm testing a peach for ripeness. This is my greatest dream come true. He is here.

The sun blazes hot. My eyes are dry. Sweat pools in places I don't even want to talk about, and now everyone's staring at me. Lou twists his Dodgers cap forward. "One, two, three . . . action!"

The camera light turns from red to green. "Hello, my name is Clementine Fountaine, and this is Laurel Hollow Farm. Our blueberries are . . . made fresh from nature . . . "

I don't want to do this in front of Rico.

"My name is . . . "

Dad shakes his head. "Do it again. Be natural."

"Hello, my name is Clementine Fountaine and this is . . . " A crow caws loudly from the pine tree across the way, and Lou shuts it down again. Pressure builds in the back of my head.

Rico looks at the birds like I don't exist.

"Cut!"

"Again!"

"Come on, *mon chou!*" Dad cheers me on like he did when I was the worst soccer player on the field, my sport before dance drew me in and claimed me.

The sun is getting higher in the sky. My headache pounds deep into the base of my skull. It says, *Too many beers.* Did Renée's mom add weights to my fake lashes? Why did I ever say *yes* to this.

"Action!" Lou yells.

"My name is Clementine Fountaine, and this is the Laurel Hollow Farm." I smile as the camera pans the horizon. I pick a single blueberry. "And this little blueberry has more antioxidants than any other fruit . . . " I stumble, unable to concentrate. I lean onto my knees to stop the swirling of the world. Blueberries rush toward me. A hand moves into my line of vision, and the world goes dark. When I finally come to, I keep my eyes closed, a lame action to make this all go away.

"It's heat exhaustion!"

"No. She's hungover!"

"She's dehydrated." Dad's hand cradles my head, his fingers firmly pressing on the underside of my skull, a physical reminder for me to get it together. I turn toward Rico. He gives me the smile that I remember so well from the shooting range. He's telling me to do it. So I do.

I pick my crumbling bones up off the ground, flick a few pieces of hay from my jumper. "Lou! Let's do it again. I'm ready." I glance at Rico, who's now busy doing his job. "I'm ready for anything."

chapter six ♡

I'M FLOATING BETWEEN SLEEP *and wakefulness, enjoying a dream so vivid I don't want it to end. It's me and Rico. We're in a dory rowing across the bay. I listen to the groan of the oars in their sockets, the seagulls cawing from above, and the chug of a lobster boat rounding the bend. Rico's strokes are smooth and strong. We pick up speed, cutting through the waves toward Mallagauh Island. My face tips toward the sun. I'm enveloped in the swirl of positive ions spitting from the Atlantic and the face of my Starstealer looking back at me.*

Roscoe howls from outside my window. My eyes fling open, disoriented. My pajama pants scrunched up my thighs. My headache has finally dissipated into a dull *ping*. Directly next to my bed is a cooler full of coconut and pineapple juice blends, Poland Spring water and wedges of watermelon. I want to crawl back into my dream and live there forever.

I remember.

Starstealer.

Here.

On the farm.

I jump out of bed and put music on, vintage Rolling Stones. "Gimme Shelter." Powder is still caked on my face, and I look like a long-lost cast member of *The Addams Family*. I suck in my cheeks, expand them like a blowfish. *What to do. What to do.* First, I wipe the old makeup off, letting the cut on my cheek get some air. It's red, but not infected. I coat a layer of mascara onto my eyelashes and smear a hint of tinted gloss over my lips. I plop down at my makeup table and twist my hair into a high ponytail. I rip off my pajamas, pull on cut-off jeans shorts and a Dodgers sweatshirt, and *bam*, back to Americana.

With twenty minutes left before the picnic, I FaceTime Trace. Her normally curly hair is pulled under a white cap, and a wide lace collar is tied at her throat. She's pure Pilgrim, and I can barely stand it.

"What up?" she asks, like it's perfectly normal to be dressed like a character from a Thanksgiving napkin.

"Other than your outfit? Wow."

Trace wrinkles her nose, and her voice clips old English. "You do not know the devil goes about in my likeness to do any hurt— that's Sarah Osbourne's quote, you know, the real witch—but if thee makes fun of me . . . my likeness will come to Massachusetts North and kick your ass."

"Maine has not been a part of Massachusetts for a long time."

"No matter . . . " She takes a sip of Coke. "How are you? You seem . . . too happy. I don't like it."

"You're never going to believe what happened."

"Do tell . . . "

I tilt toward the phone so she can see my eyes. "The guy I've been obsessing about all summer is on the farm. He's here. He's a raker."

"Listen, you've got to get this through your head. It's one thing to do a little slumming; it's something different to be lusting after the pool boy. Trust me, both my mom and my sister have done the deed with ours and, before you know it, you've got green slime growing all the way down the pool, and he's eating all of your hummus and hanging out in your study watching too much Netflix."

"Trace, this is awful. He's . . . we . . . it's not like that."

"Happened in my house. Maybe you're still rebounding from that butthead Travis. You know what they say about rebound boys?"

"Best served on toast," we quote a line from her first feature movie, *Girl Child*. We sit quiet for a minute until Trace says, "Remember ninth grade, before I was working all the time? It was the best . . . "

"When we had Miss Pippin. The perfect British drama teacher."

Trace breaks into a perfect Yorkshire accent. "Children! Children! We must focus on our arithmetic!"

"You're a nut."

"Dude, you know I'm right. It's never okay to hook up with an employee. It goes bad every single time."

"It's fine! We are all the same here in Maine. If not, you'd never go out with anybody."

"Whatever, girl . . . " She looks up from the screen. "Okay, okay . . . they're ready for me."

I press Sandrine Fountaine into Google, wait to see the regular picture of her appear. I'm shocked to see a new headshot. She's dressed in black. There's a brooding yet mysterious look upon her face. I click on it. *Publishers Weekly*. Her poetry debut, "The Seasons We Live," will be published by Festers Press forthcoming in the fall of 2017. I get up from my bed, fold myself into a plank position, and hold for thirty.

The night is perfect August, the only time of the year where the sky can turn into a true turquoise and the long afternoon light makes the sharp edges of the farm seem more like a painting than an actual place. My heart beats faster than normal in anticipation of seeing Rico.

But, I don't.

He's not milling around with the rakers waiting for dinner. I don't see him playing soccer with the guys across the field. And I don't see him walking the path from the southern raker village of Camp III.

Dad eagerly shakes each raker's hand. A group of girls, a little older than me, are sitting at a picnic table, so like Mémère and Aunt Vivi always did. I tentatively go up to them. I want to ask, *Where's Rico?* Instead, I smile and shake one hand after the next. At the next table, I finally see Rosa. Her long hair is twisted into a low braid, showing off her amazing cheekbones. She's sitting quietly at the end of the table. There's a pinched look around her mouth, I don't remember it from the start of summer.

I rush over to her. "Omigod. Welcome. I've been thinking about you . . . How was strawberry season? How's your boyfriend?"

Her eyes focus across the picnic. I twist to see what she's looking at, but I can't see. She's lost weight. "We broke up . . . " I step backwards, surprised by her cold tone. Rosa clears her throat, her eyes darting around the picnic as if looking for an escape. I follow her gaze. The very guy from the bus station is standing by José Luis and my dad. I take a step closer. Dad points to the road out of town. Rosa's eyes get glassy. She's going to cry.

Renée calls from the buffet, a pair of tongs dangling from her hand. "Clementine, get over here. We're gettin' ready."

"What's going on, Rosa?"

"Nothing . . . my friend, Pulga, he's leaving."

Across the way, the migrant worker slowly walks over to José Luis's truck and gets in.

Rosa and I watch as they drive out of Laurel Hollow, destination unknown.

My father rings the giant cowbell hanging from our back porch and raises his lemonade into the air. "Welcome to the sixty-seventh year at Laurel Hollow Farm." He waits for the applause and gets it. "We're so pleased to have you. It makes me *mucho contento.*"

"Not the Spanish." Renée hands me a potato salad spoon.

"Right?" I whisper back.

Dad continues, "While you are here, Laurel Hollow is your home."

A ripple runs through the crowd. Somebody mentions Pulga's name. An odd stillness follows. Something is wrong. Felipe is shaking his head no. I search for Rico, as if seeing him will give me the answers to what's going on. But, he's nowhere to be seen.

Dad continues, "I believe you don't get anything you don't work hard for. I'm expecting excellence in all things . . . "

My dance muscles constrict. Some of the older rakers whisper something to each other in Spanish. Another raker softly pats Rosa's back. I'm moving toward Dad before I even make a decision as to what my plan is. I jog up next to him and smile wide. "My grandmother, *Mémère*, always said here at Laurel Hollow . . . *Cuando llegan los problemas, es tu familia la que te apoya.*" I smile, hoping I get it right. "When trouble comes, it's your family that supports you . . . Please, consider this your home for the season. Let us know if you need anything. We're here for you."

"So, please," Dad shouts, "Enjoy your time here at the farm. Let's do it!"

The sun dips lower in the sky. The crowd clears. I finally see Rico. He's leaning against the barn, hair tucked behind his ears, legs crossed in his loose Levi's, hands fiddling with a long piece of grass. I move toward him, but Renée calls me back to the buffet line. I scoop potato salad onto plates. I grab more watermelon. I scan the crowd one more time, looking from each happily eating raker to the next. Rico is no longer there. Neither is Rosa. They've disappeared.

Pearson is surprisingly light on his feet for somebody over six feet tall, big boned and bulky. I jog next to him, meeting his pace step-by-step, before pushing forward for the first time ever, leading the way. I'm running away from all things yesterday, from blue hair and white chalky makeup, from Rosa stealing the guy I've been waiting for all summer. I'm running from lies—the lies I tell my father, the lies I tell myself.

The air changes the closer we get to the ocean, a phenomenon best described by my father on a trip to Kansas City, where he described living in Down East Maine as the intersection of dripping hot fudge and a single scoop of homemade vanilla ice cream. My Maine lungs like it. They push me further down the peninsula, where there's only one place to stop.

The beams of glowing, cascading light cut by the tall pines remind me of being on stage, ducking in and out of light. My feet pick a spot, grazing over lumpy root systems and emerald green forest moss. Ahead, the land juts out like a square thumb; its nail is a tiny cottage, buttoned-up tight. It hasn't been painted for years, and the wood is a defiant gray.

Pearson practically collapses into the clearing. "My God, what happened to you? That wasn't a jog, that was a sprint. I bet you were doing a sub-six." He pushes sweaty dark hair away from his forehead, making it stand on edge. His face is flushed and blotchy, making his wide eyes somehow brighter. He gives a crooked smile and pulls off his sweatshirt, giving me a faint glimpse of his abs. He did it on purpose, I know it. He knows it too and laughs. I push the secret shingle where Grandpa created a hidey-hole and snag the rusty brass key from the hook.

"This tiny house used to sit out on Little Ruggles Island. And one year, when the bay froze solid, my grandfather and a bunch of his friends put it on skis and hauled it here."

"Maine . . . "

"Maine . . . " I slip into a Down East accent. "Don't wanna have anything go to waste. Use it up. Do it. Make it right." I shove the key into the lock.

"Before we go in," Pearson stops me. "Is everything all right at Laurel Hollow last night? Your dad called my dad while we were playing golf. Dad went right into work mode, something about missing paperwork."

My ears perk up. *Pulga*? "I think they asked a raker to leave . . . I'm not sure what happened, though. He had a nickname, Pulga. Flea in Spanish. I don't know his real name."

"Must be hard."

"It is . . ."

This softness around Pearson, it's something I didn't expect. Like he's evolved into a better person than he was before. He's everything you could want in a summer boyfriend—handsome, attentive, athletic. But something is holding me back, and his name is Rico—or more specifically the ghost of the feeling when I was with Rico, under the tree.

Pearson takes a step closer to me, crunching his feet on layers of old mussel shells, hard seagull poop, and a couple of dried-out old clam shells. He fiddles with the key, his tongue sticking out of his mouth in concentration. There's a small *click,* and the sharp tangy bite of turpentine mixed with musty air itches my nose. I'm surprised when tears bubble into the corner of my eyes, melting into my sweaty cheeks.

Mémère's studio.

The thin pine floor groans under Pearson's footsteps. He moves toward the single easel holding her last painting, an incomplete seascape of only turquoise blues and sharp greens. Paintings are stacked, ten deep, one after the other. I watch his face, wanting Mémère to be respected for who she was in my world, not his. His brows furrow together, his head dips forward, studying with a surprising intensity.

"I've taken art history classes. These are good, Clem. Real good." He pulls a painting from the back of the stack. "Look . . . "

My mouth clamps together. I'm afraid if I say anything, I'll cry again, but this time, my tears will be angry, snotty tears. And I don't even know why I care what he thinks at all, because it's not like that between Pearson and me. He continues, his voice getting more animated, until I finally smile.

"Take, for instance, this one. Do you see how she uses abstract expressionism to represent the mussel shell's natural defiance in a world where getting eaten for lunch is a real problem?"

"It is precarious to be a mussel."

"Right. You have such a stand-up family. Your grandmother was a painter, your mom is a writer, and you're a dancer. All cool stuff . . . "

"She also worked for your family."

"Oh, a salty tone." He turns to another pile of paintings. "Doesn't make me feel weird. You?"

"I dunno." I touch her dried-out paintbrushes, arranged in tall blood-orange plastic cups decorated with raised golden mushrooms. I rub my finger along a shiitake. Classic, Mémère: *"Don't throw it out if it's still good. You'll find a use for it."* The same is true for the seemingly hundreds of tubes of oil paint still sitting here, waiting for her to come back.

But she won't. Just like my mom.

"You ready?" he asks. "Gotta keep the blood pumping."

"Yeah. Sure. One minute."

Pearson's eyes are on me as I flip through the paintings, from an intensive study of a lobster tail to a landscape of the lilacs in bloom. Mémère interests were always hard to follow. I flip to one more painting and stop. The dried sweat on my skin makes me suddenly shiver. After all of the abstracts, this piece is concrete and real. It's a raker, over in the corner of this very room, sitting next to the window overlooking the Atlantic. His hair is short, pushed away from his face, accenting his large eyes. His shoulders are bare. It's painted with such care, as if Mémère knew this person. I lift it toward the window, looking for her signature in the bottom right hand corner. It's her maiden name: St. Hillaire. Who is he? He reminds me of Rico, the strong cut of his chin, the angles of his cheekbones. I place the painting in the back of the stack and walk toward Pearson, who's now waiting for me out on the little deck.

"Okay, ready for the run back?"

He lifts an eyebrow. "Yeah, but maybe this time we could take it easy. You've got twenty-nine days till go time; you don't want to pull a muscle. Have you made your travel plans? New York is expensive. My buddy, Davis, he ordered a bottled water, and it cost twenty dollars. Twenty dollars for water."

"I hadn't even thought of travel plans . . . that's such a good point."

"All you need to do is tell your dad. He'll pay, right?"

"Zero sign of that right now . . . he wants me to go to college for agribusiness."

"That's rich . . . " Pearson laughs. "I mean, you're farmy, not farmish. I saw farmish girls at the fair; they've got more hay in their hair than you."

"Pearson."

"Clem."

"Don't be a douche."

"I'll try not to be a douche."

I tip my head and meet his eye. "Good. Thank you for caring about my audition. It helps having somebody else here besides Renée know about it."

"It's nothing, Fountaine." And starts jogging toward the woods.

"Rico, can you stack the rakes?"

I trip over Roscoe to get to the window, spying through a gauzy curtain, and all thoughts of going out with Pearson disappear into the abyss. Rico's hair is longer than Starstealer's, pulled away from his face, man-bun style. It's a look I've made fun of in the past, but on him . . . It. Just. Works. Rico seems taller, too, but that could be my angle or he could have grown. I lean a little further out the window, growing bolder. The dancer in me likes how he moves, keeping his core straight. Rico gathers a few blueberry rakes at a time and carefully places them in the back of the truck, his biceps flexed and defined. Roscoe saunters up to him, tail wagging in excitement. Rico rubs his ears, making the dog groan in pleasure. And I'm melting. Melting for this boy.

"Afternoon!" I yell.

Rico pretends not to see me, but I know he does by the way his mouth is fighting back a smile. I lean further out the window. "I said, 'Hey.'" He drops a rake into the back of the truck. He tips his head to me. "I said, 'hey, do we know each other?'"

He doesn't pause. "Nope. Don't think so."

"Kind of weird, because I'm sure we've met before."

He turns away. Body Language 101: If a dude turns his back to you, he's saying, 1) he's not interested and 2) he's not interested.

I catch a glance at myself in the mirror. I'm vile. Bedhead. Mascara smudge. My T-shirt is bright neon orange with a donkey head screaming, "Hee Haw!" No girl, I repeat, *no* girl is getting a guy with this lame excuse of a look. I pull my index finger under my eyes, something that would've made my mother yell, "*You'll regret that in your forties*," and suck in my boobs, so they don't press against the donkey, because hee-haw donkey boobs aren't sexy. They're not.

Much better. I'll try again.

"Do you need help? I can help you!"

He laughs, like me helping on my own farm was funny, making me want to clock him in the back of the head.

He covers his eyes with a hand to see better.

"I'm doing my job."

There's something about his voice, a little touch of California. *It's him! Why in the heck won't he admit it?*

The party! Oh, shit, shit, shit! The party! I snatch my phone from the charger. I open the selfie I sent to Pearson where I'm in my full drunken glory: bra strap showing, eyes glazed and dull, fresh blood on my cheek from scratching my face in the thicket. Those words . . .

"*I thought you were a* nice *girl, Clementine Fountaine.*"

"Did you pick me up with José Luis the other night?"

Rico turns his baseball hat around and leans against the truck. "Yeah, I was there."

"I thought we hadn't met before?"

"Did you want me to bring it up?"

"No."

A smile plastered on my face, I belt out the window. "Lemme make it up to you." He opens his mouth and gets only to "n—" when I interrupt him. "Great. I'll be right down."

I grab ripped jeans from my floor and a Laurel Hollow T-shirt from the clean laundry stacked on my bureau. I lace up an old pair of Timberland work boots. I rush down the back staircase and out the door. Rico scratches the small cleft on his chin and points to the rakes.

"I thought you were joking."

"My farm! Let me help."

"Lead the way," Rico points to the pile of rakes next to the barn.

I grab a rake in each hand. He does, too. We move back and forth from the barn to the truck, like picnic ants. I measure my movements to his: our strides are close to the same, even though he is a good four or five inches taller than me. Rico glances at me, first out of the corner of his eye. "The other night, you talked about your boyfriend."

"I did? Pearson?" I rip away a stray fingernail, giving myself time to think. Did I tell Rico that Pearson was my boyfriend? My stomach turns. Shit. I did. "But Pearson isn't my . . . "

José Luis rounds the corner, a walkie-talkie in his left hand and a cup of coffee in his right. He stops short, looking from me to Rico. He clears his throat. "Rico, a word."

Rico places his final blueberry rake in the back of the truck and walks the ten feet to his boss. They talk low. I try to listen, straining from my spot. But there're two words I hear distinctly:

Stay and *away*. There's never been an invisible line on this farm, but things seem to have changed.

I toss a rake into the back of the truck, metal scraping metal, and it scares Roscoe. He bolts directly through the screen door to the safety of the farmhouse. When I turn back around, Rico and I lock eyes. There's only fifteen feet between us, but it may as well be a million miles.

chapter seven ♡

I NEED TO DANCE, to shake it all off. I march into the studio and start hauling blueberry crates into the yard, grabbing two at a time, pushing one after the next until I've finally cleared out a third of the space. I grab a broom and sweep dust into a pile, drag an old fan out of the corner, and turn it on high. I shove earbuds into my ears and push myself through my choreographed routine, a blended mix of modern with a few hip-hop nods. I keep missing the beat. It's like my dancing has lost its heart.

I twist to the ground, thinking of the plastic heart still stuck in the bottom of my sandal, frustration welling. Nothing is going as planned. Just nothing. I do the only thing I can; I grab two more blueberry crates and head to the door, only to find Dad and Johnny pointing toward the right corner of the barn. Dad takes a sip of coffee and shakes his hand at the sky.

"The damn roof is buckling again. These old things are such a bother. I feel like I just fixed it."

I toss the crates into a pile, wipe sweat off my face with the front of my shirt.

Johnny responds, "Dev, it's been twenty years since we fixed it last."

"Things don't last anymore . . . "

"True that," I whisper to myself. I wander to where my playset once stood, out in back of the barn, beside the apple orchard, twenty feet from the abandoned chicken coop. I press my foot into the ground, feeling for the cement underneath the grass. It once kept the whole thing from tipping over. Dad yanked the playset out of the ground after it all went down, when the promise of *her* was lost and Mom was gone. Now it's an underground gravestone.

I remember when we lost Amelie. The fruit hung heavy on the bush that summer, each day full of equal parts sunshine and shade. Humidity was non-existent, since the ocean breeze cooled the air perfectly. Harvest felt easy and comfortable with the rakers buoyed by the sheer weight of the fruit. I'd finished dance practice and was heading to the kitchen for a sandwich, probably peanut butter, honey, and banana, which was my go-to in 2014.

But I could have it all wrong. Maybe I was biding my time until darkness came, so I could run around with Seb and Renée or sneak down to the Dairy Bar for a loaded Nor' Easter, a disgusting combination of every single candy in the store, hot fudge, whipped cream, and a cherry. Regardless, I was oblivious. And self-centered. And I want to take it all back. I let the memory flow over me . . .

"Clementine, she's moving! Come quick…"

I dropped dance slippers and scurried down the hall to our sleeping porch, which is like a regular screened-in porch but set up so if you wanted to sleep outdoors, you could. And since we didn't have air conditioning, somebody often did.

Mom was on the chaise, her swollen ankles elevated, her face relaxed in the afternoon sun. She's flushed and round from pregnancy, calm in a way I'd never seen before. "It's okay, touch it…" She grabbed my hand and held it to her hard belly, and I could feel my sister, pitching and rolling inside.

"Only two more months."

Mom grabbed my hand, "I've waited so long for this. I can't believe it's finally happening."

"Right? I'm ready for Amelie to come."

"You're going to be the best big sister."

"I'm gonna try, Mom."

Later that night, I woke to screams and the house exploding in activity. Mémère, sick with cancer, running to the door and helping Mom to the Jeep. Johnny was there, like magic, and he stayed with us while my family raced through the darkness to Eastern Medical Center. My sister died soon after birth, the umbilical cord wrapped around her delicate neck. Johnny held me as I cried and cried because I didn't know how much I already loved her until she was gone.

After Mom lost Amelie, it's like the berries knew. It sounds crazy, but it's true. Every single one of them died on the bush, turning gray, tough, and mummified. The entire crop was lost.

If the summer had turned out differently, would we be where we are today? Maybe instead of writing in Mexico, Mom would be happily chasing my little sister over by the rusted-out playset, now long gone. Maybe I'd have my true life beat, and I wouldn't be struggling with my steps.

My hand shifts over my necklace. One diamond for Mom, one for me, one for Amelie . . .

Johnny swats a fly away from his badge. "The roof needs some reinforcements, Dev. If you wait until this weekend, I'll get up there with you to patch it up."

Dad purses his lips together. "Let's wish for no rain between now and then."

The word 'reinforcements' sticks in my head. Maybe that's what pulled me to the Starstealer in the first place, the reason I dove into the strawberry game: because it was for his sister.

In the far corner of the barn is a stray soccer ball. I jog over and pick it up, an idea growing in the back of my head. If I can play soccer, I could play with the rakers. I could play with Rico. I pop the ball on one knee to the next. I kick it toward a crack in the foundation, gaining confidence with each hit. *Boom. Boom. Boom.*

Felipe comes out of the barn holding a new roll of boundary tape and some stakes.

"Clem, you play?"

"Hell yeah, I do." I try to pop the ball into the air, but instead it falls directly between us. Felipe laughs and drops the tape. He's all smiles, rocking his body back and forth like it's a competition. He knocks the ball a couple of times between his knees, drops it to the ground, and kicks it from the corner of his foot directly toward me.

Nervous with him watching, I pull my foot back to kick it but hit it wrong, sending my foot folding across the top of the ball toward the ground. The weight of my body flips forward as my foot tips back. It twists with a horrifying whack, and a sharp pain moves up my leg.

"Oh shiiiiitttt . . ."

"You okay?" Felipe runs to me, kneeling toward my foot. He twists it back into place. I yelp. We both watch as it starts to swell purple and blue.

Felipe's brows scrunch together "I did this to you."

"I did this to myself. Go back to work. I'll ice it."

"You sure . . . ?"

"Yes, go."

Felipe looks across the fields. "We don't want any trouble. This job means a lot to us . . ."

"Felipe. My fault."

"You're the best, Clementine."

"That's what they tell me, Felipe. All the damn time."

I drag myself into the house, hopping on one foot down the back hallway to the kitchen. I fill a bag with ice, then limp over to the couch to elevate it. I pull off my sneaker, fling it toward the fireplace. My skinny ankle is bloated and purple. I stack three pillows high and rest my foot on top. The ice is jarring at first, causing me to inhale sharply before the cold oozes into my foot. Hot frustrated tears brim at the corner of my eyes, but I push them back, gasping for air, as I stare at my phone's calendar. Twenty-six days. Plenty of time to heal. Plenty of time to prepare, I keep telling myself.

With nothing to do, I search for Rico Santiago on the web. He's nowhere to be found.

Like he doesn't even exist.

Dr. Plourde pokes and prods at my foot. "Wait it out, Clementine. It's a bad sprain. Give it a couple of days, and you'll be on the mend."

"I don't have a couple of days."

He snaps his folder shut and plops on a stool by the window. "How's your mental health?"

"Excuse me, I'm here for my ankle, not brain."

"For a girl your age, not having your mom. And . . . you seem a little . . . Let me think of the word. You seem a little chippy."

"Chippy? Is it a good thing?"

"Stressed. High-strung. Not relaxed. You seem a little chippy."

"This isn't about my mom. Why does everyone keep asking me that?"

This is about nothing going right for me this summer. I try to smile. Dr. Plourde has kind eyes and a room full of pictures of his kids and a jar of lollipops. So, I smile.

"I have my dad. That's all I need right now. I'm here for my ankle. I'm here to know if it's safe to dance on it."

"Listen to your body, that's my best advice. If it hurts, stay off it. If not, well . . . dance."

"I'm not the best listener, Dr. Plourde."

He laughs, "So your father told me."

"He's the pot calling the kettle..."

"You, Johnny, and your dad. You're all the same. Not a one of you listens."

I glance out the window in time to see Pearson jog down the street with Sierra Sanders.

I'm not sure how watching him and her makes me feel. *Is it confusion? Jealousy?* I'm not sure.

Dr. Plourde lifts my foot higher, taping it up tight. "Time is the greatest healer. Relax and see what comes next."

He reaches into a glass candy jar. "Grape or strawberry?"

"Strawberry, of course."

My ankle still hurts, but at least I can put pressure on it. I limp through the fog. It's stuck in every nook and cranny of Mount Blanc. It gathers around corners and catches on trees, resting diluted apparitions, too tired to go anywhere else. At the Beranger Library, I push into the large double doors. Inside the entryway, the smell of moldy books tickles my nose. I move down a long hallway full of mahogany cases, holding all kinds of weird treasures behind beveled glass—old Victorian dolls with still eyes and creepy smiles and a random shell collection from Mount Blanc's very own Mrs. Dora Bellevue.

I dip into the tall stacks, grabbing books from my reading list for senior year: *Return of the Native* and *Their Eyes Were Watching God.* I plop my backpack down on the table, skim through the *Return of the Native,* and come to the immediate conclusion I'm going to call my first-born son Diggory.

Ten feet from me some dude won't sit still in his work cubby, tapping his foot in a near constant rhythm. I read another sentence. How am I supposed to focus on Hardy with those soul-sucking tapping noises? There's a rustle, and the feet still, a scraping noise as a chair drags across the floor and a flash of familiar shoulders and longish dark hair.

Omigod.

Rico.

I sink low in my seat, covering my face with my book. He shoves a pencil behind an ear, gloriously oblivious to my stare, and heads out of the room—leaving everything behind. I consider the ten feet of space between me and his stuff. I glance past the magazine rack, toward the door Rico walked through. All I can hear is the slight hum of the air conditioning and the persistent *tick* of the beastly looking grandfather clock in the corner. "Rico, Rico, Rico . . ." I like how the sound rolls off my tongue. Not having the moral hesitation I should have by this time in my life, I limp across the room toward it. I grip the chair he sat in.

The view from his seat is much prettier than the spot I chose, where the only thing I can see is an old globe with a huge dent in Antarctica. Rico's view is different. It's like he's found the most visually perfect spot in the library. From here, you can see how the Boston fern drapes over the wooden stand and the mysterious smile of one of Mount Blanc's founding patrons, Adelle Le Duc, over the stone fireplace. Outside, the muted fog accents the old walnut tree in the courtyard, its limbs reaching to the sun like an Indian Buddha.

A creak of footsteps freezes me in my spot, but it's Ms. Laverdier from the Loon Nestle Gift Shop creeping toward nonfiction, leaving me with my friend called *temptation.*

Don't do it, I tell myself. It's an invasion of privacy. But my fingers have a life of their own and they dive into his things without a second thought.

Rico's laptop computer has gone to sleep. Books are piled all over the place: precalculus, world history, and psychology. *Tender Is the Night* by F. Scott Fitzgerald lies open in the center. I flip to the text highlighted in yellow marker: *You're the only girl I've seen for a long time that actually did look like something blooming.* "A romantic . . . "

I flick at the half-open backpack, creating a larger opening for me to inspect. There's a bottle of water and, in the pocket, a frayed photograph of a young Rico smiling from the lap of a woman who must be his grandmother, since they both have the same inky long lashes. The older woman's arms are tight around his skinny shoulders, and his head is thrown like she'd whispered the funniest joke in his ear. Ohhhh . . . he loves his grandmother.

The next picture is a toothy looking girl smiling wide at the camera. I flip the picture over and read the words on the back: Nina, age 5.

It's him!

"Seriously?" A voice hisses. Rico's voice.

I want the floor to open up, sending me to the bowels of the library, where ancient rotting books and old DVDs go to die. But it doesn't happen. I turn to face him, plastering a dry grin on my face. "I needed to borrow a pencil."

Rico looks like he's trying to decide how to deal with me. He opens his mouth to say one thing, shuts it, opens it again before shoving *Tender Is the Night* into his bag. He plucks the picture of Nina from my fingers.

"You don't need to be like that—" I whisper.

"Listen. I need my job."

I fight the urge to touch the perfection on his smooth skin, mixed with the right amount of boy stubble.

Madeleine Devoux, the librarian, rounds the corner glaring at both of us through thick glasses. For a librarian, this woman's got some voice modulation issues. She calls in her singsong voice, "Clementine, this isn't the place."

"It's okay . . . I'm leaving." Rico gathers his work.

I grip the table. "Don't leave because of me."

He leans toward me, voice low, in perfect library tone. "If I'd known you were Clementine Fountaine, I'd have never put down my ten dollars." He heads for the door. "I've got blueberries to pick."

Frantic with the thought of losing him again, I awkwardly limp after him, dragging my bad ankle behind me.

Madeleine Devoux gives me a harsh toddler *shush*, "Slow it down, Miss Fountaine!"

"Sorry. Can't."

Outside, the fog blurs the sight and hides the hunted. I pause on the corner of Main and Evans. On instinct, I head north, looking for the distinct, sharp edge of his shoulders. I'm rewarded by the outline of him, two hundred feet away, in front of Suds Laundromat. It doesn't take me long to catch up with him. I am motivated. I squeeze the tendon between his shoulders with my thumb and pointer finger, my personal version of the Vulcan grip, and hiss, "I can't believe you lied to me."

"Ow!" he yelps, crumpling under my grasp. I let go, immediately feeling like a psychopath. "Where'd you learn that?"

I take an awkward step backward. "Did I hurt you?"

"A little." He rubs the impact zone. "Didn't think you'd come after me. Now I know you better, you don't have boundaries."

"If I didn't have boundaries, I would've smacked you down for all the tapping. Me! I have self-control." My voice rises dangerously high. Frank Perron, from True Value Hardware, pounds on the window, yelling for us to beat it. I lower my voice and show Frank my dimples.

"See. Self-control."

"Right, like when you stole the strawberry! Exactly the moment I said to myself: law-abiding citizen."

"Dude. We earned the berry!" I wait for a family of tourists in matching yellow rain coats to pass before lowering my voice. "Why'd you lie to me? Why not say, 'Hey, fancy meeting you here?' You know, all chill."

Rico inhales deeply, as if he's considering the proper words before responding, and turns those expressive eyes up the street, like he's looking for a getaway car. I force my face to relax, starting with the angry squint of my eyes, the quiver in my cheek, before giving a cheeky half smile I sometimes use in Laurel Hollow promotions, a full combination of pretty innocence.

"Well . . ."

He tosses a lock of hair from his eye.

"What was I supposed to do? I show up here to work for my family, and *wham*, it's the girl from the fair drunk off her ass, screaming about . . . what's his name? Pearson?" *He's jealous.* I open my mouth to say something smart, but he continues: "And then there you are, surrounded by a film crew. You're not a normal girl."

I pretend to get busy looking at the Bouchard rakes in the window of the store, like I'm going to find the right thing between the mulch and the dog food. "I can't help it if my life isn't . . . I dunno . . . conventional."

He leans close to me. And I notice two more details about Rico: he's got the most beautiful under-lashes I've ever seen and a single freckle on his right cheek. "I guess I'll see you at the farm?" His voice lightens. "We can be friends. Okay?"

"Friends?" The word is dead on my tongue.

"There's nothing wrong with friends, chica."

I laugh, kind of manic. "Let's go have lunch. Come on, it's just food."

"Fine." His voice doesn't sound fine. This, I ignore, because I can very easily be the Queen of Denial. We make awkward talk for friends, who maybe aren't friends, heading on a date that's not a date. Five minutes later, The Muffin's lights cut through the soupy fog, a radioactive marvel. I hold the door open. He shakes his head. "Ladies first."

Renée kicks the kitchen door open, expertly carrying a bowl of chowder, a towering slice of lemon meringue pie, and a couple crab rolls to a maroon booth in the corner. She delivers the food like a pro and spies me. She snatches a couple of menus from an old milk crate and hightails it in our direction, effectively letting me skip the line.

Renée gives me a cool look before turning back to Rico. "And who're you?"

My grin is overenthusiastic. "This is my very own Sagadahoc Rhubarb Festival Starstealer."

Renée's pen hovers in the air, and I notice she's traced the veins on the top of her left hand with a red Sharpie marker. "Oh, right. Accomplice to the Great Strawberry Heist! I heard there's a warrant out for your arrest."

Rico shifts uncomfortably in his seat.

I grab his hand. "Kidding! She's kidding. Trust me, Johnny would know if there was a warrant out for our arrest."

"Yes. Strawberry accomplice. Mexican. Raker." He nods to Renée, which feels old fashioned and gives me a little warm feeling in my belly. "Rico."

"Right . . . so it's like you two are practically living together."

"Well, if you put it that way." A flush crawls up my neck and I give my head a quick shake. "Like, you know, the same property at least."

"Nah . . . I wouldn't say we're living together. She is in the big house and I'm in the small . . . it's more like a plantation in a way."

Renée raises an eyebrow. I brace for it. "Like slavery."

"No!" I yelp. "Not slavery. Jaysus, Renée! You make it sound horrible."

"Certainly," Renée agrees, pen poised over her pad. "What can I get you?"

Rico orders a grilled cheese and an A&W Root Beer. I order a BLT, French fries, a chocolate shake, and a side of coleslaw. Charlie frantically rings a bell at the order window, letting the entire restaurant know an order is up. Renée screams, "I hear you!" before rolling her eyes and getting back to work.

Rico leans closer to me, and I totally remember what it felt like to be sitting under a tree with him a couple of months ago. He's comfortable, like a fuzzy blanket or chocolate pie. I tuck my good leg under my butt to make me a little higher in the booth and lean forward.

"How'd you end up at my farm? It's time to fess up."

He lifts an eyebrow. "How did I end up on your farm? I dunno. Weird fate?"

"Let me guess, after you left me at the fair, you went to a fortune teller who told you exactly where I live. How perfect."

He fiddles with the sugar. "My father was a raker. He came to Maine a few years ago. He always said it was one of his favorite places on the whole East Coast."

Renée plops down my chocolate shake in a silver carafe, condensation thick on the side, and Rico's root beer before hustling off for another order.

The pause growing between us is oddly comforting, so I wait a minute before I say anything else. And when I do finally speak, my voice sounds wanting and vulnerable. "Why didn't you want to keep in touch?"

"It's hard to keep up with people, doing what I do. I start the year in Florida—strawberries, oranges, lemons. It's New Jersey in spring and Maine for summer." He's got a storyteller's voice, and I want him to keep talking for as long as possible, to make this moment last.

"Tell me about Nina."

Rico's dark eyes light up. He leans in closer, resting his hands on the table, only inches from my own, like he's about to tell me a secret. I push aside my shake and inch closer to him. His eyes are alive; I want to fall into them. "She loved the strawberry. Freaked out when it came." He fumbles with the zipper of his bag and pulls a picture out of the depths. "Nina on her birthday."

She's a kid with an impish jack-o-lantern grin sitting on a blue cooler holding the strawberry lopsided over her head like she's holding the gold medal at the Olympics.

"Adorable."

Rico plucks the picture from me. "She's a rascal."

I swallow hard.

Amelie would be almost two.

Deep in the depth of the booth, it's like we're back under the tree, me and him, with the entire world buzzing around us, and I can feel the spark growing. I *knew* it was there, I *knew* it!

This guy's energy *is* magic.

Renée sets Rico's grilled cheese down in front of him and assembles my food across the table. Rico plucks a packet of sugar from the holder and taps it on the table. I like the way his hands move. I like the smoothness of his skin. I like the crinkles around his eyes.

"What're you eating, Clem?"

I try to smile, but my lips feel stuck to my teeth. "Oh, *hi* Pearson." My butt squeezes deeper into the plastic seat, and I want to disappear. "This is Pearson. Pearson, meet Rico."

Pearson puffs his burly chest, not unlike the ridiculous rooster who attacked my Dad at the start of summer. "Nice to meet you."

"How're you feeling?" he asks, pulling the plate of fries away from me. "If you're not training, you should be at least filling your insides with good stuff."

Renée darts toward us, eyes flashing in defiance because she thinks despite Pearson's good looks, he's an ass-and-a-half. Especially after he hooked up with her friend Taja last summer and promptly ghosted her. Nothing I can tell her about him changes this opinion.

"Can I get you anything else? Pearson? Maybe a table of your own or you could sit at the counter," Renée points across the café. "There's a spot at the very end. Maybe you should go grab it for yourself."

We sit for a moment in silence, nobody touching the food. Rico's eyes move from me to Pearson, a slight quiver in his jaw.

Rico plops his grilled cheese onto the plate. "José Luis will be looking for me." He peels a ten from his wallet and leaves it on the table. I grab the money and try to hand it back to him.

"No, I'll get mine. This isn't a date or anything."

He gathers up his sandwich in a napkin and bolts for the door.

I squish around in my seat and face Pearson. "Seriously?"

I consider the very best way to pluck the freckles off his well-formed nose.

He grabs another fry and circles it through the air like an orchestra conductor. "He said it wasn't a date." He plops a twenty on the table. "Because a gentleman *always* pays." Pearson pops the fry into his mouth. "Well, that's how *I* roll."

He pushes himself up from the booth and waves to Renée on the way out, leaving me alone, so mad at myself for letting him ruin my time with Rico. It won't happen again. It can't.

Renée and I sit in front of Vacationland Pawn on Route 15. Dad's brought me here so many times in my life to fill in some of those "little financial edges" or to add some extra "cream in his lifestyle coffee." He sells weird stuff from the attic nobody cares about anymore: china dishes, some rare stamps, a signed Elvis Presley record. Weird shit. You go up to the attic, find stuff, sell it. Poof! Benjamins in hand. Hot fudge sundaes for everyone. The Fountaine attic provides.

Beside me, Renée shakes her peasant shirt away from her chest in rapid succession, staring at the greasy-looking shop. The window is foggy with a layer of dirt, but I can clearly see the outline of a red electric guitar, Cabbage Patch dolls still in their original boxes, and a ten-speed bike.

"I dunno, girl. These places kind of creep me out. What're we doing here, when we could be jumping off the dock or playing mini-golf. Beau Boudreau's going to be there. You should see him. He filled out into something amazing."

"I need a plane ticket to New York."

Renée glances at my ankle.

"It's going to be fine."

She sniffs. "Don't you have a credit card like every other kid from Los Angeles?"

"You've watched way too much television. I don't have one. I have eighty dollars."

Renée blows a bubble and cracks it. "You gotta talk to your dad. You can't be making money doing a 'real' job if you are stuck doing commercials for free. It's violating about a hundred and one labor laws."

"He calls it the 'equity of my future.'"

"They're hiring at The Muffin."

"Let's see what I can sell."

"Swim next? I've got a feeling I'm going to need to wash this place off me."

I roll my eyes toward the door, so she follows me without another word, an unwritten rule of law with us—if one girl gets her way, the other gets hers next. Inside, a small air conditioning unit chugs cool air into the packed space. Renée spies a rack of vintage clothes, makes a funny noise in the back of her throat, attitude rocketing from zero to one hundred percent in.

A young guy sits behind the counter reading a stack of old *Mad Magazines,* not the Einstein look-a-like Dad used to barter with. "Where's Dennis?"

"He's at the old nursing home on the south side of Mount Blanc. I'm his nephew, Lenny. What can I do for you?"

"I'm just looking."

"Looking to buy? Looking to sell? We've got it all here." He points to an enclosed glass case. "Class rings from all over the country, some pocket watches . . . " He picks up a jeweler's loupe and points to my necklace. "Nice . . . let me give a looksee."

My hand flies to my throat.

"Come on, let me see. I'll give you an estimate." His eyes gleam. "In case you're ever feeling desperate . . . " I take off the necklace and hand it to Lenny. He turns on a light and looks through the glass. "Whoa, flawless. Nice. The clarity is good, very good actually. Three-quarters of a karat each. This entire necklace . . . " he jots down some calculations. "I could sell this fast. I'd give you two thousand dollars for this."

The number hits me.

I hold my hand out. "I'm not ready to sell . . . " Because if I did, I'd be disrespecting the sister who never got to live, which feels like one of the most unfair things I could ever do to her.

I back away from Lenny, who's already back to his magazines. I'm about out the door when he yells, "Well, if you change your mind . . . "

The door slams.

"I won't."

In the Jeep, I wait for Renée to come out. When she does, she's carrying a large bag, sporting a huge smile on her face. She calls to me, "Success comes in unusual places!"

chapter eight ♡

FOUR DAYS LATER, I wade into the ocean, slipping through the seaweed, until I'm over my head, floating on my back, watching the sun trying to push through the mist. I feel like somebody who is hidden and wants to be found. I keep my eye on the beach, willing Rico to come find me, but he doesn't. It's only when my fingers are puckered that I admit defeat.

I limp through the woods, where the shades of green glow in the light. Moss grows all over, and ferns sprout between the rocks. I bet if Rico were here, he'd grab a piece and run his hands up the stem. I pull the beach towel tighter around my waist and look at the silhouette of the rakers meandering toward their cabins.

Felipe sees me. I strain to hear the music sneaking through his ear buds but can't get the tune. He asks too loudly, "Nice swim, Miss Fountaine?"

I scream over the music. "Yes!"

"How's your ankle?"

"Feeling a tad better!" I yell.

"Good. I was worried."

He pulls the earphones out of his ears, balls them up tight, and jams them in his pocket. I point down the worn path. "We haven't used Camp III in a couple of years. It's far from the rec hall and everything else. Do you need anything? Ice? Drinks?"

"No, things are great down there. I've got a good roof over my head; berries are flush on the vine. It's a banner season."

I nod toward his phone. "What're you listening to?"

"I've got eclectic taste. I like to start my day with some pump-it-up music. You know, like old-school Van Halen."

"Pre-Sammy?"

"Yes. And when the sun is high in the sky, well, you never know what I'll hit. Maybe Bach. Maybe Air Supply. Or even my lady Dolly."

"Dolly Parton?"

"Right. Love her. '*Working Nine to Five*'. Scratch that. For me, it's *Six to Two*."

"*What a way to make a living . . .* " I sing.

"It's not too bad. I end my day with either 'Mellow Yellow' or hard-school Atlanta Rap." His eyes get dreamy looking at his music on his phone. "Love rap."

"Felipe, can I have Rico's phone number?"

The dreamy look, *poof*, disappears. "Miss Fountaine, he doesn't have a phone. He spends all the money he doesn't send home on his computer that he uses for school. He's got mad goals, my guy, Rico."

"You mean to tell me he's the only person in Mount Blanc without a *phone?*"

"Pretty much." Felipe shoves his earbuds back in his ears. Discussion over. *Dammit*, he'd called me Miss Fountaine again.

"Felipe! Felipe, call me Clem. Or Clementine."

I'm not sure if he hears me. Regardless, he doesn't turn around and keeps on moving.

❀

I'm more confused than ever. I blare my favorite Spotify station: The Clem/Trace Jam. I flip open my computer to my dance pictures. I rotate my waist in the chair, pulling my torso in, floating my arms into the air to the beat of the music. I'm not sure what catches my eye, but I see the outline of somebody standing in the fields looking toward me. I limp over, trying to see if it's Rico, but by the time I get to the window, he's gone.

Twenty-two days until the audition, and I can fully put weight on my foot. I head out the door and into the barn with the old manure, gasoline, and hay smell. I turn right, past a rusty tractor I liked to call *Frank Beer (not John Deere)* and open the door to my dance room. I flip the switch on the wall. Despite Dad's assurances he'd get all his crap out, there've been a load of excuses: *gotta rope off the lower barrens; meeting with the Blueberry Council; Clem, I've got shit to do.*

I'm two-thirds of the way done, far enough along to jimmy the one back window open and shove a blueberry crate out through it. It slams to the ground but stays intact. Dad buys only the best when it comes to the blueberries.

About ten minutes into the job, sweat pours out of me, but it feels good to be making progress, so I work and work until I need to go back outside to stack the crates on the corner of the barn. Back inside, I've made great progress. I jump a couple of times on the bouncy floor, pulling into a hip-hop *pop and lock* and twisting into a *running man*. I grab another crate and expose a stack of cardboard boxes, too big to push out the window.

I pull down the first box and tweak it open. It's our outside projector, surrounded by movies. We've got all kinds of DVDs: *Dirty Dancing, Batman Returns, Freaky Friday,* and more. In the back corner, I see our outside screen. A plan forms in my head. If I plan a movie night for tonight, I'll get to see Rico. If I do something nice for the rakers, José Luis can't say "no."

I haul the gear to the door, and the box breaks, sending DVDs scattering across the floor.

While picking them up, I notice Mom's scribbling—you can't mistake it, she's a slob. It says: CLEMENTINE'S HOLIDAY CONCERT 2008. I plug in the projector, shove the DVD in, and project myself onto the wall.

I'm eight years old, and my body is tiny under a massive amount of black hair tied back with a huge red bow. Trace is next to me, but her hair is woven into cornrow braids, which I always wanted and never got. Even little you can see she's going to be a star. We had matching black leotards, red flowing dance skirts, and red and white tights. We look like perfect little elves, innocent and earnest as we twist around the stage to "I Saw Mommy Kissing Santa Claus." Truth be told, Trace steals the show with her sass and extra pop to her step.

But when the music ends, it's my parents I hear the loudest.

"*Mon chou* . . . bravo!!" Dad calls, but it was my mother's voice screaming the loudest.

"Killing it Clementine . . . "

I flick the movie camera off, letting those old emotions rocket through my gut before finally settling again. Mom's chair is still over by the stereo. An ugly thing from the forties dragged out of the back corner of the barn, covered with a tapestry from a hippie store in Bar Harbor. The spot she'd sit to watch my every step.

"*Hold your carriage higher, Clementine.*"

"*Crisper movements.*"

"*Are you drinking enough water?*"

"*Fabulous! Look at you!*"

We haven't spoken since my last birthday—three months ago—when she'd called on Dad's phone and he forced me to talk to her. It hurts too much. Pulling up her contact, I sit for a minute and look at her full, heart-shaped face—the only feature I inherited from her. Her eyes are pale green, framed by lashes she never bothers to tint or put mascara on. This drove Trace's mother crazy. "*Why would she do that?*" she'd always ask me, like I knew. Mom never even bothers to comb her hair, just lets it grow into a mass of auburn ringlets. Right before she left, gray sprouted at the crown of her head. "*Look, Clem! I'm turning into a crone. A woman wizened by age.*"

I press the call button and wait, but she doesn't pick up. Instead, the phone rings and rings, until her breathy message plays: "*Hola! This is Sandrine Fountaine. Leave a message.*"

I don't.

Johnny and Dad are breaking up a bunch of Laurel Hollow boxes and putting them in the back of the truck. I march up to them and hold my hand flat. "I need money, Dad. I'm going to get snacks for the movie I'm showing the rakers tonight."

"Taking initiative, Clem. This . . . it's great."

"It's our farm . . . "

"Whatcha showing?" Johnny asks. "*Batman Returns?*" He sniffs. "I'm not a true fan of the Michael Keaton Batman. I've got Christian Bale."

"Ayuh, it's the Dark Knight all the way." Dad yanks forty dollars from the back pocket of his Carhartt pants. "Get a bunch of sodas, too. And popcorn. And butter."

"Now we're talking money, you still haven't bought me my new speakers for the studio. Remember the dunking booth bet?"

"It's on the list."

"Like cleaning up the studio . . . "

Johnny rolls his eyes.

Dad tosses the keys. I snap them clean from the air. I jump in the Jeep for the trip to the store, but the gas gauge is in deep red, and the engine clicks.

"I'm on zero miles. You drove it last . . . "

Johnny yells, "Dev, I'll take Clementine, and we'll pick up some gas on the way back." He squashes the cardboard boxes like a winemaker squashing his grapes. When he's finally satisfied, he jumps down to the ground and pounds the back of the truck with his fist. "Let's go!"

Johnny and I hit the road, listening to country music on the radio. Keith Urban. Alan Jackson. The drink holder is filled with gum wrappers. All varieties: Juicy Fruit, Hubba Bubba, and even the old Teaberry Gum you can get at the candy store over in Bensonville. When Johnny's chewing a lot of gum, it can mean one of two things: he's quit smoking or he's had another breakup.

The outline of the cigarettes is pushing through his pocket. So I ask, "How's Buddy?"

Johnny grips the steering wheel, taps the brake before turning onto Main Street. I see Pearson in line at the Tasty Freeze with Sierra. They look cute together. Johnny starts talking, stops. "He dumped me, Clem. Two weeks ago. Left me for a painter from Old Orchard Beach."

His voice is full of so much pain, I hurt for him.

"House or artist?"

"House."

"Dumbass."

"Indeed."

No wonder he's been at Laurel Hollow even more lately, swinging by for a game of cribbage, staying late.

I touch Johnny's elbow. "I'm so sorry. I loved Buddy, too. Those blond curls, those abs. And don't get me started on his lobster stew."

"With all the delicious butter. You've gotta stop. You're killing me," Johnny groans. "It's not all bad. Me and your dad. Same situation. Glad we have each other."

The divorce papers were mailed to the lawyer, and Dad told me everything would be final by the end of next month. I've had a lot of time to deal with it, so I guess I'm okay, yet I find myself gently moving my fingers from one diamond to the next. They're my worry beads.

He pulls into Mount Blanc's only market, Perringdom's. It's small, with a sloping wooden floor and a large whirring fan overhead. The front window is full of local veggies, buckets of corn, a basket of green beans, and coffee cans full of local flower bouquets. There's penny candy, car magazines, cigarettes. I walk down a narrow aisle, past cans of Dinty Moore beef stew, canned peas, and cranberry sauce until I find the popcorn kernels. I grab the largest jar of Orville Redenbacher's I can find and a bunch of the sodas from the coolers in the back of the store. I turn the corner in search of butter when I hear the sprinkling of Spanish. I peek around a display of fishhooks. Rosa's pointing at a girl I've never seen before. Her voice is low and urgent. Rico's name floats between a bunch of words I don't understand, syllables banging into my ears, going nowhere. I curse my years of French and do my best to eavesdrop. I lean into the boxes of Pop-Tarts and Carnation Instant Breakfast.

"*¿Pasa algo? ¡Alto!*" I struggle with the meaning, leaning closer. They flip to English.

"I said delete the picture, nobody can see him."

"You think they'd come for him?"

"I don't know. How am I supposed to know? It's all fucked up. All of it."

"Sí..." They slip back into Spanish. I hear Pulga's name. Rico's hits me like a solid karate kick to the gut. I jump, sending a box of cinnamon Pop-Tarts slamming into the ground. Rosa and her friend step around the corner, catching me cold. Rosa's eyes snap to mine. She swallows hard, before picking up the Pop-Tarts. She slides the box into the display, her face a still mask I can't decipher. In her other hand is an international calling card and a bag of popcorn. I point out the window where Johnny sits idling in the truck.

"Want a ride back to the farm?" I turn to her friend. "We could take you, too."

Rosa's pointy chin pushes a little further toward the door. "Felicia and I were leaving. We don't want to be a bother."

Felicia shoves the phone into her jeans pocket, and I know without knowing, whatever answer I'm looking for is gone. "I'm down at Bluette's Farm. The other direction. I'm good."

I tease, "Ohh . . . the competition, huh?" It falls flat.

Rosa clears her throat. "José Luis is picking me up."

"Tell him I said 'hi'." I hold up the supplies. "And I'll see you tonight at the movie maybe. Do you know . . . will Rico be there?"

Felicia's eyes move toward the Cheerios and fixate on them like they're super interesting.

"He has a mind of his own." Rosa's voice is tentative.

"What happened to the guy from the bus station? Pulga, was it? He was on the farm, then he wasn't . . . "

Rosa took a step away from me. "He had to go."

"But why? We seem understaffed."

Felicia clears her throat, "Sometimes it's hard to have all the paperwork buttoned-up. He had to go back to North Carolina for work . . . "

"Is that why you guys broke up, because he had another job?"

"How we work, it's better to stay uncomplicated."

She sounds like Rico did back under the tree at the start of summer. I hold the popcorn in the air, knowing I'll never know what they think of me.

chapter nine ♡

JOHNNY FIRES UP THE truck and shoves a piece of gum in his mouth. I shift uncomfortably in my seat. Something's going on at the farm, I know it. The scanner radio screams. A tinny voice comes through the dispatch. *"Suspicious poacher a quarter-mile from Sawyer's Cove."*

Johnny snatches the small speaker, brings it to his lips: "LaMonde. En route."

"Ten-four, Officer LaMonde."

"What in the hell is going on?" I yelp.

Johnny's body language changed from something light to pure business. His hands grip the steering wheel tight as he guns the engine. "I'm on the clock. You're coming with."

The side of the road is a blur. We drive eighty down the long stretch of highway.

"All this for a suspicious poacher?"

Johnny doesn't respond, his eyes scan the road, lips clenched in a firm line. This is not the Johnny I know, and it kind of scares me. "Johnny . . ."

"No worries, Clem."

But this doesn't feel like a "no worries" situation. We take a corner on two wheels and bounce down a pothole-lined dirt road. I bite down hard on my tongue. My mouth fills with salty blood. A clearing looms ahead, littered with border patrol and game warden trucks.

Johnny brakes, slams to a stop. He pauses, his big hand on the door, "Stay here, Clem. I mean it. This shit is serious."

"Okay," I whisper, but he doesn't hear me. He's already gone.

I crack the door open, peeking my head higher over the dashboard trying to see through the fog. A boy lies on the ground, surrounded by border patrol agents and Maine Warden Service. There's something familiar about the slope of the thin shoulders, the tousled hair, the straight nose.

Omigod.

It's Seb.

I fumble for my phone to call Renée. She answers in one ring.

"Hello, Blueberry Princess."

"Ren, what's up with Seb?"

"Sebastian? I dunno."

"He's getting arrested."

"Ohhh . . . Classy . . . Tell me everything."

"I don't know. I can't tell. The fog is rolling in. I can barely see anything."

"Dude. I'm at The Muffin grabbing my check. Go help him."

"How am I supposed to do that?"

"I dunno! Call me after. I want all the deets."

Seb's head hangs. He's lost his swagger. He murmurs something I can't hear. I'm afraid for him. I attempt to slow down my thinking by summoning my inner CSI. The clues: we're in a tidal estuary; a long net is lying by a felled log; Seb is wearing beat-up moldy looking waders so big on him he looks shorter than his usual six feet.

I'm not judge or the jury, but the dude looks guilty. His usually goofy optimistic face is downturned, and he's not meeting anybody's eyes. A hundred feet away is a huge bucket full of whatever he wasn't supposed to be taking.

"Son, what in the hell were you thinking?" Johnny asks, before pulling off his hat and looking out at the river. "We have permits because we regulate this stuff. Just because it's there doesn't mean it's yours for the taking."

Seb says something too softly for me to hear.

I'm a trapped beast, brought back to the time when all we needed to worry about was our nightly game of Manhunt. When our only concerns were whether we were the hunter or the hunted and finding the perfect tiny place to crouch and wait. *Fuck that.* I jimmy the truck door open slightly, placing first one leg then the other onto the ground. I tiptoe across the soft grass, over to the back of the game warden truck. The bucket is five feet from me, dirty as hell, with a layer of grime that's not new. Around the corner I creep, making sure nobody's looking my way. I shiver, shocked by the dampness on this side of the peninsula but glad it's giving cover.

I drop to my belly and shimmy under the truck. The world is a sea of grass and feet. From the spot on his knees, Seb spies me. I give him the universal head shake for: *Hell to the no. Don't say a word.*

I see my answer.

The evidence! If you destroy the evidence, there is nothing to book him on!

I smear my thin T-shirt along the cool grass. I reach out, but my fingers barely touch the bucket.

"Son!" Johnny gives Seb the business. "This isn't like stealing a few apples. Elver eels are serious." He twists and turns. I'm back under the cover of the truck, a weasel diving for her hole. "The fine is more than you can make in a year."

Seb looks like he might throw up.

My foot hits something hard. A stick. I point my flexible dancer's leg and give it a long hard whack. It pops closer. A slimy cold slug lands on my wrist. *Gahhh* . . . I flick it off with my pointer finger, pushing the stick toward the bucket, and inch forward through the long grass. I'm a super spy girl, all crawling elbows, all scurrying knees, moving toward my destination.

Seb notices me.

He points one of his skinny fingers toward the water. "You've got the wrong guy . . . he's down there. I swear . . . "

Johnny stomps across the beach, the other game wardens look up the path toward the road. My opportunity is now, so I take it. I ram the stick into the side of the bucket. It teeters, left and right. It falls to its side, slippery elver eels rolling down the small hill to the tidal river. I race back and dive headfirst into the safety of Johnny's truck. The game warden, a guy named Chuck, rushes to the eels and flings the flopping fish into the river.

"What the hell happened?" Johnny calls.

Seb tries not to smile. Johnny pulls the other two officers closer to the truck. Johnny asks, "What's the going rate on elvers?"

I wiggle in my seat, sticking my head even further out the window, surprised to see the officers huddling together making a decision.

"A good thousand dollars a pound, maybe more . . . "

"The evidence is gone. Do we just let him go?" Chuck asks.

"We could still charge him. I'm sure of it." Johnny's face looks soft. I watch as he takes a miniature key from his pocket and deftly unlocks the cuffs trapping Seb's hands. "Don't let me catch you getting in trouble again, boy."

"Yes, sir."

Seb smiles to himself.

It's good to be a local in this town.

It always has been.

Johnny and I head toward home; popcorn kernels, butter, salt, and a whole bag full of sodas sit at my feet. I'm hiding my grass-stained shirt with the hoodie I found behind the seat and my dirty knees with a towel. I can't get warm. Johnny's too quiet. His lips are smashed together. The truck cab smells oddly of the fish, as if even after washing off his hands, the shame of the entire scene was stuck on him.

I rest my head on the cool glass window thinking of Seb, Pearson, and Rico. All of these boys. Would my old boyfriend Travis have stepped up for his family? He was so many things, but can I imagine him prying himself away from the game Fortnite? There's nothing about Travis Tripp who wants for anything, so he's never been tested. It's hard to compare Travis to Seb or Rico; it's like they're different species.

I twist toward Johnny. "Why'd you let Seb go?"

"We have some leeway with kids. It helps." He glances my way. I try to smile, but it feels forced and wrong. "Plus, Seb's mother and me. Your dad. We all go way back."

Johnny unwraps a piece of gum and shoves it in his mouth. I hold out my hand, and he gives me a piece. "Seb's dad is locked-up for his second drunk driving incident. But that's not the worst of it. His brother was deployed. A Marine. He died early last year. Friendly fire. He was only nineteen."

A spot behind my eyes burns hot. I knew Zach. He was always the one to fill up the water balloons for the epic fights we had at the playground at sunset. It didn't matter if you were big or little, male or female; if Zach had a clear shot, he took it. His aim was good, too. He smacked me clear between the eyes once, knocking me from the pier into the ocean. I sink deeper into my seat, letting my head rest against the cool window. The last time I saw him, he was scooping ice cream down at the Twisty Freeze. He had a missing front tooth from a hockey accident, and when nobody was looking, he'd always roll back the fake one to make me laugh. I shake the tears from my eyes.

Renée arrives in a fab Joker T-shirt for *Batman Returns*, carting a full lawn chair stuffed with a family sized bag of Lay's barbecue potato chips, a fuzzy blanket, and a winter hat in case the air cools down more. Damn fog.

I meet her at the car. "I'm worried about Seb." I want to tell her, *I'm worried about Rico, too.* I'm worried about all of it. Me. Dance. My dad. I can only deal with one thing at a time.

Renée pops open the chips and grabs a handful. "Well, if Santa had a list of kids who're currently on the *fucked up* list, I'd put him on it."

"Where do you think he is?"

"My best guess is Fisherman's Point."

I check for the eighty bucks I'd shoved in my back pocket from the stash in back of my underwear drawer. It felt right to dig into my travel money after all I heard about Seb. I can always go back to see Lenny if I need to. Plus, Dad needs to pay me for the work. It's only fair. "Let's roll."

I jump into her VW and pull the door closed. She pushes the car into drive.

"Ren, do you ever feel like you've gotta do something for somebody else or you'll explode?"

"Every day. It's endless."

My foot throbs in response, a long aching pain, moving from my third metatarsal to my heart.

Ten minutes later, we roll down the long frost-heaved road to Fisherman's Point where a couple of buildings sit on a crooked pier. The tide is out, showing off a mucky seafloor. Seagulls sit on a tower of lobster traps, glaring at us from the top of a shrink-wrapped sailboat that still hasn't made it to the water. I see Seb's rusty truck. He's here, for sure. Old familiar smells of low tide bite at my nose, reminding me of chemistry class: sulphur and salt. Twenty feet from us, the door pushes open, and there's Seb.

He looks as dirty as he did earlier; his curly hair is stuck to his head, his clothes muddy.

"Clammy. NeeNee. Come on in."

Renée gives him the once-over. "Jaysus, dude. Jump in the ocean or something. You stink."

"I appreciate your cruel honesty."

She rolls her eyes but follows him in. It's cool and dark in the shed. A dirty-looking fridge hums like it's working doubly hard. The walls are covered with fishing nets, lines, and poles. Tools hang on the back of the door: wrenches, hammers, drills. Faded posters from *The Dukes of Hazzard* line the far wall, and a stuffed twenty-two-pound lobster hangs from a hook in the ceiling.

"To what do I owe this pleasure?" Seb asks, hands on his skinny hips, looking me dead center in the eye. Like he doesn't know.

"Just wanted to say hi."

He pulls out a warm Bud Light from a torn case. He hands it to me. I take one. So does Renée. We stand awkwardly.

"Why don't you keep your beer in the fridge?"

"Because it's where we keep the worms and the fish bait."

I force the warm beer down my throat. It's awful.

Seb's laugh is kind of harsh. I wonder how many of those warm beers he's had. "Fine. You wanna talk about it? How you spied on me today?"

"Is that what we're calling it?"

His freckles disappear under the flush of his face.

"I don't need your help. I've got my life in control."

Renée smacks his arm. "What's your problem?"

"Let's go watch the movie . . ." I pick up a rusty-looking oyster knife, steel blade, wooden shaft, letting my thumb press into the tip. My mother once told me she and her friends would cut themselves with pins, pushing their blood together. Blood brothers and sisters. Something we three are definitively not.

Seb, the maestro of the bait shack, waves a Bud Light in the air, his pupils barely dilated. He's snookered. He belches and pounds his chest like an old man. "You think you can come back and start putting your nose in *my* business. Well, let me tell you something—wait, what the fuck happened to your hair? It's blue! Weirdo!" He shakes his head. "So, yeah, Blue Hair, I don't fucking need help. I asked for it once. You did nothing. Come to think of it, it might even be your fault I had to resort to what I did."

Renée fills her cheeks with air. "No good, Seb."

The oyster knife's shaft is cool in my hand. "Excuse me?"

He practically spits at me. "Don't act like you don't know. I asked you for a job at the farm, Clem. And shit-diddly happened."

Renée slams the Bud Light can with her foot. "What did you want, her to drive up like Publishers Clearinghouse and yell at your front door, 'Congrats, you're a blueberry raker!'"

"Good point, Renée." I twist to Seb. "Do I look like I do the fucking hiring? I don't. I have the power of a flea at Laurel Hollow!"

"Come on, Renée," Seb practically spits. "We all pretend to be the same here. But we're not. It's time to get real. She gets to breeze into Mount Blanc, spending all of her time doing squats with the Smith asshole."

Seb sniffs and looks out the salty window to the fog bank rolling back in.

"I'm out of here," I turn to go, sending a deep-sea fishing pole clattering to the ground and not bothering to pick it up.

I slam the money onto the table, sending old shells skittering across the floor, impaling Andrew Jackson's nose with the tip of the oyster knife before whipping around and getting right up into Seb's face.

"You know something, Seb. This is bullshit coming from you, this *I'm a small town boy* crap. We *all* have our problems, and you can either be a victim or not."

By the time Renée and I got home, I can see the final images of *Batman Returns* being played on the outside screen. Dad didn't wait for me. Soon, the rakers are all heading back to their bunks for the night. Morning comes in early at Laurel Farm; they know this better than anyone else. I missed it all for Seb. A friend I thought I had but don't.

chapter ten ♡

I PULL ON DANCE clothes and head to my studio, my muscles practically quivering in anticipation since it's been so long. I might only have three-quarters of my space, but I'm going to use it. The main spotlight illuminates the center, leaving the corners in shadows. There's a long line of mirrors—used to perfect every move, monitor every step.

The floor gives under my feet as I walk over to the sound system, still creaky with one blown-out speaker. I fiddle with it until it sounds halfway decent, turning on "Dreams" by Imagine Dragons.

My body moves without thinking.

I'm a marionette.

Somebody else is pulling my strings.

And I escape into the music.

I twist. I kick high. The beat shifts. Flashes of Mom watching me proudly from the shadows haunt me. The look of wonder on her porcelain face, like she didn't want me to know how much she lived for my every movement. But I know she did. At least she did once . . .

The music intensifies. It radiates through the cells of my body. I twist in the air, and something cuts loose, leaving me yearning for things to be back the way they used to be. The music shifts. I move across the room and back again.

We had so many great moments here in Maine. Picnics, just the two of us. Singing to the snails. Hiking up Mt. Blue. I meet the beat. My head dips and curves.

For all the blueberries did for us, Mom couldn't stomach the little blue gems or any berry for that matter. If she had one bite, hives would push up through her epidermis to create red screaming flaws on her perfect skin.

The song slows, and I come to stop in the middle of the floor. I'm no longer alone. Rico stands at the door, his intense eyes capturing me in my spot.

"Hola," he breaks the tension without effort, allowing me to escape his gaze. I grab a towel from a basket near the wall and wipe the sweat from my forehead.

"You could have said something sooner . . . " My voice croaks, not sounding at all like I intended, too honest and raw.

"Why would I stop you?" He steps further into the room. "You're amazing."

It's exactly what my mom always told me, which unleashes the raw spot in my heart that I keep bottled up, because nobody wants to deal with that piece of me. Tears bubble in my eyes, and I try to hold them back. "Nope. Don't come closer. I'm a mess."

He doubles-down and steps closer. "Amazing."

There's a huge sweat stain on the front of my shirt between my boobs, which makes me cry harder. Not so attractive.

"Did you follow me in here?"

He lifts a can of Bug Gone Spray and kind of shakes it at me. "Mosquitos." He steps across the wooden floor toward me, his eyes holding mine. "Come on. Sit down. Tell me about it."

"Okay."

We sink to the floor together, leaning against the back wall. I'm hyperaware of the six inches between our legs. The three inches between our hands. I could touch him with a mere flick of my wrist. My eyes are still hot and wet. An embarrassing hiccup escapes my lips. "You've seen more of my emotions than any other person I've ever met. It's like every time we're together, you get to see another crazy side of me."

I see the tiny flecks of gold in his dark eyes. "I'm a natural therapist."

"Oh, really?"

"Nah, been around."

And suddenly it's too much. I break free of his beautiful eyes and instead study a trio of freckles on top of his hand. "I'm sorry about lunch at The Muffin . . . "

"It's fine. We all know guys like him. Guys who don't like competition." His hand moves a half centimeter closer to mine before it springs forward twirling in the air. "Tell me about all this. The dancing. It looks serious."

"Before I was my dad's go-to social media star, I was a pretty serious dancer. I started at age three, and I danced five days a week until last year. It was my everything. All my best friends did it. And my mom was there every step of the way."

"My sport is soccer."

"I played for a bit. I'm awful."

Rico shrugs, "No matter. It's about being together on the field. Tell me more about what happened with dance."

I pulled my T-shirt over my nose for a second to wipe away the sweat. "I don't know where to start. Things were unraveling last summer. My parents were fighting. Tension. It was everywhere. I went off to the Bates College modern dance camp, and when I came home, she was gone."

He bites at his lip and lets out a visible exhale. I know before he even tells me that he misses his mom, too.

"I haven't seen my mother in eighteen months. I came here to meet up with my father, but he . . . " The cord on the side of Rico's neck throbs, and his voice gets far away until it finally catches and he stops.

"What?"

"A massive heart attack while picking oranges in Florida. Died right there on the field."

Tears bubble in my eyes just thinking of it. I wipe them away with the back of my hand. "Oh no. Were you there?" His dark eyes focus on the specks of dust floating in the one sliver of light.

"I'm sorry."

"Don't be."

I bridge the final gap between our fingers and hold on. He responds by twisting his hand into mine. And in this moment, I have more in common with this person than anybody else I have ever met.

"Let's meet later."

"Clementine, I don't know."

"The answer is yes. It's gotta be . . . "

We look up at the same moment, our eyes meeting in the mirrored versions of ourselves, and we both, at the very same time, nod our heads—yes.

Three long hours later, I wait for Rico at the edge of the blueberry barren. He's late. Fifteen minutes late to be exact. In the distance, I watch Paddy O'Brien's lobster boat, the *Cindy Louise*, being chased into port by a flock of seagulls. I fiddle with my phone, texting first Trace and finally Renée. I try to put into words the intensity of Rico's eyes looking at me in the mirror but don't know how to say it without being creepy, so I hit delete.

A text from Trace pops in.

> T: *I've been attached to a trapeze all day. I be flying. What up?*
>
> Me: *Last month you were learning disco. This month you're levitating.*
>
> T: *Your Facebook live post was on fire. Sign with my mom!*
>
> Me: *I'm waiting for Rico!!!!!*
>
> T: *Remember the pool boy. Don't do it.*

A branch cracks. It's Rico! I shove the phone deep into my pocket.

He's fresh from the shower with wet hair tucked behind his ears, his thumbs hanging from the back pockets of loose shorts. He must know the effect he has on me, because the smile on his face is growing with each step. The closer he gets, the more I sink into my spot. He stops, smiles at my outfit: a lace sundress and my high-top Converse sneakers. A perfect mix of girly and skater chick. I curled my hair, letting it fall in soft waves around my shoulders and rubbed kohl eyeliner over the top of my eyes to accent the corners.

When he finally speaks, it's huskier than usual and I like it. "Every time I see you, it's like you're somebody different, like you have different channels." He pretends to twist a fake remote. "*Click*, crazy carnival chick. *Click*, commercial superstar. *Click*, library deviant. *Click*, dancer."

We twist toward the path.

"Where're we going?"

'It's a surprise."

"I don't like surprises."

"Do you like weird places in the woods that surprise you?"

The crush I have on this boy settles into my intestines, a flicker of nerves. And, honestly, I don't know what to do about it. So, I do what I always do when the uncertainty and excitement get going. I talk. I tell him the history of the farm and my grandparents. I tell funny stories of my dad's sister, Aunt Vivi, and the time she fell off the Laurel Hollow Organics float during Mount Blanc Days, flipping in the air and landing perfectly on her feet like a champion gymnast. Rico, in turn, tells me about the first time he was stuck in a snowstorm at the end of last year's apple season when Felipe dive-bombed into the snow and hit a stump.

"Rookie mistake."

"Right?"

We move in silence for another forty feet, dipping deeper into the forest. The temperature drops. Rico plucks a piece of bright green moss from a boulder, leaving pieces behind like we're Hansel and Gretel and he might need help finding his way out. He's magically dark. I tease him about it. He teases himself.

I touch my necklace, feeling the coolness of the three stones, letting them settle in next to my clavicle.

"Tell me about it."

"Huh?"

"The necklace you're always fiddling with . . . "

My cheeks warm. It's like he sees through me.

"Nobody has ever asked me about it before, you notice *every-thing* . . . " He waits. So, I continue. "When I met you, and you were talking about your sister, well . . . my sister . . . When my mom found out she was having a girl, she ran out and bought this for me." I hold it up so he can see. There's a small diamond for each of us." I lift the clasp, where a red ruby sits. This represents my dad. Hidden from view but still close. My parents waited for her for years. They did in vitro and everything. But she died at thirty-six weeks. I never even got to meet her."

He's quiet for a moment, processing my story. "I'm sorry they lost her."

I worry briefly that I've shared too much, until he reaches down and grabs my hand, something that came so naturally my heart wells.

"Almost there . . ." I say.

Rico squeezes my hand. "Can't wait."

We round a bend, and the conversation immediately falls away. Rusty train cars sit settled into the earth like a village of abandoned old houses. A well-worn path loops around the clearing, connecting the giant steam engine dead center to the aloof caboose over in the corner, practically in the trees. Everything is rusted a solid red, softened by the tall grasses weaving through grates, wheels, and spokes.

"It's a train graveyard," I say.

"A train graveyard. As in, a graveyard for trains?"

"Right." I kick at the steam engine's massive wheel, surprising a baby mouse who scurries frantically across the path and into the tall grass on the other side. "It was like this in 1947, when my great-grandparents moved here. It's the Maine Timber Line. They must've gotten new equipment and abandoned the old here."

Rico picks up a rusty railroad spike like it is precious. He holds it up to me. "Think about it. This train might have transported wood anywhere. Like the Smithsonian or Chicago Cubs Stadium." He rests the spike on the wheel of the train and folds his arms together and goes existential. "I think about the fruit I pick all the time. Like maybe it's served at a wedding or maybe a baby is trying it for the first time."

"I've never thought of it that way." I follow the dirt path past an old passenger car toward the largest steam engine sitting at the highest point of the clearing.

He grins at me. "What if your blueberries were somebody's last meal?"

"Like death row? Kinda morbid, don't you think?"

"In some ways, it is. But think about it. They can pick anything. It varies from person to person. A bucket of KFC fried chicken. Filet mignon with French blue cheese. A bowl of fresh strawberries and cream."

"I'd have a hot fudge sundae, with homemade whipped cream, nuts, and a cherry. I'd eat it. I'd order another."

"Two sundaes?" He doesn't sound sold.

"Well, if you didn't have to live with a stomachache, wouldn't you?"

"No. I wouldn't." He grabs a rung on the side of the engine and climbs on like he's sitting on top of a horse. He motions for me to join him. *So, what's a girl to do?* I grab the first rung and slowly climb up until we're ten feet off the ground. I flip my leg over and allow my back to slowly melt into his chest.

He whispers in my ear, "My last meal would be a bowl of my mother's beans and rice. Sometimes it's the simplest stuff you miss."

"All this food talk, I should have brought snacks."

We're quiet for a minute, each lost in the view from atop the train. He shifts, not sure where to put his hands; he finally rests them on his knees before slowly inching them toward me.

"My mom used to read me this book called *The Little Engine That Could.*"

Rico's eyes light up. *"La Pequeña Locomotora Que Sí Pudo?"*

"You read it, too?"

"Sí…" He whispers in my ear and points to where the sun is dipping lower in the sky.

"Do you see it? The dragonflies?"

I don't see at first. Then, suddenly they're everywhere . . .

"No, damselflies. How amazing . . . "

One lands directly in front of us. Translucent wings, its body a bright turquoise blue. The bug considers us, like we're the most interesting thing she's ever seen, before darting away toward the bug party.

"Migrating . . . "

"It's too soon."

Rico leans in close, points to a young maple tree struggling in the corner. Its leaves are already turning yellow. "No, it's happening. It's already changing."

"We can make the rest of the summer damn good."

"Maybe . . . "

I chant a line from *The Little Engine That Could,* turning *I* into a *we,* because I'm not so alone anymore.

"I think we can, I think we can . . . "

He joins in.

"I think we can . . . "

Darkness is settling in Laurel Hollow when Rico and I arrive on the barrens. He steps closer to me. I raise a single eyebrow like I do when I raise the stakes playing poker.

His eyes squint in consideration. "I know we're in a complicated situation, and I might regret this, but I've got to see you again." He scratches his chin, not taking his eyes from me. I resist the urge to place my hand on the side of his face. He touches the blue streak in my hair, giving me a chance to sniff his lovely mix of shampoo and boy, and I lean in closer as if it'd keep him there. "Meet me at the end of Angel Ave. There's a path. 4:30 tomorrow?"

"I'll be there."

"Good." Rico steps backwards away from me and doesn't turn until he hits the first clump of blueberry bushes. He trips, catches himself, and twists toward the raker camp. I watch until he's only a speck in the distance, a perfect image moving into the dusk of August. On their own, my hips twist in a figure eight, and I feel the beat of being with Rico invade my nervous system. I go directly to the dance studio and practice some more.

Later, Johnny's distinct honking laughter fills the air. I tiptoe up the thin stony path to the back door of the sleeping porch, obscured by a lilac bush, and peek inside. As usual, he's fully dressed in his uniform. His bucket hat sits on the floor, next to his gun holder. Dad's wearing cut-off shorts and a Laurel Hollow sweatshirt.

"Dev, we're doing the best we can with the boy. His real name is Saul Miguel. But he's so small. Jaysus, he's only eighteen."

"An adult in the eyes of the government, but a frontal lobe like every other dumbass who made a bad decision . . . Remember all the stupid shit we did."

"Yup . . ."

"Like the time we broke into—" I slam the door open, and Johnny jumps in surprise. "Clementine, you scared me!" Johnny pours himself another drink. My nose twitches from what smells like cigarette smoke. Dad pushes the Styrofoam box of barbeque ribs under the chair with one swift kick. A bottle of Seagram's 7 Crown Whiskey hides near a row of red potted geraniums. I flutter around the room, much like those damselflies, moving from deadheading the African violets to neatening up the magazines on the table—in alphabetical order from *Blueberry Today* to *Secrets of Bees*.

Dad rests his hand on his flat stomach. "Your old buddy, Seb Michaud, swung by today." I meet Johnny's eyes, a little feeling of apprehension skittering across my forearms. "He's going to jump on the farm, to help harvest for the week. Johnny, the boy reminds me of us back in the day. He's got a hunger for doing better, like a true work ethic. Like Mount Blanc style."

"And why do you think Seb is like you two?"

Johnny takes another sip of his whiskey. I kick his leg.

"I'm not saying a word," he finally whispers.

Dad raises a glass as if giving a toast. "Working Mount Blanc style means, no matter what, you do what's right for your family, your farm, and your town." Johnny and Dad fist bump.

Johnny finishes Dad's thoughts. "It's obvious. There are times in life when you gotta make a decision. Maybe a decision that isn't popular, but you do what you do, 'cause you gotta do it."

"Like I did at the commercial?"

Dad shakes his head and drops into the chair, "Hungover, that's sure as hell not Mount Blanc style. It's L.A. style. Not impressive. Johnny, she's dating Pearson Smith. Can you believe it?"

I give Johnny the crazy sign, circling my finger around my ear. Johnny roars with laughter, before turning to me wild-eyed.

"You're shittin' me, right? Seriously, Clementine?" He points to Dad. "And you! You think this is a good idea? After the way Christine put you in your place every time you tried to talk to her when we were kids? Every single stinkin' summer." I lean closer. "You should've seen her, Clementine. Back in the day, Christine would move through town like a blonde Massachusetts goddess, wearing her designer this and that. She called your dad a Canuck!"

Johnny turns to Dad, who's chewing on a bone, not unlike Roscoe. "Come on. Don't tell me you don't remember."

"We were kids."

"She was racist and elitist, and—"

"We've all grown up."

Johnny releases the second button of his uniform and shows off the white T-shirt underneath. "I sure as shit hope so."

I grab a rib from the container and gnaw on the smoky meat. "Wouldn't it be amazing if we didn't pay attention to this town's social hierarchy, for one night?"

Dad rubs my head. "I love your innocence."

Johnny takes another sip of his drink. "No. It's golden. You be you."

I shake a rib at them and take another bite. "Good plan, boys. I'm gonna *be me* for the rest of the summer. On that note, Dad, I need some more cash for some incidentals."

He hands me a twenty.

"Not enough, Dad."

"Has to be enough for now."

I shove the twenty deep into my pocket and listen as their words jump back and forth through time, stories so intertwined it's tough after a while to keep track of who is talking. *Just* the way they like it.

chapter eleven ♡

ALL EVIDENCE OF DAD and Johnny's bender is gone. The whiskey is stashed away—what's left of it, anyway. The ribs were sucked to the bone and put out to pasture next to the bushes, per tradition, like it didn't even happen. A single Gerber daisy sits on the table to suck up residual cigarette smoke, because now that Dad's thinking of his sins, he's going to go full force into health mode. A truck lumbers past the sleeping porch, shaking the wide floorboards, a sign it's finally time to open my eyes. There's a text from Mom: *Did you call?* And a text from Trace: *I'm fucking coming! Six days, baby!* I snuggle deeper under Mémère's hand-knit blanket.

Right before I fell asleep last night, Johnny said, "Dev, I miss Buddy." And Dad's response, "It's all about love, isn't it?" It's a perfect memory to start my day, a mantra even: *it's all about love, it's all about love.* I stretch myself into full wakefulness, spreading my legs out wide, bending into a forward fold.

The only thing left behind is Johnny's border patrol bucket hat, which hangs from the chair post. I push off the little corner mattress, cocooning myself in the blanket, and pad over to it. I've always liked Johnny's uniform, especially the hat. It's so much a part of him; I almost feel it *is* him. I shove it on my head, liking the feel of it.

The blueberry barrens spread out like a desert, smooth and flat. The air is filled with the sweet aroma of berries ripe on the vine. What I learned last night is both my dad and Johnny didn't let life get in their way as kids. Johnny was the first guy to come out in his high school, and my dad didn't give a shit about who thought what; he blissfully went about his day, getting it done.

All I can think about is Rico's *"I think I can."*

And then Pearson's *"You sure as hell can."*

Johnny's and my dad's *"You be you."*

An idea bubbles up in the back of my neck, turns, and whispers in my ear, *"New York? What's he going to do?"* I push Johnny's hat down even tighter and head to Dad's office to drop it off for safekeeping, and, while I'm there, I may—or may not—book a ticket to New York. Down the hallway, I look both ways to make sure Dad's not around.

I nudge the door to his study open and stop.

It looks like a group of monkeys had a kegger. An old banana peel is five feet from the trash. Pieces of paper are scattered all over the place; notes on organic fertilizer, crop rotation, and new smoothie ideas are piled on top of his desk. A tower of bills is stacked up neatly in the corner, unopened. Mom always did the books for Dad. His brain wasn't meant for such a concrete task. I touch the computer mouse. The screen comes to life. I search "United Air" and log in as my dad. Everything is ready for me to autofill my flight to New York City for my audition. Boston direct to NYC. I click the credit card on file.

I'll tell Dad I'm on set with Trace in Massachusetts. I'll fly out of Logan. Take an Uber into the city. Do my routine. Fly back to Trace. If I get in, I'll deal with my father. If I don't . . . well, he'll never know.

This feels wrong for a quick moment.

It might even be illegal.

But Dad *does* owe me from the dunking booth. He owes me big time. Two hundred dollars to be exact. The confirmation appears with a satisfying *ding*. I take a picture of the confirmation and delete it from Dad's email. I won't remind him again about the stereo speakers. We're even-effing-Steven. I turn to leave, and my elbow catches a manila envelope on his desk. It falls to the ground, scattering cashed checks across the floor. That handwriting? It's my mother's. I pick up the closest check. The signee: Sandrine Fountaine. Paid to: Devon Fountaine. Five thousand dollars in April of 2016. I squirm in the chair. I find another check for two thousand dollars. Another for ten thousand. For all Dad's been bitching about Mom, she's been supporting the farm. And since the last date was four months ago, I gather the money is coming to an end, which is why he's flipping out.

Mom never mentioned sending money, so I always assumed money came from Dad. *But what if that wasn't true, which is why he's freaking out about the farm?* The memory of the last time I saw her floats in my line of vision: a Ghost of Shameful Past inviting me to relive our last day as a family. She'd flown back from Mexico, looking stronger than ever. Smooth, tan skin pulled tight over her runner's body. I remember the dress she wore was more feminine than usual, a billowing thing that seemed to float as she moved. She wanted to talk, to explain what happened between Dad and her. But the fact she'd left when I was at the dance intensive . . . a bitter, jagged pill.

I glance at the clock. Only eight hours, thirty-two minutes, and I'll be with Rico again. It's the only thing I care to think about. But something is still nagging me. I rifle through Dad's folders, looking for the one I saw at the start of summer. It doesn't take me long, and I find it. I sit down, searching for Rico but stop at Pulga. There are red letters across the top: "*Incomplete application —refer to ICE.*"

ICE. Immigration and Customs Enforcement.

I rush through the papers and find Rico's. APPROVED is smacked across the top. Rico is good.

Five minutes later, I ram earphones into my ears and put on The Killers for the quarter-mile drive down the dirt road to the raker's village. It's a street of cabins, a bath house, and a little recreation center my grandparents built when they first bought the farm. I drop two buckets of icy drinks to the ground, sending a tsunami of cold water down my calf and into my running shoe. The entire place is empty. I consider the cabins. The windows are like spun sugar you see on fine desserts, thin and cloudy. I cup my hands to either side of my face and peer inside: two bunk beds on either side, little hooks on the wooden walls holding shirts, a tiny table with empty coffee cups.

I hear somebody talking. I yank out the earbuds.

I recognize José Luis's voice.

"Something has to be done. The conditions . . . I don't care if it's an overflow situation . . . Okay . . . Okay . . . I get it."

Footsteps get increasingly closer. I grab the drink buckets and haul ass toward the rec center, ice-cold water splashing down my calves. So. Cold.

"Clem?"

"Oh, hi! I didn't see you there. How're you, José Luis?"

He bridges the distance between us. It occurs to me it's my job to make it seem like I didn't hear a thing. "Can you help me haul the drinks to the rec center? I keep spilling. It's cold. And kind of heavy."

"I'll take it for you."

"So nice of you." I grab a Coke. I crack it open and take a sip. "Is there anything I can do for you as a thank you? Dad's totally got me on the clock today."

He looks at me kind of funny.

"No, we're good here in the village. Have a great day, Clem."

Across the yard, Rosa wrestles a water cooler into a wagon. I'm struck, once again, by how beautiful she is without a trace of makeup. Her delicate bone structure gives her the right number of angles and valleys but it's her skin—a creamy light brown, a hint of blush to her cheeks from the heat—I'd love to have. My lily paleness is the bane of my summer.

I persist. "I'll bring the four-wheeler around and drive it out to the fields, so you don't need to carry it."

"Sure," she responds, her voice sounding like Hayley Turner, my lab partner from Honors Bio when we had to dissect a fetal pig: like she'd rather be anywhere else on the planet.

I want to ask Rosa what's up because I'm a girl's-girl, but I don't. Instead, I play polite. "I hope you're having a good season on the farm. Have you gotten into town at all? You should try The Muffin." She nods at appropriate times and even smiles an answer once in a while. Is my English too fast? I slow down. "Seriously, they make the best chocolate shakes."

She shifts toward the field. "They'll be looking for me . . . "

"Stay right here." I jog up to the barn, grab the keys, drive the old four-wheeler out of the barn. We bungee the cooler to the hitch rack, and I hand her the helmet. "Climb on backwards and hold on! We'll be there in five minutes."

Her eyes dart from me to the ground. "Maybe you should wear it."

"No! I'm fine. It's more dangerous back there. I don't want you falling off or anything." I rev the engine, warming her up. "Come on, let's get to it."

She settles the helmet over her head and fastens it tight before climbing on. I drive standing, hopeful I'm about to see Rico earlier than I initially thought. "They're all in the western field."

Rosa smashes into the back of my legs; we are like strangers on a tilt-a-whirl ride, straining not to touch. I see a dip in the ground and yell, "Hold on!" We each float into the air and slam back down. "You okay?"

"*Sí.*"

I easily find the picking area. It's quartered off by long pieces of string so the rakers know exactly where to rake each day. Rico is in the very far corner. He doesn't look my way, keeps harvesting berries like I'm not even here. I follow suit and pretend I don't know him.

Felipe tiptoes over the bushes and grabs the other side of the cooler, lightening Rosa's load.

Felipe spies me and stops, glancing over at Rosa, who gives a quick shrug to her shoulders. Other rakers stop raking. I swallow hard. What is going on? I wasn't sure.

Seb's lanky body moves toward me.

"Look at you!"

"I got hired this morning!" He plucks off one glove, then the other. His face is bright red, making him look like a real-life Jolly Rancher. "This is hard work. Don't let anybody tell you differently." He helps himself to water, and I notice the way his Adam's apple bobs up and down his neck when he swallows. He snorts water out his nose.

"What is it?"

"Don't wear that." He points to the hat on my head. "Freaks people out. You might as well chant 'Build the Wall' and invite them to line up with their work visas for inspection." He shakes his gloves.

"Omigod, I forgot!" I snatch the hat off my head. My face burns hot. "No wonder . . . "

Seb laughs. "The hat lives on the corner of Get Out of Town Drive and Booted Lane."

"I didn't mean to . . . "

Fifteen feet from me, Rosa's whispering something into Felipe's ear, her hand cupped artfully over her mouth. Whatever she's saying to him, he's shaking in agreement.

Seb holds up his rake into the air. "No worries, you're showing them who truly is boss: The U.S. of A."

"Shut up, Seb."

"This one's on you, Clementine."

I turn back to Rosa, but she's already moving down the field, a Bouchard rake dangling from her hand. Fifty feet away, Rico pours his berries into a crate, hopefully oblivious but probably not for long.

We're meeting in three hours.

I hope I haven't blown it.

My current Facebook Live has immediately taught me two things. One, it's awkward as hell to be talking into the abyss and, two, it's awkward as hell to see yourself on the screen while talking into the abyss. I try to smile, but my lips feel dry. Truth be told, I'm getting more and more nervous by the people tuning in: Jane from Toledo, Keiko from Vegas, Val from San Juan. There's twenty people, now thirty people, *shit no*, seventy-five! Dad gives me a wild thumbs-up from the corner of the kitchen.

I hit the record button.

"Welcome to Laurel Hollow Organics. My name is Clementine Fountaine. I'm here to show you how to make our signature blueberry smoothie. It's a blend of our local berries, yogurt, and a few other special ingredients . . . " Somebody hits the love sign on the bottom of the post, and hearts float across the video screen. "Oh, look . . . "

Dad steps closer like he might need to save me.

"Okay!" I slap my hands together, refocus, fiddling with the blender. "Dump in one cup of frozen Maine blueberries . . . " I start to gain some confidence. "Fun fact about wild Maine blueberries: way back in time, Native Americans promoted growth by burning the fields . . . " I hold up a cup of yogurt. "Yogurt. Delicious for the gut flora." I hold up a butcher knife like a ninja. "This is one of our secrets . . . fresh mint." I slam the mint down and chop like the Swedish Chef on *The Muppet Show*. "Did you all know Maine blueberries helped feed the Union Troops during the Civil War?".

Chop. Chop. Chop.

"Nice detail!" Dad whispers across the room.

I sprinkle mint into the blender and deftly hold the honey jar to the camera. "We have our very own beehives here at Laurel Hollow. They're important to pollinate the berries. My grandmother used to say blueberry honey is full of earthy goodness. She called it the elixir of the land." I squeeze the blueberry honey into the blender. A loud, blurting farting noise makes me jump. "Excuse me," I joke, "But, seriously, folks, any honey will do."

Hahahahahah goes across the screen. I stop. The person commenting is none other than my old boyfriend, Travis Tripp. My face burns. I stutter. "Now po-o-o-ur in a little water, about a cup and a half . . . " Next, my old bio lab partner's face grins from the corner of my screen, next Lila from gym class, and finally Georgie from dance. "Finally, hit blend."

Brrr . . .

Trace's Facebook picture brightens the corner of my screen: *Trinny. Travis. Let her work!!!*

Sam from Virginia writes: *Is that the Trace Taylor?*

My head is hot. I pour the drink into a willowy spa-like glass Dad ordered special from a website called ElegantLiving.com. I fasten a spring of mint to the top. It falls. I do it again. Hold the smoothie into the air.

"Take a drink," Dad urges.

"Cheers!" Two hundred viewers are watching. I lift the smoothie to my mouth. It smells kind of yeasty and sour. I take a drink anyways. It's awful. My eyes bulge. It's the yogurt. It's sour! I can't get it down; it spews out of my mouth onto the counter. Dad races behind the camera.

"That's all for today, folks! Remember, Laurel Hollow berries are the best!"

We sit and watch as our followers count drops and drops. My phone blows up with all my St. Andrews friends teasing me. "I told you I wasn't ready for social media greatness."

Dad puts his hands on my shoulders. "You were fantastic until the end. Life is a journey, not a sprint."

I wipe up the mess. After a day like today, my only hope of redemption is Rico. I hope he shows up for the date. He's got to.

chapter twelve ♡

I SMOOTH A WRINKLE from my sky-blue cotton shirt and tie it at the waist. I walk, slow and steady, down Angle Street, a place full of small 1930s bungalows and capes. Most have lobster traps piled high out back and buoys hanging off drooping fences. There's nobody around except a skinny-looking cat lying in the sun. The dead-end street has a tiny path—the kind kids use to cut across town—worn down to hard, smooth dirt.

I grab a wormy apple off the ground and mindlessly play "twist of the stem." With each twist, you think of a letter of the alphabet to find the letter of your love. "A, B, C, D, E, F, G . . ." The stem falls into my hand. I fling the fruit into the woods; it splats on a tree, *karumph*. Besides the tap of a woodpecker, I can't hear anything other than the trees dancing overhead.

Another couple of feet down the path, I notice something weird in the center of the trail. It's a clipping from a blueberry bush tied with a little ribbon. I step further into the woods. There's another bundle fifteen feet away sitting on top of a rusty old wheelbarrow. Branches bite at my arms. I grab the last tiny bundle tucked into the midpoint of two conjoined-at-birth trees. In the stillness, strands of guitar float through the air, growing in tempo until they seem to be coming from all sides. I call into the willy-wacks, "Rico?"

The music stops.

"Over here."

Disoriented, I follow the lichen-covered rock wall to an intricate stone patio. I take in each piece of diamond-shaped stone, placed in random sunbursts about thirty feet across. It's crumbling in spots, overgrown for sure, but mostly intact. Ten feet from me is a cracked marble pool full of pennies, being guarded by a headless Poseidon. At the far corner, next to a trellis sagging with roses, Rico puts the guitar down and stands. He's wearing a light T-shirt over loose jeans and flip-flops on his feet, but his eyes flutter away from me, like he, too, is feeling suddenly awkward.

"Pretty amazing, right? Felipe came here with a bunch of local girls; they said it's an old mansion site burned in the 1930s. The name is French. La Bat Retrat?"

"It's called *Battre en Retraite!* Which means 'the retreat.' My grandfather told me about this place. It was owned by a bootlegger who had raging parties out here, like people getting naked and wasted Gatsby-style. One night, it burned to the ground. Rumor has it the authorities put an end to it. Like, 'Oops, I dropped a match' type of end."

"Seems like prohibition was an intricate game of cat and mouse."

"Aren't most things?"

My face flushes.

"Want to go exploring? It might be fun."

"We could or . . . " Rico points to a blanket on the far side of the rose bush. He grabs my hand, and it's so commanding it throws me off balance. I follow him past the smirking, crumbling Poseidon to a little nub of land. The view: a tiny sliver of the blue Atlantic over tall pines. We're completely hidden. And I like it.

Rico pulls sandwiches wrapped in wax paper and potato chips out of a paper bag. They are classic Maine Italians: a slice of ham, a slice of cheese, a layer of tomatoes, chopped onions, green peppers, black olives, and sour pickles on top.

"An American choice."

"When in Maine . . . "

I pop an olive into my mouth and eye the sandwich.

"I don't like onions."

"Something new every day . . . " He piles his onions on a leaf. I place mine on top of his. We eat our sandwiches, slipping into small talk. He tells me he wants to be a doctor, and I learn his GPA is way higher than mine. We discuss all things soccer. How he misses being on a team, but it's okay, he'll play again. We talk about California and the wonder of the potato burrito. He doesn't get my obsession with The Cure and Rage Against the Machine and The Replacements. We compare favorite episodes of *The Office* and *Parks and Rec* before moving to books we both loved and hated. He loved *The Outsiders*, I hated *The Adventures of Tom Sawyer*. We both like peanuts. We both hate scrambled eggs.

"If you had twenty-four hours with nothing else to do, what would you do?"

"Easy. I'd play soccer again."

"I saw you, the first day you came. I couldn't stop watching you."

"That was before I knew you were here."

"Okay, keep going. Twenty-four hours."

He closes his eyes for a moment. I like the way his lashes curl upwards, the slight pull of his mouth as he thinks. "I'd hike the Precipice, in Acadia; there's a bird who nests there, the peregrine falcon."

"You're a birder?"

He pulls a small notebook out of his back pocket and drops it in my lap. Written in his neat handwriting is his list of birds: chickadee, tufted titmouse, bald eagle, hawk . . . he's got pages and pages of birds. He pulls the book from my fingers and flips to the last page. "Look, I saw a hummingbird this week. In Mexico, we say they're magic, they bring joy. Do you know when I saw one?"

"No."

"Right before I saw you dance."

"Right."

"I did. It's true," he says stubbornly, like he's hurt I didn't believe him.

The afternoon sun crests the trees. Rico scoots his butt lower on the blanket. Not one to miss an opportunity, I move down next to him. The earth feels good and solid underneath me.

We don't talk for a good five minutes, just lie together under the sun. "Rico, today . . . "

He doesn't let me finish, practically shushes me in the process. "I don't want to talk about it."

"We've talked about so much else." There's a raw place in the back of my throat. "Do they hate me now? Does Rosa? The hat was stupid and Seb . . . he's a dumbass."

"Seb's okay. He showed up. And he worked. He worked right there along with us . . . Many Americans won't do it."

I shift uncomfortably.

"Without you and your dad, well, I'd be somewhere else right now. Not with you."

I roll on my side, taking him in from this angle, the perfect shape of his brow. "You always this charming?"

"Ladies, be warned."

We grow quiet. A woodpecker pecks away at a tree: *peck-peck-peck-peck* . . .

"Imagine working hard for a single bug?"

"I can imagine working hard for many things."

"Rico, is this weird for you? Being with me?"

"My aunt believes the power of the mind can make change."

"You didn't answer my question."

"Think about it. What if the mind could cure cancer? What if it could project us to places we want to be?"

I prop myself onto an elbow and poke him with my finger. "I don't want us to be weird."

He scratches his perfect chin and looks at the sky. "My aunt believes you can change the tracks of your brain from negativity into positivity. All of these feelings are choices."

"You're not going to talk about this with me?"

He squeezes my hand and holds on. "She used to do this thing with my cousin. They'd watch a rainstorm heading their way, and she'd have him concentrate hard on moving the storm to her crops if they needed it and away if they didn't."

"That's crazy."

"Don't be negative." Rico points to a cloud. "Let's try to move a cloud." He points to a cumulus puffball in the sky. "It's heading north; let's make it go south."

"Holy kumbaya."

"Clementine. Turn it south."

"Rico, this is a weird pick-up activity."

"Concentrate," he whispers.

"Fine." I stare at the cloud, willing it to move in another direction. It stubbornly floats north, but a large piece does break away like the shape of an elephant's trunk.

"It's okay. Have faith."

"Move. Move. Move . . . "

The air shimmers, pushing against the cloud, until, finally the cloud eases into the other direction.

"Look. It's happening. Don't quit now."

"I won't."

Like magic, the wind shifts northwesterly and the cloud dips south as though we willed it. It fills me with an odd piece of hope.

I roll toward him, propping my head up on my arm. He swallows hard but doesn't move. I'm not sure who moves first, but when his warm lips finally meet mine, they're soft as those clouds. I forget about all of the things I haven't done right because there's no way things can go wrong with a kiss like this. I lose myself in the very essence of him, not noticing the storm clouds building until the rain is finally pouring down.

Twenty minutes later, I'm soaking wet in the middle of the family room, unsure of exactly what is going on.

Dozens of pink daylilies in matching creamy white vases sit by the fireplace. Sharp yellow roses are bunched near the window, and a trio of purple orchids sits at the end of the counter, regal and snooty in isolation. On the end table by the couch, there's not only carnations shaped like a ladybug, but also a little cat made out of freaky, itsy-bitsy miniature daisies. A sneeze blows out my nose so fast it hurts my ribs.

"Dad!" I run to the bottom of the stairs. "Is Mom okay? Aunt Vivi? Why does our house look like a funeral home?"

He opens his bedroom door. He's freshly showered with his hair slicked back, and I can smell his Old Spice aftershave from here.

"What?"

"The flowers, Dad. Did somebody die?"

"Why do you always need to go so negative?" My head snaps.

"So everything's okay? Are we starting a flower business? Because it seems a tad off-brand."

"Did you read your card?"

"They're mine? Who the hell would do this?" I practically trip over Roscoe rushing back to the family room. This stunt has Travis Tripp written all over it. He's probably worked his way through every single girl from St. Andrews still in town and now misses me. All I want to do is bolt back across the blueberry barrens, through Mount Blanc, and down Nestle Lane to our spot on the blanket—Rico and me.

I fumble with my bag for the phone.

"What're you doing?" Dad rocks back and forth on the soles of his feet.

"Texting Travis I don't accept his apology."

"Don't think these beautiful flowers are from that bozo. I think they're from somebody else." He gestures to a card sitting by the roses. "Read the card."

"Oh, you've read it?"

"Maybe . . ."

I snag it from the stems. A thorn digs deep into my flesh; blood bubbles to the surface and falls onto the white envelope. I rip it open with my thumb and hold the card in the air. "It says, 'I'm feeling good about your progress! P.S.'."

"Somebody wrote a P.S. without a P.S."

Dad looks at me slyly from the corner of his eye. "Pearson Smith."

"You totally know these were from Pearson. Why would you want me to go out with him after what Johnny told me about how horrible Christine was to you growing up?"

Dad screws his eyes together. "Trust that relationships bring us to places we need to go, which is why we're going out tonight with the Smiths. Forgiveness is key. In life and in business. Go get ready."

"You can't be serious."

"I am! Go get dressed."

I do as I'm told—for the moment, at least.

While getting dressed for dinner, I watch out my window as Rico plays in an impromptu game of soccer. He moves faster than the other players, pushing the ball ahead before kicking it sideways so Felipe can score. It strikes me there are two kinds of players in this world: some take stardom for themselves, while others are comfortable passing it along.

An hour later, Dad and I arrive at the Seaman's Club. Dad flips the visor in his vintage Ford Mustang that he takes out of the barn only on special occasions. He slicks back his brows, making sure every hair is in place. I peel my sweaty thighs from my seat, straighten my sundress, and adjust the straps of my sandals. I glance up at the clouds beginning to break from the afternoon rain shower and will them back together, wishing I had the power to conjure a little tsunami to save me. But all of today's magic is gone, and I'm powerless to move the clouds.

"Clementine, come on," Dad urges. I get out of the car and sink into the grass. My sandals are instantly slimy and wet. This whole thing feels wrong, like I'm cheating on Rico. But even as I think it, we don't have any agreement between us. We're friends, friends who've kissed. So far, that's it.

Out of seemingly nowhere, Pearson leads the way across the grass, loose tie around his neck, jacket over an arm, ruggedly handsome as always. Christine Brommage Smith pulls my dad into a long embrace, and I notice a black smudge on the far corner of her ass. This pleases me. I imagine Mémère in my ear whispering, *Madame Merde*, which translates nicely off the tongue as *Mrs. Shit*.

"We're so glad you could make it." Christine turns with forced cheer. "Clementine, you look lovely."

"Thanks." Fake dimple.

She purses her lips in consideration and scans the setting. "Maybe you and Pearson wouldn't mind posing down by the river." She points down the path with the miniscule white rocks. "It's so beautiful. I think I've even seen this spread in *Maine Life*."

"I don't . . . "

"Look, the sun is coming out just in time. Clementine looks the best in long light. Take the damn picture so I can get a cocktail."

Pearson rolls his eyes but obeys. I follow him to the small inlet down by the water where a huge pot of petunias overflows toward the ground. My nose tickles with the smell of diesel fuel from the boat trying to dock behind us. The parents get crazy about posing us in front of the water, getting the meandering boats perfectly into the frame. And I'm trying to figure out exactly what is going on here.

Pearson grins. "You like the flowers I sent?"

"They confuse me."

"Why?"

"Dude. You filled my house."

"I'm proud of you. You've worked hard."

"Is that all?"

His voice lowers an octave. "Yeah. Well, I kind of feel bad about ruining your date."

"You didn't ruin my date."

"I didn't help your date."

"You didn't."

"Clem."

"Pearson."

"I miss you, my little workout buddy."

In my bag, my phone is exploding. "Let me check . . . " I have message after message.

Via text:
Trace: *The commercial dropped. Looking good girl.*
Mom: *I always knew you were a star!*

Via Snapchat:
Timbo: moons me with my picture in the background on his television
Travis: gives me the peace sign from a smoothie shop on Bellevue that uses our berries

Pearson clears his throat.

His mother calls, "We have a no-cell policy here."

Dad chimes in, "I'm thinking wedding photos, Christine. Fall 2024, maybe down in the south banks of the Carolinas, an outdoor wedding, an open bar! Maybe a signature drink?"

The adults grin wide. I dodge a demon child trying to escape his exhausted parents, a bright red lobster lollipop in his grimy hand.

The kid jumps hard into the Boston Whaler, sending it forty-five degrees starboard and yells, "Safety first," which sounds more like "suffy fist" due to a mild speech impediment. I like his thought though. I could use a life preserver right about now.

Christine sinks into her thin cardigan. "I bet Dave is waiting for us inside. He's allergic to mosquitos."

Dad shoots a dimple her way. "They never bite me."

"Why?" she teases.

I take one last look at my phone.

Via Instagram:
A DM from a stranger: *Yo. Blueberry girl! Wanna lick my berries?*

Ew . . . vile. Trace has told me the dark side of being a public figure. Seeing it for myself doesn't make me want to go into the business, not at all.

We all squish into the small entryway. The hostess motions politely toward the dining room to a table overlooking a swirling high tide. Mr. Smith saunters over from the bar and shakes hands all around. Dad and the Smiths settle in, martinis all around. Pearson pretends to be interested in the nuances of the oysters: Nonesuch River in Scarborough, Pemaquid Point, John's River in Damariscotta. Like there is a big difference in the fleshy mollusks. His perfect ears are flaming red. He's mad. I can tell.

I touch his arm. "Listen, thank you for the flowers."

"It's okay, Clem. They're only flowers."

I hide behind the menu, trying to decide between baked stuffed shrimp or the buttered lobster tails, not liking the shift between us. The restaurant is growing dark, making it seem smaller, cozier. The walls are covered with black and white pictures of local food from the fields, streams, and oceans. Dad sees me looking and points toward the mahogany bar at the far wall.

Mr. Smith takes a sip of his cocktail. "The boy, Pulga. I couldn't get his paperwork in order. He's being extradited to a facility in Dover."

"Are you talking about Rosa's Pulga? The guy who left the farm on the first week of harvest?"

Dad quietly takes a sip of his martini.

Pearson shifts next to me. "I'd go lean protein, stay away from the fried stuff."

Mr. Smith fishes out the olive from his martini. "Well, the law is the law . . . "

Christine rolls her eyes. "If I had a penny . . . "

I shift in my chair, trying to focus on the menu.

Dad says, "Clementine, those pictures are from Laurel Hollow." I resist the urge to pluck the olive from his martini glass and, instead, walk across the sloping floor to the photographs.

Pearson's heavy footsteps follow behind.

I'm not sure where I fit between these worlds.

I pull onto my dance toes and twist my hips toward the wall. Pearson and I both take in the picture. It's a group of rakers happily standing in front of Camp III, the further camp we use only for overflow. It looks to be around 1950 via the outfits—loose cotton dresses and khaki pants, and everyone's wearing wide-brimmed hats to keep off the sun. It's a cozy house with a swooping miniature front porch. There's a huge barrel-shaped barbeque grill with steam rising up in the air in an artful plume. Somebody must have said something funny because all of the rakers are laughing. One looks familiar. I lean in closer.

"Omigosh! Pearson. Look . . . it's the guy from my grandmother's studio. He's there."

Pearson loosens the tie around his neck. "Sometimes answers are right in front of us. You need to know where to look. You got your wish; the guy was a raker, like you thought."

He squeezes my hand. "I sent those flowers because I wanted to." He turns and heads back to the parents, leaving me alone. Across the room, Dad beams like the brightest light in a dark harbor, and I wonder, once again, what I've gotten myself into.

chapter thirteen ♡

EVEN THOUGH IT'S CLOSE to midnight, I pull on running clothes and slip out under the light of the moon. I follow the farm road looping around the fields. I dip lower into the blueberry barrens when the rumblings of fatigue force me to finally slow. I hear something, faint at first, but there, a slow gentle strum of a guitar rolling from Camp III.

Rico.

The sound of the guitar leads me like the Pied Piper himself, pulling me through the gate. I run past a mosh pit of entwined trees and race the last forty feet out of the woods. I gasp, realizing the cozy picture of what Camp III used to look like is long gone. Now, sixty years later, it's disorderly, a second thought, not as loved. I recognize the tiny cabin sitting in the camp's epicenter from the picture I saw at the restaurant. Once ash white, it's now peeling gray. The back porch has fallen in. Around it, broken down trailers and barely habitable mobile homes sit haphazardly.

"Construction, my ass," I whisper to myself.

"Rico . . . " I whisper softly into the darkness, hoping and praying for a response, not knowing which camper to approach. "Rico . . . "

"In the pop-up," somebody yells through a window, voice clogged with sleep.

"Who's out there?" Another person barks. "It's almost midnight. Get some sleep!"

"Sorry."

I listen until I hear the notes of the guitar once again form into a melody. Anticipation grows as I see the soft light glowing in the far corner of the site. I practically skip the last fifteen feet and stop short. People are talking inside. He's not alone.

The door creaks open. I jump further away. Rosa steps out of the trailer in a simple tank top and pajama pants. A throaty giggle bubbles from her perfectly formed mouth. She murmurs something I can't understand in Spanish.

"Mañana," Rico replies from his perch on the small counter, totally shirtless.

I don't know what to do. Rosa twists her head. Rico's hair falls across his temple, and a cheeky smile is on his face. Rosa spies me and yelps, "What . . . "

Rico's eyes meet mine.

Deer in the headlights.

Hand in the cookie jar.

We freeze.

Time stops.

Rico shakes his head, his dark eyes a warning. I wish frantically for the world to swallow me whole. Rosa breaks the silence.

"Hi, Miss Fountaine. Can we help you?" Her voice sounds like a teacher I once had who made me feel naughty for asking to go to the bathroom.

"Clem, please. Call me Clem. Sorry to have bothered you."

I twist toward home, turning my ankle in the soft earth before diving back into the woods. I run, run, run away from Camp III, leaving Rico and Rosa for good. When I'm worn to the point of dropping, I slow down, catch my breath. I climb to a little knoll in the massive rock overlooking the fields. I fold my knees into my chest and wrap my arms tight around them like a hug. I suck in the cool night air. A needy child, my lungs demand more oxygen than usual.

I watch as the moon travels to the edge of a cloud and pauses, its light glowing from the perimeter, a slim line of glowing silver in the darkened sky.

Mémère hovers on the edge of my dream. I know she's there, but I see only a flash of red skirt and sturdy boots as she moves around the vegetable garden in the late afternoon sun. I pluck one green bean after the next from the scrubby vine, placing each in the flat woven basket we use for collecting dinner every summer. I get bored of beans and jump two rows over to the carrot tufts, so enjoyable to pull from the warm ground.

"Only a few, Clem," Mémère says, "gotta let some of them grow."

I tug the carrot out of the ground, brush dirt away with my thumbs, and take a bite. It's crunchy and lightly sweet. Aunt Vivi sits five feet away on the dusty old plastic lawn chair we keep in the corner of the barn. Legs stretched out, slim ankles hooked together, dark hair piled on top of her head, thick sunglasses over eyes. She's going on and on about Bart, the finance guy she's dating in NYC, how even though he dresses in a suit every single day, drinks tea, and sometimes wears a bow tie—she can't resist him. She likes how he orders saag paneer at the Taste of India, extra cheese, extra spicy. She likes how he takes his shoes off in Central Park and digs his toes into the green grass. She likes how he admires Prince. The late singer, not the royal.

"What's wrong with you, girl?" Mémère scolds.

Aunt Vivi pulls off her glasses. "I'm not supposed to be in love with a guy from Goldman Sachs. Seriously, it's pretty far from all this."

Mémère's throaty laugh surrounds me. "Like it's something you can choose. You love who you love, you can't help…"

Aunt Vivi laughs. "You should write bumper stickers."

Mémère yanks a head of lettuce from the ground. "Maybe I already do."

I search the pile of shoes for my Birkenstocks until I finally find them in the back of the closet, next to the paintball guns Dad uses to shoot the groundhogs who like to eat his garden. I pull them out into the morning light. I flip one over and use a pencil to gouge out the plastic heart that's been living in the comfort of my sandal sole. One last quick jab and it skitters across the floor and under the electric heater. I leave it there amongst the dust bunnies to think about how it's let me down.

Renée and I lie out at the beach, side-by-side, on large beach towels. It's eighty-two degrees of sunny perfection, a slight breeze out of the west. The only other people on the entire beach are a mother with her two young kids, clamming over on the low tide line. They're screaming and laughing and throwing sand at each other. Renée scratches black polish off her little toenail and fumbles in her bag for Coppertone suntan lotion. The scent is so my mother. It smooths nicely over my thighs.

"When's Trace coming?"

"Tomorrow morning."

"Exciting! America's sweetheart here in Mount Blanc."

"She wants a place to disappear to."

"Well, this is the place. I'm practically see-through." She motions toward her long torso with not a hint of a tan, even after hours of trying.

"At least you look cute in your bikini."

"I like all bodies," Renée muses. "Gave it a lot of thought after my art history class last year. Those Rubens! Do you know the painting *The Three Graces*? Naked daughters of Zeus! Virgins, dancing in the garden, rocking their curves. One represents radiance, the other joy, the last flowering. Those girls embraced it." She scrunches a skirt into a pillow and settles in. "I'm not sure I'm flowering this summer. Plus, I'm still a virgin. No prospects in sight."

"Maybe it's for the best."

"Why? You've done it, haven't you?" She leans on an elbow, studying me with her green eyes. I squirm under her gaze. She notices and pokes me hard. "You have."

I'm careful with my answer. "Yes, I have. I did. But there was something about it. Renée, it wasn't right. I knew it as soon as it happened. I tried again . . . Maybe I didn't love Travis. Maybe our chemistry was off. I don't effing know."

"That's not the first time I heard that. But I've also heard when it's right, it's right."

I think of Rico. "When my body says, *'Yes!'* the universe says, *'Hell no!'*."

"What happened?" Renée doesn't bother to open her eyes. "Pearson or Rico?"

"Both."

"Better to live than to have nothing at all."

"Not supportive."

"It is."

Renée turns over onto her stomach. Her eyes slowly close, giving me time to think. *How could I believe so strongly about Rico, about the initial connection, only to have him go off with Rosa?* It doesn't make sense. But one thing is for sure: the way he looked at me last night, he didn't want me there—not in the least.

My phone rings. My hand jerks. I fumble for it. It's Johnny LaMonde.

"Bonjour," I say, trying to infuse some enthusiasm into my voice.

"Clementine, you seen my hat?"

"It's in my dad's office. I left you three messages. Didn't you get them?"

Johnny's truck door dings open, footsteps across gravel. "I'm swamped, Clem. Things have gotten busy. We picked up a kid your age trying to sneak over the border to Canada. He was all alone, from Syria. Got all the way here from Portland by himself. Made me think of you, which made it extra hard."

"Horrible."

"Awful. Poor guy said Canada is his only hope." Johnny is quiet for a moment.

"Where were his parents?"

"I dunno. He didn't exactly want to be my best friend."

My mouth feels dry; my toes curl in the warm sand. "Your job can be hard, huh?"

"Yeah darling, my job can be real hard," he pauses. I hear him take a long drag of one of his Camel Lights. "Clementine, would you tell me if things weren't good on the farm?"

"What do you mean?"

"I heard a rumor. I'm sure it's nothing."

"Mom always said rumors are like ghosts: you can't chase them if you can't see them."

"Ghosts can catch up with you, trust me . . . "

"So, yeah, the hat's at the house."

Johnny cuts me off, "Clem, somebody mentioned seeing you around town with a boy. Said he was a raker? Is it true? Because if you are . . . "

"I'm not, but if I was, it would be nobody else's business but my own. Jaysus, first you have all kinds of things to say about Pearson. You didn't like Travis either."

"Clementine Joan Fountaine, don't get salty. Travis cheated on you. Pearson's a snob. Well, his mother is anyway. It's just . . . "

"What?"

"The rakers. They can have . . . complications, Clementine. Real ones. Ones you can't even dream of—like this boy from Syria."

"Oh, trust me. I get it. I live with my dad. Always going on and on about the work visas—"

"Clementine . . . " His voice is a warning now. It's not something I'm used to hearing from him. Even on the day we went after Seb, he didn't sound like this. "Be safe, okay. It's all I'm asking of you."

With the sun warm on my face, I answer as truthfully as I can at this very moment. "Done."

I squeal into the parking lot, late for Zumba and rush to the door. Margie gets downright pissy when you come in late. Down near the pier, about seventy-five feet away, Sierra's got her middle finger in the air and she's giving it to somebody. Her voice is getting louder and louder. I scoot further out on the sidewalk, so I can see exactly who she's screaming at.

It's Pearson!

Pearson's taking up space, his legs wide, shoulders hunched forward like he's talking low. This seems to make Sierra angrier; she pops him in the shoulder.

"Hey!" I holler. "Everything okay down there?"

Like two kids in trouble, they both fold their arms over their chests and take a step back.

"Sierra, you good?"

She twists toward me, sassy-pants as always, her blond hair shining in the sun.

"Yeah, I'm done here."

"Me too . . . "

Pearson jogs up the hill toward me, but I turn to head into class. He beats me to the door and holds it open.

"What was that about?"

"Nothing . . . just having a little conversation."

"Didn't look like something little . . . "

Pearson smacks me with a towel. "I think she's on her period."

"You know that's offensive, right?"

Pearson opens the door to the Odd Fellows Hall. I follow him down the stairs, trying to catch up with him, but he's fast, and before I can, he's joined Ruthie at the front of the class. His big burly frame moves in perfect step to Ruthie's eighty-year-old bird bones. I move to the back of the class, swiveling my hips to Chuck Berry without enthusiasm.

Has this summer robbed me of my "life rhythm?"

Because I feel dead inside.

chapter fourteen ♡

ON THE WAY TO pick up Trace, I swing by The Muffin for much-needed coffee. Like that will make it all better. It's busy inside. Renée carries plates piled high with blueberry pancakes, puffy omelets, and runny-looking eggs Benedict. The pick-up bell keeps ringing, ringing, ringing. I march from the take-out coffee bar across the restaurant and grab two orders of corned beef hash from the order window. Heat pulses from the kitchen in a spray of thick greasy air, courtesy of the slabs of bacon and sausage sizzling under metal weights.

Charlie screams at me like I actually work there. "Hurry up, Clem. Table twelve is waiting." He slams the ticket into a spike.

"Which one?"

Renée pulls up behind me. "Over by the window. And *thank you*."

I walk slow, so as not to drop the glistening toast hanging from the side of the plate, and make my way toward the table, where two little raisin ladies—complete with frosty cotton-candy hair, liver-spotted hands, and bifocals—wait. They smack their lips at me in unison as I plunk it all down at the table.

"Are you planning on eating all of it? Honestly, Rose, you might explode. "

"Gotta get filled up, Pat. Heard we're having a big star fly in today."

"People are people." Pat twists her tiny frame. "Do you have any hot sauce?"

I leaned closer. "Who is coming?"

"Trace Taylor. Do you know her? I loved her in *The Sevens*."

"Never heard of her . . . " Pat said.

"But, how . . . "

Rose ushers me closer. "I was listening to those boys over there. The ones with the big cameras. It seems they're here to spy on her. They said a picture of her in her bathing suit is worth $750. Min-i-mum."

Pat pushes her mug toward me. "Can you get me more coffee? Along with the hot sauce . . . " She coos at me. "I love the hair. Some say blue hair isn't in . . . " She pats her grays.

"But I don't believe it."

This cracks Rose and Pat up.

"More coffee, please."

"Fine." I jog across the checked floor behind the main counter. Grab the coffee pot and fill up the line of guys sitting there in their work clothes before heading back to the old ladies, Tabasco and coffee carafe in hand. Pat doesn't waste any time dousing the hash with sauce and digging in. Rose eyes me up and down.

"Do I know you? Wait, are you? I got it. Clementine Fountaine! Your grandmother and I were the best of friends back in the day." She lifts an iPhone into the air and snaps a picture. "I've seen you on television. Maybe . . . " She bobs her gray hair toward the paparazzi, "They'd be interested."

I back away, very slowly. "Nope. I don't think they would."

Rose raises her eyebrow and snaps another. "I'm hoping to get to Orlando this year. Didn't your grandmother ever tell you winter is awful in Mount Blanc. Bone-chilling cold, nothing going on but Netflix and chill."

Charlie dings his bell at the window. "Food's up."

Renée comes over to relieve me of the coffee pot and shoves a warm blueberry muffin into my hand.

"Rose, Clem's gotta go. She's got blueberries to pick."

Rose gives a little wave. "Oh, those blueberries and those rakers. Ooh, la la la."

"Stop it, Rose."

"Whatever, Pat. You remember exactly what happened with Lee."

I lean in closer. "Are you talking about my grandmother?"

"Sorry. I'm old. Secrets float around my head; it's tough to recall what exactly can be told and what should stay hidden."

"Truth." Pat fumbles with the creamer. "Can you help, dearie?"

I pull the creamer lid off and hand it to her before moving to the door as fast as I can, but not before glancing back at the guys with the cameras waiting for my best friend to arrive.

The plane dips low in the sky, pushing against the crosswinds, tipping to the left, tipping to the right. The propellers roar as it drops onto the runway like a rock skipping over water. The side door pushes open, stairs roll out, and there she is, my one and only Trace Taylor. Her hair is pulled away with a headband, making a hair halo around her face, the perfect mix of her Irish mother and Jamaican father.

She squeezes me so tight I sound like a frog when I say, "Trace, you're not in Hollywood anymore!"

She points to the runway. "You should've told me. I almost grabbed the barf bag when I saw it."

"Been there, done that."

"The runway is dirt." She points to it again, like I don't see it.

"Yeah, I know. But at least you didn't need to take the bus from Portland."

"Gosh, would I love to have Sasha come here," she says, referring to our mutual friend back home who thinks traveling coach is pretty much like licking the sandwich counter at Subway.

"I have an idea: we could film it—you know, like a short—and do a slow release. Let's call it *Travels with Sasha Saswell.*"

Trace is applying to film school at NYU next year. She can't wait to get behind the camera instead of in front of it. Now I've had my own experience with it all, I can't blame her one bit.

"Let's get this vacation going!" She lugs her suitcase to the Jeep. I hand her a hat. "Put it on. They're already here."

"Spies everywhere, my friend." Trace tilts her head and considers me. "You've lost weight, and you have a pinched look around your eyes. Your raker? I told you it was a bad idea."

"I never listen," I repeat the truth for the second time today; my voice sounds low and gravelly. Trace must finally hear something she's not ready to touch. She peers out the window at the tunnel of trees as we push out to the far corner of the blueberry barrens.

"It's beautiful, Clem." She points to the tall plants filling the ditches on either side of the road, huge plumes of flowers growing thick and strong toward the sun. "Those golden flowers, I love them."

"Goldenrod. It's a weed."

"Humph. Still beautiful."

Funny, a weed is a problem for every farmer. I wonder faintly once again about Johnny's question and what kind of weed has seeded on our farm for him to call and ask about it. I push the

Jeep faster. If there's anything I know about weeds, it won't be long before they multiply.

And one thing's for sure: with Trace Taylor here, this town's about to get real small.

I leave Trace's suitcase by the stairs and usher her into the living room we hardly use so that she can get a sense of the old farmhouse. Her mouth drops, and she gives a little spin. "It's all Claudette Colbert and *It Happened One Night*." She snaps pictures of Mémère's porcelain pig collection, *"La Cochon,"* in the corner cupboard, before touching our vintage 1920s curtains with fringe, which always reminds me of an old flapper dress. She tilts her head back, inspecting the painting of Hotel Frontenac in Quebec City in the snow. "Is it an original?"

"Indeed."

In the kitchen, she stops short at the obnoxious display of flowers still shoved into every nook and cranny of the new addition. "You guys open a flower shop?"

"Pearson."

"Rich boy with rooster? Say no more." She takes in the field through the windows. "I can't believe I've never been here. After all this time. It's like another world."

"Well, we're almost in Canada."

Out the picture window, the rakers stop at the far corner of the field. "There they are!"

Trace and I rush to the window.

"I can't see them," she whines.

"They're right there."

"I'm short-sighted."

"You have to see him. Once you see him, you'll get it."

"Do you have binoculars?"

I open the window for a better look. Felipe jogs over to the truck, his ever-present earphones in his ears, and stacks blueberry crates on the ground. Seb is fiddling on his phone. José Luis barks orders to him to get to work. Rico is bent over raking. Rosa is twenty feet away. Further proof I've lost him. But it doesn't mean I'm not going to have my best friend spy on him.

"There!" I try to point him out to Trace.

"I still can't see. I need glasses. From this angle, all of this fuss doesn't seem worth it. Especially when you have a guy who cares about you so much that he bought out a flower shop for you. You've seen the rom-coms! Always go with the flower guy!"

"Argh!"

I leave Trace at the window and trip over a vase of roses, which sends a river of water across the floor. Roscoe, hearing the commotion, saunters in and takes a drink. In the far corner of the room, I grab Dad's paintball gun from the closet and hand it to Trace.

Her eyes grow wide. "Girl, I'm a pacifist."

"Use the viewfinder like a normal person."

She shakes the paintball gun at me. "Normal people don't act like this."

"Take a look at Rico, and I'll tell you everything."

"You're a train wreck." Trace pulls the gun to her eye as she peers through the finder.

"Rico is in the middle."

"Does he have an apple face?"

"That's Seb."

"He reminds me of Ichabod Crane. He's got the biggest Adam's apple I've ever seen. It's like a plum. Why didn't they call it Adam's plum?"

"Trace . . . " I plead.

"Fine," She moves from person to person until she finally lets out a loud whistle.

"Omigod. He's James Dean meets Ricky Martin."

"Right!" I rub my itching nose. "Now you can see what the fuss is about."

"Oh, I see alright."

My nose seizes.

Achoooo!

A deafening *BOOM* shakes the entire room.

Trace drops the gun, and it's like I'm truly awake for the first time all day.

"Not a paintball gun!"

"Holy shit!" I scream, seeing the gun for the first time. "It's a Winchester 1300!"

"Look out the window. Did I kill somebody? Did I kill Rico?"

All the rakers race toward the house, Rico is first in line, followed by Seb.

Dad rushes into the room. "What in the hell was that? It sounded like a gunshot." He spies his rifle on the ground. Dad snatches the gun, dropping the shells out the chamber with the ease of a sniper. They hit the floor with a delicate *ping*.

"What the hell, Clementine!"

"I thought I was giving Trace a tour of the fields via your paintball gun viewfinder." I face my father, whose only movement is the quick flare of his nostrils, in and out, in and out. "You didn't tell me you had a loaded gun in there!"

Seb pokes his head through the window. "Well, hello Trace Taylor. I heard you were in town. Bringing a bit of Hollywood to this part of the world."

"I'm so sorry." Trace looks dazed, and a dark bruise is building on the side of her cheek. "I've never touched a real gun." She takes two steps backwards, crushing a rose with the heel of her boot.

"Hold on, sister. I think you need to sit down," I pull her to the couch.

Dad goes into full-blown this-didn't-happen mode. "There's nothing to see here. Everyone! Blueberries are waiting. Let's get on with it."

Rico's intense dark eyes don't leave mine. And despite it all, a connection to him is still there, like an invisible cord tying us to each other. "You okay?" He asks me, like we're the only two people here.

"Yeah," I whisper, hoping what I see in his eyes is real. "I am."

Trace sits at my makeup desk inspecting her shiner. "Dude, I look so tough. Like I could take down the world." She gets up, fires a karate kick into the air, and falls directly into attack mode, hands-up and eyes screwed together like she's trying to kill me.

"It's a beaut." I inspect the hues of purple and yellow skin in the corner of her eye. "I think you need more ice. It's puffy."

"Nah," she twitches her cheek for special effect. "I'll be fine. And I kind of like it."

"I'm glad you're here."

"Me, too." She pushes me over to the side of the bed and climbs in. "I think it's time we discuss your love triplets." A fly darts around the room before landing on the wall, exhausted from looking for a way out.

"Love triplets?" I repeat.

"Yeah, your love triplets. I've been here for roughly five hours now, and as far as I can tell, you don't give two shits about Travis. So, he's essentially out. Not included. Thank God, because he's a man-whore anyways." She lifts another finger. "Let's talk about Seb. I think he likes you, too. But I agree. He seems shady. He's kind of like . . . lemme think . . . " She snaps the air. "Remember Chris in sixth grade, how he used to flip out for no reason whatsoever?"

"Sure. He's the guy who flung his metal lunch box on the wall before screaming at the entire class . . . "

"I found out this summer Timbo and Carson used to break into his lunch box and put weird shit in his sandwiches."

"Actual shit?"

"No. It would have been too obvious. The day of the incident, they put a dead lizard in his ham and cheese, but once they got going, they said they put all kinds of things in there. A frog heart from bio. A plastic eyeball."

"Gross! They told you this? Poor Chris!"

"Yeah, this summer. Down at the beach. They were all stoned and proud of themselves. I got so pissed I left and messaged Chris that I finally understood." A lump grows in the back of my throat because Trace truly is the best. "Anyways, Seb reminds me of a combination of Timbo and Carson. It's like he's an instigator."

"How do you do this?"

"What?" she asks.

"Arrive. Nail personalities in one look."

Trace gives me a look. "You can't play different people if you don't study them."

The wind outside seems to pick up, as if Rico were wishing for the mood in the room to change from negative to positive. It envelops us like a cool gift. Trace arranges my comforter artfully over her goose-pimpled legs.

"And Rico?" I ask.

Her deep throaty laugh fills the room.

"Girl, you're in TROUBLE. The way he looked at you. I don't know what you think you saw or what you did see, but his eyes said he's crazy about you."

"How do you know?"

"Umm . . . freaky intensity focused on your face not your boobs. He's a keeper, but I'd also bet he's got secrets."

A phone buzzes. Trace gives me an apologetic look. "It's my mom." She gives a quick wave and pads out of the room to the nook overlooking the farm.

I stretch out long on the bed and follow the crack in the ceiling over to the old water mark by the window. I stretch my legs over my head, point, and count to three. I push Mom's number. She answers immediately, like she's been waiting. "Clem?"

"Hi, Mom."

There's a rustle; she covers the phone, sending whomever it is she's now dating out of the room. I wait, like I always do, imagining her sitting there wearing something long and flowing. Flip-flops on her feet. Hair piled up on her head, held together by a chopstick. Or, if she's desperate, a pencil.

"Sorry. I'm here. I've missed you. I saw you called. I left you messages . . . "

"I know."

Awkward silence.

"Clem, you can't be mad at me forever."

I can.

"How's your novel?"

"I'm almost done my first draft. The story is falling out of me. It's like shedding skin I didn't know I needed to get rid of." She chokes a laugh, and I can hear her drag a chair across the floor. She will speak on the phone only if fresh air is involved.

"You want to talk about the boy? Is he a raker? Yes? I can already tell he is." She gives a low whistle. "He is delicious looking."

"Huh?"

"It's on CelebrityToday.com. It's you and a boy who looks to me like a raker. A very good-looking raker. I have you on a

Google Alert. I get all the info about you. Sorry . . . it helps me stay connected."

I want to tell her, *Mom, I've been Googling you, too. I've been keeping track.* But, instead, I'm struck dumb by the onslaught of information pouring through my head. Rico and me online? Doesn't make any sense. I snatch Trace's iPad from the corner table and quickly go to CelebrityToday.com to find a picture of me and Rico together in the field. I'm leaning into him, with my hand on his chest, and he's laughing at something I said.

Holy crap.

Now the world knows.

"It's okay, Mom. It's over."

"Doesn't look over. Clem, is your dad pushing you too hard? Do you need to come live with me for a bit? I can rent a bigger place. I know your dad's on edge, honey. He's trying hard. And you dating a raker will do absolutely jack shit nothing to help."

"You can't tell me who to date. You're not here."

She doesn't say anything, for a moment.

"Clem, you made the decision. I told you I'd come back and rent a place for the summer. You told me to stay out of your life."

"I was mad."

"I invited you for Christmas, bought you a ticket, and you bailed at the last minute."

"Dad needed me."

She laughed. "Yes, he always needs somebody. Mémère. Vivi. Johnny. And nobody questions it. Now he's doing it to you. What's going on there?" I don't know how to answer her, so, as usual, she keeps talking. "How's dance?"

I can hear somebody whispering in her ear and her classic response: "Fuck off. I'm talking to my daughter."

"Mom . . . "

"Your dad is not exactly flexible. Your ONLY shot is not pissing him off any more than you usually do. You've worked for this your entire life. You making online buzz with a raker, it violates all kinds of labor laws. You're his boss. You've gotta be careful."

"I will."

"Good."

"I've gotta go. Talk soon, okay?"

"Love you."

"You too, honey."

The phone clicks off.

Trace being here and the conversation with my mom. It's a good energy hitting Laurel Hollow, swirling round me in an invisible force field of creative energy and positivity. I pick up the iPad with the pictures of Rico and me. He's looking at me like a love story, like it's real.

Trace and I haul lawn chairs, old comforters, and a cooler full of seltzers back behind the barn and settle in. The farm feels too quiet tonight. There's no bonfire going on at the raker village, no pop-up soccer games under the light. The whole raker village is silent and oddly dark, but the stars are blazing.

I crack my seltzer open and take a drink. "The deal in Down East Maine is we don't have the light pollution we have in California—or Boston for that matter—so it's a purer experience." The stars scatter across the sky, cascading into the horizon. If you study them, you'll see each one is different. Some stars have a weak quiver while others blaze strong. Just like people.

Trace is kind of quiet as she settles in. "It's a masterpiece . . . "

"This time of the year, me and Mom would watch the meteor showers. Every time you see one streaking through the sky, you make your wish."

"I thought you could wish only upon a star, not a meteor."

"Princess bullshit."

Trace snuggles under the blanket, searching the sky. "You know what bugs me about princess stories? It's the idea of being saved and who saves whom."

"You mean how the prince is always the savior? Like Mr. Darcy saving Elizabeth Bennet? Like Atticus Finch saving Tom?"

"Ninth grade lit again?"

"I remember sitting there thinking, *why can't Elizabeth be the hero*? Why can't she save herself? Or Mr. Darcy, for that matter . . . "

"I'm not trying to save Rico from anything. Before this all happened, he was saving me. It's an impossibly perfect relationship. He's the best person I've ever met."

"I know." She pats my hand. "I know . . . "

"What am I going to do when he leaves?"

"You're going to go kick butt at your dance audition, finish your senior year, and figure out what you are going to do next."

"But, Rico . . . "

"He's got his path. Enjoy today. It's all we can do."

"Alright, princess."

She leans back on the blanket and puts her hands behind her head. I join her and look deep into the Milky Way where a long streak of light breaks up the sky. It feels like a path toward so much we don't understand. Despite it all, it's there for us, every time we look into the sky; no matter what is going on here on earth, it's the same.

chapter fifteen ♡

OUTSIDE A BUSTLING BLUEBERRY processing plant, I wait for the commercial to start. I'm worried my makeup will melt before we get this show on the road. I don't stand out much since I'm dressed "factory chic," with a flannel shirt and loose jeans, giving me time to take it in. Pick-up trucks arrive, carrying crates of blueberries from as close as Cherry Harbor and Bensonville and as far away as Blue Hill and Bar Harbor. My bench vibrates due to the huge blueberry sorting machine working away inside. It's consistent and oddly comforting, so I rest my head against the cool brick and wait.

Lou's inside, charting angles, setting up lights. Dad's a peacock, chatting with every single person he sees. Dev is a pointed man, driven to exhaustion, dead set on his goals. But he also takes time to talk to people. He leans in, keeps eye contact, makes them feel special. *How's the crop? What do you think prices will be this year? How's it going with the heat and the rain? Wicked awful.*

I hold the conversation with my mom close to me, not wanting to share the thaw I feel in my heart. No more talk about auditions, no more talk about money. I get it. His fate is linked to the blueberries in a desperate way now. Just like the rakers. I know money is good. A couple of hundred dollars a day usually. If you convert it into pesos or Guatemalan quetzal, which so many workers do, it's considerable. One thing's for sure, we couldn't do any of this without them.

Crates and crates of blueberries are lined up right outside the factory waiting for their turn. Neatly locked into each other, they remind me of the Legos I used to play with as a kid. I liked how they'd snap together with a satisfying click. For whatever reason, the building blocks of my summer are starting to push together in a much cleaner version of connect the dots: José Luis's whispers at the raker village, the way he wants me to stay an arm's length from all of them; Johnny and his warnings; Rico's inky dark eyes taking me in yesterday, the complete opposite of the night before at Camp III. Something is up. I'm sure of it.

A Bluette's truck pulls up. Felicia, the girl I saw with Rosa, is in the front seat. We meet eyes. She looks away.

A Laurel Hollow truck pulls in and, despite all the uncertainty, a small wave of hope rises. *Is Rico in the truck?* Instead, I see Felipe's ever-present bright smile and Seb's mop of hair.

Dad is on them in a second, urging them over to me.

"Come have a soda or something to eat." Dad points to me, like he did when I was five. "I learned my lesson with this one. We've also got plenty of snacks. I owe you as much after her best friend almost killed you all in the fields yesterday."

"Dad!"

Seb leads the way, his knobby knees winking at me. Felipe pulls off his Yankees baseball hat and smooths his hair away from his forehead before heading my way.

"What're you doing wearing a Yankees hat in Maine? You could get beat up."

"Or I could get shot."

"*Touché.*"

Seb bops me on the head with a closed fist.

"Hair!" I warn.

He backs off.

"What were you thinking? Playing with that gun? My bloody life passed before my eyes . . . "

I think of Zach and what a gunshot must mean for Seb. I put my hand over his.

"You're lucky my Uncle Jimmy wasn't there. He's always packing, he might have returned fire."

"Very funny."

Felipe jumps in. "Hey, I've got an Uncle Jimmy who'd do the same darn thing."

I flip the cooler open, "Want a Coke?"

"Never say 'No' to a cold Coke."

"I never say 'No' to a beer," Seb waves away a fruit fly. "But whatever, I'll take a soda."

From inside, Dad's voice grows louder, more animated, as he explains the final vision of the shoot, which, naturally, is different from Lou's vision. Seb scratches his moppy hair.

"Heard you went to Camp III the other night." He burps, pounds on his chest, "Excuse me. Anyways, people are talking about it."

I look pointedly at Felipe who gives me a *Don't ask me* shrug.

"Did Rico tell you I was there?"

"No, Rosa did."

Hearing Rosa's name, Seb lights up. "Dude, Rosa loves me. Doesn't she?" He points his Coke at Felipe. "I can tell by the way she looks at me."

Felipe lifts his shoulders to his ears and down again. "Dude . . . "

"Stop it. Rosa's going out with Rico. I saw them together."

"What?" They say together, looking at me like I've got two heads. They crack up, reminding me suddenly of my dad and Johnny, two weirdo peas in a pod.

"Okay. Stop already."

But Felipe can't stop. He giggles until it ends in a small hiccup. "We were having a birthday party for Rico last night."

"And you weren't invited," Seb says, not apologetically, which would have been polite.

"But I went for a bit."

I refrain from letting my face crumple into something mean and bitter. Felipe seems to sense my energy and takes a step back. "We can't invite the boss's daughter to a party. You get it, right? How complicated it all is." Felipe takes a sip of soda, obviously searching for the best words. "Plus, Rico doesn't like a fuss. Not his style. He's more of an undercover type. You know, keeping it all on the down low . . . "

Dad pounds on the window. "Five minutes." I give him the thumbs up and turn back to Felipe.

"Plus! Stating the obvious, but haven't you noticed Rico and Rosa look alike? Or are you being racially insensitive?"

"What the fuck are you talking about?"

"They're cousins, Fountaine. First cousins. They grew up together in Mexico. Rico's mom is Rosa's guardian." He leans against the processing plant and takes a thoughtful sip of his soda. "It's exhausting. All their little family talk. Rosa all the time going on about missing her *quince.* She thought about it every single year since she was a little girl. How when she turned 15, she would wear a fancy dress, like her sisters did. Did you know she's the youngest of seven sisters? Crazy."

"Are they all as pretty as she is?"

"Dunno," Felipe shrugged. "Never seen them."

Relief is a clear blue river. I feel buoyed and lighter than I've felt since *Battre en Retraite,* where Rico told me anything was possible if I believed it.

"Is the *quinceañera* her birthday party?" I ask.

"Fiesta de quince años." Felipe says. "Sort of, but it's more than that. It's kind of confusing. The girl is the *quinceañera*. The party is the *quince.*"

Seb burps, loudly. "Excuse me. I heard all about it in the fields. It's kind of like being a debutante here in the States. Big puffy dresses, teased hair, you know, girl stuff. My mother loved the movie *Gone with the Wind.* That chick, Scarlett, I bet she was a debutante. And, honestly, she was pretty and everything, but I bet she'd be a bit much to handle. Racist as fuck, now that I think about it."

Today has taken such an odd turn.

I scanned my memory for that movie from film class. "She didn't give a damn, right?"

"Nope. That was Rhett. Best line in the entire movie." Felipe shakes his head back and forth like one of those bobbleheads, smooth and consistent, a little smile on his face. "Can't believe you thought they were dating. Rosa and Rico." He crunches his can and tosses it through the air, hitting the recycling bin dead center.

Seb pats me on the head again until I yell, "Hair!" He stops.

Dad, looking pleased by the huge smile on my face, holds the door open. "I knew adding some sugar to the cooler would do the trick. Positive energy is radiating off you, *mon chou!* Good to see."

The factory is oddly cool and damp. Blueberries are dumped through a machine resembling a harp and then shaken through to a conveyor belt. Workers pluck every leaf or piece of wood still hanging on before all the berries move into the freezing room for processing.

"Let's do this." I yell to Lou, humming Dad's little French song on the way to my X on the floor.

Lou waves his glasses at me. "You're looking better than last time, girl."

"I'm absolutely fabulous," I say, meaning every word.

chapter sixteen ♡

THE SKY IS A pearly blue with strands of whispery clouds morphing from one design to the next. It's a lesson in perspectives, and I can't help but think it's all a sign. Back home, the house is quiet except for the soft hum of the dryer and the distant squawk of a seagull.

I toss my Timberland boots into the back of the closet, sending old wooden yardsticks into an instant sword fight before falling dead to the floor in a jumbled pile. I move from window to window, searching for a glimpse of Rico. But I don't see him, so I haul on my running clothes and do a quick stretch. I sprint along the edges of the barrens, pushing faster into the ground, until I see him stacking crates of blueberries onto a truck. He's sweaty, wearing a bandana over his head, a T-shirt cut off at the sleeves. He twists to grab another crate of berries, so I dive on him.

"Whoa . . . !"

I wrap my arms around his waist, tip my head back, studying his perfection—the cleft in his chin, his long lashes, the hollows of his cheeks.

"I heard it was your birthday."

"Clem, no big deal."

"No! It is! Meet me at the beach. Today at four. I've got a surprise for you. Be there. Okay?"

I kiss him on the lips and go back to running like I hadn't paused there. He didn't answer me. All of which I still took as a definitive YES.

It's twenty days until the audition. I rush into my studio, play Imagine Dragons, and roll through my dance routine. Over and over, committing it all to muscle memory. Seb pounds on the window and gives me a goofy thumbs up. I give him the finger, and he laughs. I start the routine again . . . And again. And again.

Rico is my rhythm, the beat in my heart, the extra some-thing-something I need for my audition.

I go again.

And again.

Until each step is perfect. Until each twist is smooth and strong.

Mémère always said, "*Fight for what you want.*"

Aunt Vivi always said, "*Be fabulous.*"

Mom always said, "*Dreams are the makings of a life well-lived.*"

Sun illuminates Aunt Vivi's vintage 1950s pink pansy wall-paper. Every single piece of Trace's luggage sits wide open, and clothes are spread across the floor.

Trace groans. "I'm sleeping!"

"It's almost noon. Get up."

"It's only nine o'clock Pacific time."

"You've been in Massachusetts for the last three weeks."

"Rumors."

I stick my finger into my mouth and make a loud slurping noise, an old sleepover trick she perfected back in elementary school, and slowly make my way toward her ear. She nabs my finger mid-air. "I will not be wet-willied today, you freaker . . ." She tilts her head, inspecting me. "Makeup looks good, nice hair, but it seems like there may be more to this Little Mary Maine Sunshine." I grin wildly, trying to get a word in, but she keeps talking. "Dude, sleeping here is the best. The sound of the ocean. The soft air . . ." She pads over to the mirror. "I think my skin looks better. What do you think?"

"I was wrong. Rico isn't with Rosa. Get this: She's. His. Cousin!"

Trace arches into a long stretch. "The old cousin confusion. You're not the first to make that mistake. I heard the same thing happened to Rosalind. She flipped about one of Zander's Instagram posts. Turns out . . ." she pauses, because it's always dramatic effect with her. "Grandma's 95th birthday."

She lifts an artfully sculpted brow.

"Come, we're gonna bake him a cake."

Trace lifts out of bed. "Ohhh . . . I love cake."

Thirty minutes later, we arrive at Renée's house, a forest-green cape with a sagging roof and crooked porch, to bake the cake. There's a small plaque on the door that reads *Captain Eben Crowley Homestead Circa 1787*. As always, the walls vibrate with music, making the thin myopic windows shake to the beat. We climb worn stairs and into the closed-in back porch. It's flat out ready for the next storm to hit. L.L.Bean boots sit in a neat row on the floor, and rain coats hang from nails on the wall. Renée's brother Justin's soccer bag is open, showing off all of his dirty socks.

"Hello!" I nudge the door open an inch.

"In the kitchen." Renée lowers the music to a reasonable decibel.

We dip into the narrow hallway, along the creaking floor-boards until we hit the cocoon of Renée's kitchen. Trace gives an astounded Renée a squeeze around the waist because she's so short. Renée, not a toucher, looks at me for help.

"She can't help it, she's a hugger." And she knows how to dif-fuse her stardom when she wants to. Trace admires Renée's outfit, one of her Nana's old yellow housecoats with the huge hibiscus flowers—pure sixties, pure fun—and flip-flops. I'm proud of who Trace is, a badass television star with the attitude of a friendly camp counselor.

Trace squeezes my face. "Look at her! She's glowing. Rosa is Rico's cousin! She's had the same stupid-ass smile stuck on her face all day."

Renée pushes her fringy bangs from her eyes and cocks an eyebrow at me. "Happens all the time around here. One time at driver's ed, I thought this guy was flat out *fine*. Turns out he was my second cousin. By marriage. But still . . . "

"You guys! Stop it! We're here to bake."

"I'm well ahead of you. As always." A Betty Crocker cookbook sits in the center of the peeling, navy blue Formica. I read the recipe through splattered batter, and we get busy putting together the ingredients. Trace slams the eggs on the counter and dumps the yolks and whites into a ceramic bowl.

Renée nods in appreciation. "We could use you at The Muffin."

"I played a kid baking star on a show that never saw the light of day, but I learned how to break a good egg." A shrill beeping noise blares from the police scanner. "What is that *noise*?"

Renée wipes the tip of her nose with the back of her hand, "It's Grampa DuCharme's police scanner." Static fills the room, and a voice crackles, *"Dispatching Unit 737 to Highland Lane for possible theft of cow."*

"10-4." It squeals.

Trace's mouth drops open. "You mean that's the po-po? No freakin' way! Possible theft of cow? Who steals a cow?"

"Somebody hankering for some cheese." Renée stirs the cake one last time before dumping it into a prepared pan, turning, and popping it into the oven.

Trace put her hands in the air in protest. "Girl, if you're taping one of those ridiculous reality shows, I'm not playing!"

"Sorry. It's true. In Mount Blanc, a lost cow is as good enough reason as any to call 9-1-1."

Trace's fern-green eyes grow wide. "Hysterical."

"I'm gonna write it in the book." I make my way toward the rust-colored shag with a concave seat strategically placed by the window so no matter the time of the year, you get the best view of the bird feeders. I grab a pen from the Mason jar and pull the generic spiral notebook open.

Renée rubs her hands on a towel. "It's bad luck not to write it. You don't want Pa's ghost sweeping in and kicking your ass."

"Don't listen to her. He's a good ghost. He comes only for New England boiled dinners. Even dead, he's got a thing for corned beef and cabbage."

"I'm sorry. Maine's beautiful, but it's weird. You both, in particular, are weird."

I read aloud to Trace.

"May 7, 1993. Police dispatched to Olive Ave for a lost one-eyed Chihuahua." She smiles wickedly, so I keep going. "December 24, 2015. Report of a man in a red suit dangerously tiptoeing across roof on Main Street."

Renée says, "You haven't been here for Christmas since your grandmother died. You should come back."

"Read another one!" Trace asks.

"Okay," I flip to the last page. "August 12, 2016. Shots reported at Laurel Hollow Farm. Police dispatched to the area. Suspect questioned and released."

"Oh shit," Trace grabs the book from me. "I didn't see any police. Did you?"

"Nope. Who do you think the suspect was?"

"I'm assuming the only other choice would be somebody in the raker village . . . "

"Hold off." Renée, who'd been quiet, finally chirps in. "What're you guys talking about? You blasted somebody with a gun? For real?"

"She had me spying on Rico with the viewfinder."

"Not normal." Renée sniffs.

"My family has been doing it for years. Plus, I thought it was a paintball gun. Dad likes to shoot the deer if they are eating the berries or the birds. Whatever. Just to scare them away."

Renée plucks a towel off a hook and furiously scrubs the counter. "This shit gets worse and worse. You know what I'm pretty fucking sick of? Every time something bad happens in this town, they immediately assume it's the migrants. I overheard people talking . . . these two clowns from the hardware store. You know them, Clementine. Jeff and Timmy Mitchell. Graduated a couple of years ago. Their dad owned the Happy Dogs Garage . . . they were going on and on about crime rising in the summer and who's to blame."

Trace quickly writes down the cow in the book. "In a town like this, I'm not messing with your ghost grandpa or this bullshit attitude." She finishes, slams the book shut, and tosses it back on the table.

"It seems like a place as pretty as this shouldn't have to deal with racist BS we sometimes see back home."

"You talking about Lucas? Did it happen again?"

"Yup, last week. He was going fifty-one in a fifty-five. They pulled him over anyway."

Trace's brother, who has never hurt a fly, has been pulled over ten times as much as most people we know in L.A., and it's not because he's any different than Travis—who drives like a reckless idiot—or anybody else. It's because he's a black kid with a black Porsche. A kid who paid for it himself with money from his own modeling gigs.

"Okay, stop. Trust me, if the Mount Blanc police did anything wrong, they'd be hearing from me." Renée shakes her head. "Not right."

We all nodded to each other. God, do I ever adore these girls.

The cake is not two, but three layers of pure pastry perfection, encased in a mocha frosting with little sprinkles on top for fun. I have a copy of Dave Eggers' *The Heartbreaking Work of a Staggering Genius* in my backpack. Roscoe follows me until he sees a squirrel and he's gone. A gentle rumble of a truck brings me back to reality. I turn half-expecting to see Dad or José Luis coming from the northern field, but instead, it's a black Suburban. It's sleek like a shiny show pony, so out of place with our regular farm vehicles. It even has tinted windows—obnoxious in Maine where it's hot for only a couple of months—and it makes me feel off-center. A vehicle like that might as well have fallen from Mars.

It dawns on me.

"Pearson!" I scream. "What're you doing?"

Oddly, the window doesn't roll down, and Pearson's big head doesn't pop out. I try to decipher what looks to be a camera being held up to the window. It's the paparazzi! They shouldn't be spying on me, and they sure shouldn't be spying on Trace. I march in the direction of the SUV, trying to hold the cake upright, and yell, "I don't give you approval to take or post pictures of me! Plus, this is PRIVATE PROPERTY."

A mouse darts in front of me, tail swirling. I jump, the cake teeters back and forth, before crashing to the ground in a sickening thud. I sink down and try to piece the cake back together as you would a puzzle, but it's impossible to fix. Seagulls step forward, bold and hangry monsters. I curse nature as I pull leaves and twigs from the sides of the cake, getting frosting all over my T-shirt and the side of my shorts.

"Umm. I don't want to butt in, but you okay?"

It's Rosa. From this angle, she looks like Wonder Woman of the fields with her dark hair and a sprinkling of gold spangled bracelets hanging from her wrists. She clucks her tongue at the cake like an old lady, making me smile.

"I bet it looked nice before . . . " Her eyebrows lift, and I sense she has a smartass comment deep inside her begging to be set free but, instead, she says, "Was it a birthday cake? For Rico? He'll love it anyway. For him, it's always the thought."

Rosa notices the SUV. She gets incredibly still, and the corner of her jaw quivers, like I've seen Rico's do.

"Do you know them?"

"I think it's my friend, Pearson."

"No. I don't think—" There's a touch of uncertainty in her voice.

"Let's have a Marie Antoinette attack?"

I gesture to the crumbled cake, but Rosa isn't Trace or Renée, so the question falls flat. She takes a couple of graceful steps away from me, like Rico did at the rhubarb festival. I scoop cake into both of my hands, cupping it together like a snowball, but when I turn to hand it to Rosa, she's gone. I drop the cake and turn at a forty-five-degree angle to block the SUV in the middle of the street, not sure of my plan but seeing the outline of two guys inside.

"Pearson! Cut it out."

The window finally opens enough for me to see the outline of sunglasses.

"We're here on business."

I'm propelled back to the time where Trace and I kicked apples into the street, and a passing officer pulled onto the sidewalk in front of us, making us feel like criminals. I fight the urge to flee; instead, I pull back my shoulders and take a step away.

"Are you talking about the gunshots? It was me, a mistake. I don't appreciate you poking around here. Nobody was hurt; the gun was legally registered. It's time that you leave."

"A mistake, huh?"

"Yes, truly."

I'm shocked as the window rolls down all the way, and a camera pops out at me, crisp hundred dollar bills splayed out like a hand of cards.

"We're looking for Trace Taylor. Any leads would be appreciated. We'd pay five thousand. Wait, are you the blueberry girl?"

I blink, not sure what to make of what was happening. But I could use some money for my audition in New York.

"Yeah, I'm her. Clementine Fountaine. Curious, how much would it be for a picture of me?"

"We could do three hundred."

"Trace is five thousand dollars. I'm three hundred?"

"She's famous . . . you're a two on the radar. You're *looking* to be famous . . . "

He holds up three hundred dollar bills to me. "Strike a pose. We'll take a few, and the cash is yours."

I pull my hair down from its bun, letting my blue fall across my face.

"Give me the money first." He hands it to me. I run out to the blueberry fields and jump as high as I can go. The paparazzi snaps and snaps.

I feel dirty. But the cash for New York feels perfectly clean in my hand.

I wipe cake off my knee, shove the cash in the pockets of my cutoff jean shorts, and roll up my sleeves. I smooth my hair behind my ears, adjusting my necklace, and lick my dry lips. I pull the wrapped book from the backpack and carry it into the wooded area. The light dims under the weight of the tree canopy. I find Rico sitting on the felled log, dark hair tucked behind his ears, strong shoulders drooped over his hands fiddling with a blade of grass. He pushes over, nods his head to the spot next to him. I scoot in. Our arms touch lightly. He flips my hand over and follows the lines of my palm.

"Want me to tell you your future? It's an old trick I learned from my grandmother." He points to the main line of my hand, running like a tree from the base of my palm up toward my middle finger. "Look. This one is your fate line." He waits, thinking. "Look here. This is the line where you can tell if you're ruled by your head or your heart."

"You know the answer already."

"Heart."

I fix the crushed silver ribbon into a semblance of cheer and hold the gift out to him with both hands, like an offering. "Can you palm read this?"

He scratches the scruff on his chin, eyebrow cocked in surprise. "For me?"

"Maybe . . ."

"Let me guess, it's a box of chocolates?" He takes it from my hand, wiggling each side softly so the paper groans and crinkles.

"Stop it. You know it's a book by feeling it."

"Books are my favorite . . . " He neatly rips the ends of the paper with the side of his thumbs and sincerely says, "Thank you. I could use some insight from a staggering genius."

"It's about a college kid who ends up needing to take care of his little brother and how he handles it. But it's not sad. It's beautiful."

He softly rubs the corner of my hand with a strong thumb. He starts at the base of my palm, heads left, pauses, and starts again. "Your luck line is strong, Clementine Fountaine. You will go on to do great things."

"Keeping the faith . . . " I keep my hand perfectly still, so he doesn't release it. I notice the wide space where the lines don't meet. "Wait. Tell me more about the gap in my luck."

"We all have blips on the screen."

"You're equating my luck line abyss to a computer?"

"I guess I am. Some days it's best to hit restart."

"Good advice," I yank Rico's hand to me, studying his palm, like he studied mine. There's a long smooth burn dead center of his hand, completely healed and pink but blocking the fate line for all time. "Burned it when I was little. My fate is uncertain."

I shift uncomfortably. "I'm sorry about the other night. For showing up at your trailer uninvited."

"It's fine." His mouth forms a hard line. "Clementine, if things were different . . . "

"Right. I get it. If I weren't the boss's daughter."

"If you're gonna say it like that. Yeah."

Pressure is growing in the base of my skull. "If it were the school year, we'd all be in the same high school together. Right? There wouldn't be any of this me and you and you and them bullshit."

Rico's belly rises and falls in a gentle flow, but I can see clearly that he's clenching his jaw. "Dude, it's true."

"Clem . . ."

I've never heard his voice sound exasperated. "What?" I ask.

"We're not picking teams for dodgeball or jockeying for smart lab partners. All of us rakers are here to do a job."

"I'm here to do a job." My voice sounds petulant even to my own ears. I shoot forward, turning toward him.

"But your job doesn't have people depending on you."

"The hell it doesn't." I stand to go. "Listen, I can tell this isn't working out. We're obviously two different people from two different places."

Rico shakes his head. "No."

"No?"

He stands up. "No, I don't want to fight with you. I didn't not want you at my party. I didn't want a birthday party. Turning eighteen without my mother and my sisters, I didn't want any of it."

I grab his hand, searching the lines for his fate but get lost in the intersection of lines going in every direction. "What're you looking for?"

I open my mouth, close it again. "Who got questioned by the police?"

"Me and Felipe. It was fine. Over quick. José Luis made it right."

"Why not tell them it was Trace?" I ask, incredulous. "She's the one who took the shot. Plus, it was a mistake!"

He half smiles, but it doesn't lighten the mood. "It doesn't matter. I'd rather take the trouble than pass it along."

"Rico, you can't carry the world on your shoulders."

He pulls a clump of frosting from my hair.

"Mocha, my favorite."

chapter seventeen ♡

DAD SHOVES COFFEE ONTO my bedside table and flips my shades. I open one eye, look at the clock, and croak, "6:45 a.m." He points out the window as if I can see through the thick dense fog settling in, turning the early August day cold and raw.

"Valdenisia leaf spot disease in the far corner of the western field. We're starting the burn before it spreads."

He's gone before I can even respond, his footsteps on the stairs a staccato melody trailing into nothing. The farm is alive with too-fast activity, almost as if somebody has ramped up the speed of a video. I scan the fields for Rico but don't see him; instead trucks with Bluette's Organics logos head toward the eastern fields. A diseased crop is bad for *everyone*. It's all hands on deck.

The coffee is down my throat in two gulps, old cut-off shorts pull around my hips. I yank on a Red Sox sweatshirt and twist my heavy hair into a high bun in case I need to burn the crop. I'm halfway down the stairs when I remember Trace. I push Aunt Vivi's door open. Trace is curled up in the fetal position on the far corner of the bed. Her long lashes flicker; she pushes up to rest on her elbow. I shove the coffee mug into her hand. "I need you. It's the berries . . . "

Her eyes flash open. "I'm up."

I dig through her expensive jeans and designer T's. "Go to my room and to the back of my closet. You'll find old clothes there. Hurry."

Any other day, she'd make a smart-ass comment about always looking her best, but today she runs down the hall for my clothes. In the kitchen, Dad's phone is in one hand, and his walkie-talkie in the other. He holds a finger into the air, and says, "*Oui*, send the fire trucks in case it gets *d'emblée*." He doesn't even notice he's broken into French. He sees me and barks. "Get your boots, a bandana for the smoke, and meet me at the fields." I do exactly what he says and, five minutes later, I'm out the door into the cool foggy air. Through the mist, I see only outlines of people marking the field like a crime scene.

"More here," somebody yells. "More here, too."

Lower profits for us means lower profits for Rico, and all the rest of the rakers because there will be no blueberries to pick. The bounty of the season, and the loss, is ours together. I duck under the caution tape, yellow as a school bus, and crouch low to the ground. I tip the leaves to expose the fungus. I feel sick. The spots are littered across the green leaves like the freckles on Seb's face. Haphazard and dominant.

José Luis calls, "Over here, Clementine." He hands me a pile of stakes and gestures wildly to the other side of the field. "Pound these along the edge."

"Wait. How much did we lose?"

Dad scratches his head, looking pointedly over the field. "At least three acres, maybe more."

My head whirls from the gravity of it. I quickly calculate in my head. Six thousand pounds an acre times three . . . eighteen thousand pounds of blueberries. Thirty feet away, there's a commotion, a flash of fire as the controlled burn starts in the far corner. Dad has a bandana tied over his face, making him look like a petite

French outlaw. He fires a torch, and the greasy smoke scratches at the inside of my mouth and nose. I'm brought right back to the time I was eight years old, crouched in the cubby above the stairs, watching my dad and my grandfather burning the south fields. Mémère came to find me. Today, Trace does.

"You weren't kidding?" Trace holds her shirt over her perfect nose, blocking the plumes of dark smoke blowing our way.

"It's the only way to stop it."

"What can I do to help?"

"Seriously, I have no idea."

I cough into the crook of my arm. Trace steps away. I can feel a shift when the rakers from both our farm and Bluette's notice Trace Taylor. I'd forgotten *The Sevens* was such a big hit in Mexico and Central America. Her name passes from one person to the next, a game of Spanish telephone, raising the tension to a frenzy. I see flashes of cameras cutting through the fire, capturing America's sweetheart in the moment. The sun burns through the fog, allowing me to take in the entire field for the first time. Rico stands directly opposite us, holding a burner in his hand.

A raker behind me asks, "Hey, *es eso*, Rico Marquez . . . " I twist around and see a guy roughly our age staring at Rico, his eyebrows screwed together, his mouth a crooked sneer.

I turn away from the gray smoke invading my lungs, pulling my bandana over my mouth. "That's Rico Santiago."

"Sure . . . " His voice mocks me. When I turn again to confront him, he's gone.

A pick-up truck screeches to a stop, and I see a bunch of guys from town join in to help. Ben Rogers, Sam Allee, and, lastly, Seb. They grab shovels and start building a trench to contain the fire. I motion for Trace to follow me, and we each grab a shovel from the back of the truck and dig into the soft earth. There is no joking or flirting or anything else but work. Renée arrives ten minutes later with drinks and snacks from The Muffin. My stomach grumbles. I feel weak from skipping breakfast.

Trace whispers, "Look . . ."

"What?"

"Look . . ."

Between the smoke and the lightness of fog, Rosa stands on the highpoint of the field on a large boulder. She peers at the fire, chin tipped defiantly to the sky, blueberry bushes burning around her. Her hair is pulled away from her face with a bandana, making her look like the *Girl with the Pearl Earring*. Trace snaps a picture with her phone. Rosa's beauty is in sharp contrast to the carnage of the half-burnt area, like she's an agricultural goddess who's been sent to Maine to protect our fields.

And through the darkness, Seb has noticed her, too. And he's as transfixed as we are.

From my vantage point at the corner of the field, I take a long sip of water. My fingers are caked with dirt and soot, so I pull off my bandana and pour water all over it. I scrub first my face with both my hands, until my face feels cool and clean. Though, no matter how hard I scrub, something in my gut tells me things aren't right. It's the berries, I think, peering across the charred-out section of the barrens, still steaming like an overcooked steak.

I can't help but notice the unaffected blueberry bushes, how alive they are, despite it all. Honeybees buzz toward their hives. A flock of sparrows swoop into the air thermals, oblivious their habitat has been altered, pivoting to the east.

With the fires controlled, Trace offers to pose for pictures. The line is long, but being a pro, she keeps smiling for each and every picture. José Luis was there, so Rico kept his distance, but

I catch him glancing at me, and every once in a while, our eyes meet. I resist the urge to fling myself at him, to let everyone know we're together, but I don't. I respect his boundaries, even though I don't agree with them.

Dad wraps an arm around me. "You've done the Fountaine women proud today. Mémère, your mom, Aunt Vivi . . . they'd all be so proud. You got in there, got your fingernails dirty. And look! Trace is like the cherry on top for the crew. Things are going our way, Clementine. I feel it."

"Thanks, Dad."

Dad pushes back his hair, pointing to a guy walking toward us, a camera dangling from his neck. "The *Bangor Daily News*. Could you . . . "

"You already told them yes, didn't you?"

He lifts his shoulders like a little boy I once babysat, who kept stealing jelly beans from his sister's Easter basket.

"It's been a long day, Clem. Good news is good news."

"Fine . . . "

Over my dad's shoulder, I notice Rico getting a lemonade from Renée. She says something funny, and he throws back his head in laughter, showing her a lightness he doesn't often let people see. That is, until he twists and comes face-to-face with the Bluette's raker who called him by a different name. His face deflates into something still and tense.

Dad grabs my shoulder and pulls me toward the reporter. "Clem, meet Andy Flemming, *Bangor Daily News*. He'd like to ask us a few questions."

I try to smile. Rico's shoulders are ramrod straight, but his head has twisted down, like a goat about to headbutt his opponent. Rico's mouth is moving, but I can't hear him. I mindlessly answer Andy's questions. Rico is getting up in the Bluette raker's face. I lean into my dad, smile wide into the camera. My job done, I move toward Rico, who's already walking away from the group, heading back toward Camp III, too far away for me to catch.

Seb saddles up next to me, dirt smudged over his right cheek, smelling of stale beer and coffee. "Hey, did you hear about the fight?"

"What was it about?"

"I dunno . . . It was mostly in Spanish, but Felipe told me it was about a fight in Mexico and stuff I wouldn't understand. I told him I understand local bullshit. I mean, honestly, you know I do. There was the time when I was totally disrespected in the semi-final game against Blue Hill . . . "

Seb keeps talking, but I stop listening, my eyes straining to watch Rico as he slips into the woods and out of sight.

Eighteen days until the audition; I'm trying to hold my focus, but truth be told, my obsession with Rico is overriding everything in my life. Trace and I push through a vinyasa flow, moving in unison to a plank. I think of Rico's body language as he was talking to the raker from Bluette's. Trace braces against the floor, sweat dripping from her forehead.

"Did you hear about the thigh reading trend on Instagram? The signs of your life are written in your left thigh—or maybe it's your right, or maybe right under your . . . " Trace gives me a half-smile, and I can tell she's not sure what to think of my mood.

I force my nervous system to steady and realign, but it's not happening. I dig deeper into a downward dog, stretching myself to the limit before slowly dropping my head down to the ground and lifting my foot into the air. I suck my stomach in to feel the burn, thinking of the alternate last name the guy called Rico. We push forward to chaturanga, my back cracking as I move into position, remembering how when I searched for Rico's paperwork, it was clean. Rico Santiago's paperwork passed the audit. Beside me, Trace groans and falls.

"I can't keep up with you." She rolls to a sitting position and readjusts her tank top over her lean belly. My phone pings. Trace snatches it.

Renée: *Party tonight in the cove. 8 p.m.*

Trace types in a string of emojis: heart, beer, smile.

Excuses as to why this is a bad idea are about to roll off my tongue when Trace, as usual, reads my mind. She wags her finger at me. "Oh no, you don't. We're going. You're going to have fun." I fling a leg out in front of me, bending flat to the ground, stretching out my hamstring. "So, you lost some berries. It's kind of like filming an entire scene and scrapping it. Shit happens."

"Something here is off . . . "

There's a small knock on my door. Dad steps in. He's showered recently, and his hair is still damp and wet. His voice tone is low, and the vein on his forehead pulses. "Can I talk to you?"

Trace whispers, "I'm going to give you two some privacy." I shake my head into a tight *no*, grabbing frantically for her arm, but she's gone in a Zen second, leaving me to face Dad alone. He doesn't say anything immediately. Instead, he takes over my route, from the curio to the window and back again.

"What is it?"

He holds up his phone and shakes it at me. "First, there is a picture of you covered in cake. It's all over the place. Now, two hours later, there's this." He holds his phone into the air. "'The Blueberry Princess has a new Prince!' And I, for one, don't like hearing online about my daughter's love life. Especially when the person you're going out with works on the farm."

202 • The Space Between You and Me

I suck air deep into my lungs. "I met Rico at the rhubarb festival. I got to know him. I didn't march around the farm hitting on rakers."

"Oh, you got to know him, did you? Second, obvious problem—he's supposed to be working for me. That's why he's here. To WORK."

Steam blows out my nose. "Let me get it straight, for clarity." Dad's eyebrows snap halfway up his forehead. "When you were a kid, a teen. Right here in Mount Blanc. You worked every second of the day? Right?"

"I—"

"Ridiculous. You can't pick blueberries 24-7. It's impossible."

"Don't you get all high and mighty. You have NEVER had to worry like I worry."

"Right. My life is perfect. My mother ditches me. You make me the star of the brand, when all I want to do is dance—which I pretty much no longer do. Plus, all of my friends get to keep leading their lives while you insist I come here every summer and expect me to become a nun . . . "

"I never liked Travis."

"You never liked any of the guys I've gone out with. Except Pearson. You'd like me to go out with him. Pearson doesn't even like me."

"He does like you. His mother says he talks about you *all* the *time!*" He emphasizes "all" and "time" like I should believe him. Dad sits down on the corner of Trace's bed. He still has some soot under the fingernails of his left hand. "I don't want you getting hurt. This can't end well. Plus, he's leaving. The rakers always leave. It's what they do. It's how they live. Don't set yourself up for heartbreak."

When I don't respond, he steps toward the door before twisting back around to face me. "I've got to be very clear with you. Everything you do affects OUR brand. Don't fuck it up. We lost thousands today. We can't afford much more."

"Note taken."

"Clementine!"

"I got it, Dad. I got it." After he's gone, I offer a deep *"OMMMMM..."* into the universe.

chapter eighteen ♡

RENÉE ARRIVES RIGHT ON time for the party at Broad Cove, wearing loose Levi's and a peasant shirt. She takes one look at me, her eyebrows a question under her fringy bangs. Her mouth opens to ask me something but stops with the slight shake of Trace's head. I'm not sure I'm happy or sad that these two seem to share the same brain—like Johnny and my dad, oddly enough. All I know is the air feels thick with summer and burnt berries.

We march through the woods to the beach, where the party is already humming at a slow clip. Kids are setting up chairs around the crackling fire, and backpacks overflow with snacks, bug spray, and beer. Not so different from the party at the start of summer in the barn, back when I didn't know Rico was at Laurel Hollow, and summer was still full of promise, not the sad decline of a season coming to an end.

Nervous energy surges through my body.

"I invited all the rakers," Trace says.

"Good." Renée and I say in unison.

We grin at each other.

Renée says, "The usual suspects are coming. All the townies, the summer kids, Seb and his crew, plus the rakers. Epic."

Trace grabs her arm. "I'm going to try to just blend in."

"Yeah, okay!" I laugh.

Trace sniffs the air. "My God, it's lovely here."

"I know," I say quietly. "It really is."

Trace adjusts her tank-top and shoves sunglasses across her eyes. "Incognito."

Immediately, the ringleader of a group of sophomores—a little blond bombshell with china-doll blue eyes—pulls out her iPhone and snaps a picture of Trace, who immediately strikes a pose to her "good side."

"Cut it out," I say quietly.

She shoves her phone in her pocket, like it didn't even happen. I'm tired of phones and their consequences. I resist the urge to rip it out of her little fingers and delete the whole thing. But I know her fate is probably on the same trajectory as Rose and Pat from The Muffin, so I let it be.

Trace's mouth drops as she takes in Beau Routhier. His lobsterman vibe is normal to us—sun-bleached ashy hair, rugged build, Red Sox hat on backwards. But, to her, he's an exotic beast. She strolls in his direction, and he holds a bucket of Maine crabs up to her. He'll keep her busy all night trying to get meat from those things. Renée unpacks her contribution to the party: a package of hot dogs to roast over the fire and a six-pack of beer purchased by her older brother, Justin, a guy who doesn't believe in drinking age laws—or in growing up, for that matter. Per tradition, contributions—a towering mix of random snacks—sit on the picnic table near the tail portion of a boulder we all call Whale Rock, due to the bend of its head.

Across the way, Pearson's eyes don't leave me, I feel them burning into my back, watching, watching. The fire pops, sending burning embers floating through the air. Renée calls for Sam Allee to help her cut sticks for the marshmallows somebody plopped down on her chair. Out of the corner of my eye, I see a bottle of Fireball, Maine's favorite whiskey, being passed around while the smell of marijuana is coming from the woods.

Felipe grabs a bag of chips and yells to Rosa. "They have your favorite, Fritos Chili Cheese!"

On the other side of the party, Rico waits for me, the shadows accenting the hollows of his cheeks and the sharp slope of his nose. Warmth oozes up my neck. He motions me over to him. We no longer need to play shy. We just are. I meet him where the water laps at our feet and we're alone. I can barely see the rise and fall of his chest, and I don't know what to say.

I grab a rock and skip it across the bay. I close the space between us and dip my head. I can feel his heartbeat, a steady drum, like he's synced with the earth. It's so different from mine, which seems to race or slow down at any given moment. I press closer.

"What happened today between you and the guy from Bluette's?"

"Calaca? I mean, Carlos Esteban? We'd all call him 'Skeleton' in school. He was so skinny, couldn't gain weight. He was ahead of me, a couple of years, but we knew similar people."

Awareness of all the things I don't know gnaws on the back of my throat. I twist and pull him to me.

"What're you doing?"

"Trying to match heartbeats."

"Why?"

"I want to remember it."

"You're weird."

"I know . . ."

There is so much I still want to know about him: every friend he's ever had, the things that were important to him at five and seven and ten. I press closer, listening to the *thump, thump, thump* of his blood beating through his body.

"Clem. It's okay. Everything is going to be fine."

I wrap my arms around his waist, pressing my ear harder into his chest. He pulls me toward a crevice of a rock, where we hide from the party going strong only seventy-five feet away, a party that seems to be getting louder and louder.

He lifts my chin, looks me dead center.

"I saw Pearson watching you. It'd be easier if you went out with him. He's not a bad guy; he might even be a good guy."

"Stop it. You'll be jumping on the apple harvest. Then onto Christmas trees, if you stay in Maine. If not, if you go south, maybe I can meet you."

I rest my cheek on his shoulder. A boat chugs across the harbor. He squeezes me tighter, and we both lean into the smooth cool rock. He still smells a little bit like smoke mixed with a dash of pine. It's intoxicating, the smell of him.

The party is getting louder. More people talking at once. A rise in tempo, like the change of beat at a concert.

"Did you hear something?"

"Nope," I lie, but the rumble gets louder. Rico tilts his head. My temples hurt. No. I don't want to leave this moment. We both hear it, the distinct shout. "Oh, hell no, you don't."

Oh, shit. Renée...

"Wait . . . " I urge Rico. But he's already pulling away from me.

"Don't tell me what to do." Seb's voice. "Go back to planning another outfit that makes you look like the freak you are, Renée!"

My ears prick. I wait for it.

"You—of all people to call me a freak. All I said was you should stop hitting on Rosa!"

And suddenly it's me breaking away from Rico, stumbling down the path toward the fire. The size of the crowd has doubled, and everyone is frozen in place like they've been tagged in the statue game we played as kids, not sure what to do. Rico pulls to a stop next to me. Renée is standing in front of Felipe and Rosa, who look like they don't need her help at all, but she's there anyways.

"What's going on?" I yell.

Nobody answers.

"Ask your friend here." Seb's freckles are all screwed together into one lump above his nose. He points to Rosa. "She's the one flirtin' with me, acting like she didn't."

Felipe's chest puffs out; his eyes are laser focused. He lifts a finger in the air and yells. "SHUT THE FUCK UP SEB."

Pearson brings a beer to his lips, taking it all in. Rosa stands tall, the fine lines of her face glowing in the firelight. Her cheeks are flushed and blotchy. Behind him, Sierra raises a phone. A hush falls across the party, broken only by a quick sharp pop of the fire.

"Rosa, you okay?" Rico's tone is more serious than I've ever heard before. I block him from coming closer, like a mother holds a little kid from crossing the street, my arm taut across his chest.

My eyes fly from Rosa to Seb. "Did you hurt her?"

Seb wipes his mouth with the back of his hand. "No." It was a weak denial, and I didn't believe him.

Rosa is holding her left shoulder with her right hand, like she needs to stabilize it. Hair falls from her braid, framing her face and accentuating her eyes. "I'm ready to go back to the farm."

Felipe paces back and forth looking like he's about to unleash a can of whoop-ass on the situation, his hands slamming together, his muscles constricting against the fabric of his shirt.

"Can we all calm down?" I plead.

Pearson reaches for me, but I pull away. "Clem, it's not your business."

"Excuse me?"

Seb steps toward Rosa. "Felipe, you gonna take her side? You see us in the fields. You see her flirting with me. I know you do."

Felipe cracks his knuckles and rocks from one leg to the next. Seb's face skewers into a half-eaten rotten piece of fruit.

"Just how many beers has he had?" Somebody yells from the crowd.

Rosa's voice is clear. "I don't flirt with you."

Seb tips a beer to his lips but doesn't drink. Instead, he lifts the cup to Rosa. "No worries, I'm too good for you anyway."

Rico vaults forward, tackling Seb from the side with surprising force. Seb's head slams to the ground with a crack. They twist, rolling for footing before getting back on their feet, two bull moose locked in battle.

Seb swings at Rico, who ducks. Rosa screams, "Stop!"

Rico grabs Seb's shirt taut and gives him a swift kick to his shinbone. His mouth moves in words I can't hear or understand. The rest of the party spreads out making room for the fight.

Trace pulls Rosa away, but she won't take her eyes off Rico.

"Stop it!" I rush forward, but Pearson grabs me and won't let me go. "Clementine, I don't want you to get hurt. Rico wouldn't want you to get hurt either."

Rico pushes Seb backwards into the party. Seb stumbles before getting back up with a piece of firewood. Rico pushes his hair away from his face. "Don't you ever disrespect my cousin again. Got it?"

I yank myself from Pearson and dive into both of the boys. "Fucking stop!" I throw my hands in a T, holding them apart. I see Trace hovering. She's always got my back.

Seb's breath is sour on my cheek.

Rico's heart beats fast.

Seb belts Rico in the face. I pull my fist together and slam it into Seb's chin. In turn, he pushes me toward Pearson. I fall to the ground, dig in like a bull, and get ready to charge when Pearson steps in front of me, holding me back with his body.

"Get Rico out of here," I yell to Felipe. "Rosa, too."

"Sure, get the *bitch* out of here!" Seb screams.

Rico's arms pull back, and he strikes Seb in the cheek. There's a crack. Seb falls backward, landing inches from the bonfire, his head smacking into the ground.

Sierra and her friends scream and pull him away from the fire.

Pearson yells, "You boys heard Clem. Go."

Rico listens, following Felipe away from the party back toward the raker village. Trace leaves with Rosa, but not before turning and yelling, "I've got lawyers for this kind of bullshit, Seb!"

"Yeah, miss fancy Hollywood! Fuck off." His eyes are wild.

"And you, Clementine. We all know you're one generation off from being a migrant yourself. Don't know why you cruise around here thinking you're better than everyone else." Seb hucks bloody spit toward my foot.

My finger flies into the air. "Yeah, so's everybody else here."

Seb rubs his nose, smearing blood across his face. "You're going to be sorry . . . "

"Clementine," Renée barks, taking command of the situation with her voice. "It's enough. He's hurt."

I grab a flashlight, turn it on, and beam it into his face. His eyeballs are round as dishes, glassy as a silverfish. "Oh, Jaysus. You're hurt."

"What do you expect?"

"Listen, my dad is weird about press. We can't have any more trouble."

"Well, you shouldn't have brought us all here." Seb grabs his sweatshirt off the ground before storming down the moonlit path back toward town. "Seriously, go back to California where you came from."

"Happy to, Seb."

I look around the clearing, littered with cans and chips scattered like autumn leaves, and I think what a mess we've made.

chapter nineteen ♡

ROSA AND TRACE ARE sitting on the back porch under the porchlight. I elongate my neck, straining to hear their soft conversation, but they're too far away. Renée stumbles in the dark beside me and lets out a little *yelp*, warning them of our arrival. Rosa stands—leaving Trace seated with the night moths flickering in the shadows—and steps forward to greet us. I take a quick inventory of my vital signs: blood pressure currently stable, oxygen saturation low. Home. Laurel Hollow. It fixes things.

Rosa wipes her nose with the back of her hand. "I need you to know why this was hard for me. For Rico . . ."

"You're fine now. Seb was being an asshole."

"Rico's reaction. It's not *just* about Seb. It's about much more. Things happened in Mexico, changing everything for both of us."

I turn to Trace, looking for reassurance. Her eyes haven't left Rosa's. "Tell me what's going on!" she pleads.

Rosa was tentative at first but grew stronger as she told her story. "Where I'm from, you're expected to grow up a lot faster than you do here. And it can be for ugly reasons. Even our most loved traditions have uncomfortable assumptions wrapped up in them. When I was a girl, I dreamed of the big party I was supposed to have when I turned fifteen. It's not just a personal ritual; it's something the whole family celebrates and works toward. For years, saving money. Even the poorest families are expected to host a big party . . .

"A *quince* is like a wedding with no groom. It takes the same amount of planning and saving. It's seen as a sweet, innocent time of transition, but it's normally very stressful for the family. I saw the debt my cousin's family got into, and that's when the fantasy started to change for me. As I grew older and it was coming closer, I started to think about what everyone would be celebrating and I realized . . . it wouldn't really be me. It's just your physical self. That basically you have the body and womb of a woman. That you can be treated as an adult. But it grew complicated for me." Rosa speaks more softly, deflated, like one of those dolls whose string you pull is winding down.

"I was thirteen years old when the men came to my village. One of them wanted to marry me. And if I didn't, they'd take what they wanted."

Renée spits. "When I was thirteen, I spent my entire summer watching *Pretty Little Liars* and knitting a blanket for my bed. I didn't have to worry about some asshat getting up in my business."

Rosa steps close to me, so we're eye to eye. "Clementine, Rico fought back. He was only sixteen, but he fought. He wouldn't let the men take me. Rico, his mother, they hid me. Even though it could have gotten them all killed. Thirteen weeks. They pulled strings and got me a work visa. That's why I came here . . . "

My knees buckle, so I steady myself on the porch railing.

"You mean . . . you and Rico got work visas *together*?"

Her voice is soft, yet steady; like a spoken word actor telling a memorized story, she knows every word by heart.

"The cartel doesn't like it when they don't get their way. Word got out Rico pulled favors. He had to go. He hired a *coyotaje* . . . " She lowers her voice a full octave, her accent showing clean through, and I fall into her eyes, noticing for the first time how old they look.

"Wait, what is a coyote?" I ask.

Rosa shrugs. "A man you pay to get you over the border. Rico should have asked for asylum, but he didn't. Instead, he ran to a place that would provide for his family, just like his father did."

Images hit me from all angles: Rico recoiling from the very first rent-a-cop at the fair, the fierceness of his positivity, the way he didn't want to talk about being questioned by police. It shows how terrifying it's all been for him.

"But I've seen his paperwork . . . " I push past Rosa, racing into the house to my father's study, tearing through his files of papers atop his messy desk. My mind was racing. There was an audit. ICE came.

They came and said we got a B+. A B+ is good.

I push aside a group of bills and find the raker paperwork underneath. I go immediately to S. Rico Santiago. I haul ass back to Rosa, shoving the paperwork into her hands.

"Look," I insist, pointing to his social security number. "Right here."

"It's fake."

"Fake . . . but how?"

Her eyes shift to the shadows. "Yesterday in the field . . . the SUV . . . I'm worried it was immigration. They've been poking around after the gunshot. When Calaca came, I couldn't believe it. He was on the soccer team with the guy who wanted to take me. He might tell him. And tonight . . . the fight."

"Why would he tell?"

Rosa sighs. "We are all here because we need something. Opportunity. Money. Safety."

Trace cuts in, "Wait, if Calaca is here, he understands your point of view. Right?"

"I don't know. I'm scared for Rico."

"Don't go there. I'm sure it'll be—" Renée hisses.

A truck blazes down the driveway, crunching to a stop right in front of us. Johnny's beard glows in the radio light, and I can see a cigarette between his teeth. "It's Johnny LaMonde. My dad's friend."

"Look at the license plate," Rosa whispers, "'For US Government Use Only.'"

"Let me talk to him alone."

Rosa turns toward Camp III; Trace grabs her arm and ushers her inside.

Johnny puts the truck in park. Dad's bedroom light pops on from the front corner room. A cool breeze whistled through the trees.

Blood is speckled on the sleeve of my jean jacket. Seb's blood.

Johnny comes through the door without knocking and stands in front of me, shoulders straight and imposing, hand on his hip, inches from the holster holding a gun.

"We need to talk, Clem."

"What about?"

"About Rico Santiago—I mean Rico Marquez . . ."

My heart sinks to my knees.

Johnny holds up a piece of paper, eyes dull and flat. "There was no use lying. I've gotta ask you a question . . ." He lowers his voice, "And you and I have always been straight with each other."

"Right."

"The boy your dad told me about earlier today. The one you're dating. Is that Rico?"

I can't tell what Johnny's thinking. He rubs his hand along his beard. "And he's the very same one you lied to me about when I heard all the rumors."

"It's hard . . ."

Snot gurgles in the base of my throat as I hold back tears.

"Clementine, your boy is undocumented." He pulls out his pad of paper, tapping it on the door. "Flagged by ICE on July 14th. Seb Michaud has filed a report against him. He's at the hospital now, pretty banged up. Somebody found him collapsed in the street, bleeding from the head. I heard it over the radio. They have witnesses confirming the entire thing. Sierra Sanders' father works at dispatch. He called it in, too."

"Did anyone tell you what Seb did? It's like he gets a free pass for all his bad behavior and Rico gets in trouble."

"The law is the law, Clem."

"It wasn't for Seb. He stole the elvers right from the water. You can't do it, Johnny. I'm telling you, you can't."

"Clem . . . "

"Johnny, give me a little time."

He smooths his beard and narrows his eyes at me before turning away and grabbing his radio. "LaMonde at Laurel Hollow. No confirmed sightings of suspect. Will update at twelve hundred hours."

"10-4"

There was one time when I was little, Johnny pushed me on the tire swing hanging from the giant maple. As soon as I hit the pinnacle of height, the tire broke free, hurtling me through the air, a little Clementine cannonball crashing to the ground.

I'm hurtling.

I'm getting Rico. Right now. I'm going to do it. I stomp up my stairs. Trace opens the door wide. She gestures to Rosa. She's a rare bird who can cry with no sound, a perfectly peaceful look on her face.

My breath is fire. "I need to find Rico. Now. He's in big trouble. Rosa, I'm so sorry."

"It's all getting worse," Renée whispers. "Sierra taped the fight."

She hands me the phone. I click the video, and the clearing springs to life. Sierra captured Rico slamming Seb to the ground. His foot coming out for a kick I hadn't even noticed before. It's damning. It's incriminating.

And Pearson shared it, too. "Fuckhead."

I fire off a text demanding Pearson pull it down. But he doesn't respond.

Rosa's hair is wild around her face. "If I'd been nice to Seb, if I'd . . . I don't know . . . "

Renée lets out a whoop that can only be described as a battle cry. "You aren't put on the earth to be of service to any guy who decides he wants to claim you." Renée grabs lotion from my shelf, only to hold it in her lap. "It's so complicated. Seb has a hard life, too, with his dad in jail and his brother passing away."

Trace points her finger in the air. "But it doesn't make it okay for him to metaphorically take his penis out and try to hit us all over the head with it."

The room closes in on me.

I shove clothes deep inside one of Dad's old duffle bags. I pluck my white billowy sundress out of my closet, the one I wore to Pearson's house. I grab a bathing suit, sneakers, and a couple of T-shirts. I yank open my underwear drawer and snatch the money I saved for New York. The audition no longer feels important. A kid's dream.

Rosa looks so much like Rico I can barely stand it. "He's with Felipe in his trailer at Camp III. You're running, aren't you?"

"Just until I figure out—"

"—Dude, you don't have a plan?" Renée interrupts. "This won't help anything."

"I don't have time to keep talking. No. I don't have a fucking plan, but I'm going to get one. And fast. I can't waste any more time."

Trace flings her credit card on the table. "This came up in a pilot I filmed last year. You need to go digitally silent. Take my phone, too; nobody will be able to find you. You can make a plan once you hit the road."

I stand in their feminine energy, so glad to have it back at Laurel Hollow Farm, and hope for the best.

I'm out the back door in a flash, stumbling past Johnny's truck through the darkness, running under the stars to steal my Starstealer. The keys dangling from my hand, I jam the Jeep key into the lock.

Roscoe howls.

"Shut, up!"

He howls again.

"*Shhh . . .*" Johnny and Dad race out of the house. They both look like hell. Crumpled and dirty and mad.

"Clem, what're you doing?" Dad yells from the porch. "It's 1 a.m."

"I'm taking the time I need to process this bullshit." I jam the gas. Johnny gets in front of the Jeep. "Johnny, I'm going!"

"This isn't some bus you can hold up by being cheeky."

"Hell yes, I can."

Johnny's eyes are huge. He turns on me. "You know I can keep a secret, but this is real shit, Clem. You could end up in jail."

"Listen to me. You never saw me, Johnny. Give me twenty-four hours. It's all I ask of you."

Dad grips the side of the door. "You're so much like your grandmother."

He shows me an old picture. It's the man from the art studio. This time, my grandmother has on a simple yellow dress with small flowers, and the boy is all smiles.

"Flip it over."

I turn the picture over to see Mémère's looping handwriting: *Leonore and Andres.*

"What the fuck is this, Dad? And why're you sharing secrets right now?"

He pulls out his wallet like he's going to give money, mucks around a little before pulling out a yellowed piece of paper. "This is him . . . "

BANGOR DAILY NEWS, 1946.
Andres Diaz, 19, Puebla, Mexico, died in a tragic accident at Bristol Apple Farm. No charges filed.

My brain overloads. Too many things for one day.

"What is this? Why are you giving it to me?"

"Listen, I don't feel good about this either. When she was dying, it's all she could talk about. Andres this. Andres that. She said that Andres was her biggest regret. She made me promise to protect the rakers. For her, I'm letting you go."

"Oh, you're letting me. Because you know I'm going anyway."

"This isn't a good idea," Johnny rubs thick hands through his hair.

Dad steps away. "You stop her."

Johnny turns his back to me. "I can't."

❀

Five minutes later, I'm on the back way to Camp III on an abandoned logging road full of pits and valleys. I park and use Trace's phone flashlight app to lead me. I've never driven here, and this angle is different. I'm surprised to see an old camper with the roof fallen in just sitting there. Two eyes stare at me from inside, a raccoon looking for food. I freeze, and it scurries away. My foot hits something hard. It's an empty can of B&M baked beans, and, from the look of it, it's been here since last year.

Ahead, Rico's pop-up. I bang on the door.

It opens a crack. It's Felipe. "What're you doing here?"

"Let me in."

"I dunno," Felipe gnaws on a hangnail, trying to block my way.

Rage bubbles in me. "Don't make me go through you."

Felipe's hands go into the air, and he backs away from me.

"It's fine," Rico's voice comes from around the corner.

I cram past Felipe. Rico's home is sparkling clean, but the trailer itself is awful. Synthetic cotton falls out of cushions like stuffing out of a Thanksgiving turkey. It's warm and musty in here, so cramped I'm instantly claustrophobic. A water stain shaped like Rhode Island covers the entire ceiling, a miniature kitchen stove's rusted in places, linoleum curls from the corners. A first-aid kit sits open on the mustard-yellow table, and one of those disposable ice packs hangs off the side of a little bench. Rico sits on the edge of the countertop. Three small Band-Aids cover his knuckle, and he has the purple glow of a burgeoning bruise on his jaw.

Felipe looks away. Air feels like it's knocking out of me, my lungs crumbling inward. I can't find the words. I lean onto my knees, gasping for air.

"Panic attack? Oh sheeeet." Felipe yelps.

Rico's voice is soft. "She knows."

Felipe hands me water. I take a sip, snot bubbling again in the back of my throat, but I don't care, it all comes out: "You spend all kinds of time telling me stories about your sister Nina and your mother and all of your memories back home in Mexico. But you left one big hole in your story—"

"—It's easier for me not to talk about it."

"Bullshit. Easier for you?"

Somebody from another camper yells, "Shut up!"

Rico doesn't move. His face is very still. I cup his cheeks in my hands.

"Rico, they're coming for you. Immigration. They know."

Felipe is up in a flash, shoving shirts into a bag, grabbing his laptop, books, and toiletries.

"It's all going to be fine," he says.

"It's not going to be fine if you're deported. We only have a little time."

The whole experience unnerves me. It's knocked my chakras out of whack, detaching them from my body. Rico and I peer straight ahead. Lost in thought, oblivious to the roadside farms. I zoom up further in my mind and envision all of Maine and then New England, until I can see the whole Northeast. I go higher until I can see the entire country and can connect the dividing line between California and Mexico.

I grip the steering wheel tightly. A suicidal fox crosses our path, so I veer right and slam on the brakes. "What happens when, I mean, if you go back to Mexico? Your family? Will you have enough money? Will you be safe?"

Rico shifts in his seat, considering my question. "Are any of us safe anywhere? Seb? Do you think he feels safe?"

I blink, stunned. I haven't once, in my entire life, thought about whether I feel safe or I don't feel safe.

It's been a given for me.

Rico cups my chin, his eyes kind even as the world is unkind to him. "That's the way it's supposed to be . . . every girl in the world should have that safety."

"But Rosa didn't."

He rests back in the seat and peers up into the sky. "No. She didn't. But it's not your fault."

We sit in silence for a minute.

"What do you want to do with the time we have?"

"Be with you . . . with Rosa. It's all I really want . . . "

My lower lip quivers. "Even now, you're looking out for every-body else. What about you, Rico? Who's looking out for you?"

"I've got you for that."

"Well, welcome to my bubble of protection."

He gives me a crazy half-smile. "No place I'd rather be."

It's 3 a.m. I find a place for us to sleep in the far corner of a public beach parking lot. I put the Jeep into park, and we both stare at the moon across the water. Music plays softly on the radio; it's too happy sounding, so I turn it off.

"Rosa told me what happened to her."

Rico's voice is low, almost guttural. "It's my fault. I was playing soccer for my school's team. I was good. Better than good. I got recruited to a private school, away from my village. My mother, she said, 'Go, take the opportunity. Make us proud.'"

"You were recruited that young?"

"Yeah. All I did was play. Every day." He fumbles in the front pocket of his backpack and pulls out a photo. "See, there I am, freshman year." He points to a picture of him in the back row. "This boy. He was my best friend. Ivan Munez. His older brother was in the cartel. He'd come into town and see our soccer games. One day, my mother brought Rosa to see me. Ivan became obsessed with her, but we . . . my family . . . we don't get involved in drugs. So, when they came to get her and said he wanted to marry her, it's not what he meant . . . " He shakes his head as if he's trying to shake off the memory. "She would've been pregnant by the time she was fifteen. Married or not."

I try to imagine a world where a teenager is truly in charge of anything, but I just can't. I grab first-aid cream from the glove box, squish some onto my finger, and rub it on his chin. "Your mother? What did she do?"

His voice kind of breaks. "It was horrible. She didn't know what to do. I didn't know what to do either. It felt dangerous for all of us, and the word on the street was they were coming for us."

"You were young."

"My mother told me when I was a little boy to never live in the past. It does no good, having hope for the future is the only way to live." He continues, his voice whispering in my ear. "Look up there; it's the same sky as it is in Mexico. Our place doesn't define us. We do. That's what I chose to believe at the drop in the desert . . . "

A meteor streaks through the darkness. A good luck sign, I hope.

I wake up to kids banging on the window. It's morning. Almost ten. I frantically look in the mirror, scrubbing the mascara from under my eyes and twisting a ponytail holder from my wrist to capture my wild hair. Next to the Jeep, a family is getting out of a minivan with a blow-up raft, cooler, and a full tent. The phone rings; Rico's eyes flutter open and then close again. The phone rings again. I fumble for it. I'm disoriented by the bright sunlight.

"Hello." I slink out of the Jeep, walking barefoot to the water's edge.

Trace whispers, "The Maine State Police are here."

My stomach rolls. "Right now?"

"Johnny is covering for you, but this is serious. He cornered me and told me to get you the hell home."

"Nooooo . . . Rosa okay?"

"Sort of . . . "

Renée grabs the phone, "When Seb passed out in the road, he was rushed to the hospital. Clem, Rico's eighteen. He's an adult. The juvenile court can't protect him. Too many agencies are involved. Johnny says he'll be lucky if he doesn't go to jail. It's being considered an assault."

"You've got to do something. Talk to Seb. It was a fight at a party. Tell him to not press charges!"

The tide licks the edges of my toes. A seagull dives into the ocean, grabs a fish, and flies away. I glance at the Jeep. Rico's still sleeping. It's time for him to get up. We've got one day, and I want to make it the best it can be.

I take a deep breath and tell Renée exactly what I need her and Trace to do.

chapter twenty ♡

IT'S SIMPLE TO HIDE on Mount Desert Island, the home of Acadia National Park, Bar Harbor, and other quaint villages. Tourists linger, stopping for homemade pie at the church. New Yorkers dip in and out of small shops. Others head for the park to bike or hike or picnic. I'm wearing a Cubs hat I found in the parking lot to cover my blue streak. Rico tied a bandana over his shiny dark hair. Incognito. We look like vacationing campers—not teenage runaways—at the Seal Cove Diner. I'm famished, so I attack my blueberry pancakes, bacon, and side of fruit. Rico sits quietly in front of his Western omelet, holding a cup of black coffee. He's focused on the comings and goings of the parking lot.

"I don't think I can eat."

I fumble across the table to grab his hand, thinking how far we've come since the rhubarb festival. "Johnny is one of my best friends."

He sniffs.

"Is Rosa okay?"

"Yes. And Felipe is too."

"Seb?"

"I'm going to make the next twenty-fours the best it can be for us. Let me do this for you." He pokes at his omelet. I hold up my hand, fingers wide. "I've had five great days: the one I met you, the train graveyard, our picnic, your birthday, and TODAY. Despite the bullshit, we're gonna make the best of it. Eat, so you can enjoy it. Come on, say it with me. I think we can . . ."

A smile pulls from the corner of his mouth.

"Little Caboose . . . "

"Now eat."

He leans over the table and pokes his fork onto my plate and grabs a chunk of pancake, puts it into his mouth, and chews.

"Delicious."

I'm in a countdown with Trace's credit card and phone and a vehicle that can be easily tracked, but it's a perfect day for a last day. Seventy-six degrees. A slight breeze coming off the water. Golden sunshine. And the best part, without any eyes on us, we don't need to keep us secret.

"What're you smiling about?" Rico asks.

"I'm oddly happy."

"Me too," he says. "Which makes no sense, considering."

"It was just a punch, Rico."

"It was more . . . all of it. But I'll stand by my actions. I needed to do it for Rosa. And I got to meet you."

My smile is butterscotch pudding.

We creep forward in line in traffic and then take a right into the parking lot for the Precipice Trail. The most dangerous hike in Acadia.

Rico shakes his head, the first bit of real life coming back to his eyes, and I realize he'll be an amazing doctor or soccer star or whatever he chooses to be.

I swallow. I hope it's that easy. I think of my California friends, with every need they have attended to and every mistake put right and polished clean. *You want to be an actress? A lacrosse player? The lead of the play? Go for it!* I think of Mom, paying for all my dance lessons, the outfits, the pointe shoes.

He reads my mind.

"Have you ruined your chances with your dad for your audition? It's going to be hard to come back from being on the run."

"There is this old movie called *Thelma and Louise*. He loves it. Wants to road trip with ladies on the run."

"Just because he likes something doesn't mean he wants his daughter to do it."

We sit quietly for a moment. He tilts my chin toward him. "Listen, I'm not hiking unless you stop right now. Having goals, dreams, it's what keeps us going. It's like, without them, we're just a shell of a human . . . "

The phone blows up in my pocket, one *bleep* after the next, I excuse myself and run toward the outhouse across the parking lot.

Hands shaking, I quickly put in Trace's passcode.

It's Renée:

R: *The paparazzi picked up the story. It hit the Associated Press. The local news just left.*

R: *Your mom has called your phone about twenty times. She says if you don't call her back, she's flying to Maine on the next plane.*

R: *Seb's out of the hospital. He's on concussion protocol. I talked to Justin. He'll be waiting for you at 32 Acadia Drive.*

R: *Pearson pulled down the video, but it's gone viral. Sorry...*

I text back:

Me: *Stall my mother. I'll call her soon.*
Me: *Have Trace work the media. She's a pro.*
Me: *How's my Dad?*
Me: *Thank you!!!*

Rico walks toward me. I shove my phone deep into my backpack, remembering when he told me about the peregrine falcons and how seeing them represented hope.

"Ready?" I ask brightly.

He rolls up his T-shirt sleeves over his biceps and heads toward the trailhead, not bothering to stop to read the sign on the side of the trail. But I do.

THE PRECIPICE IS MAINTAINED AS A NON-TECHNICAL CLIMBING ROUTE, NOT A HIKING TRAIL. ATTEMPT THIS ROUTE ONLY IF YOU ARE PHYSICALLY FIT, WEARING PROPER FOOTWEAR, AND HAVE EXPERIENCE IN CLIMBING NEAR EXPOSED CLIFFS AND HEIGHTS. PERSONS HAVE RECEIVED SERIOUS INJURIES AND OTHERS HAVE DIED ON THIS MOUNTAINSIDE!

He grabs my hand.

"It's fine."

"Doesn't look fine!"

"Come on . . ."

We hike to the first cliff. I grab a cool metal rung and step from one to the next until I scurry over the first obstacle. Rico is ahead of me, cheeks red from the effort. We push further up the rock slab until we get to our first cliff walk across the open rocks.

I glance down to see a forty-foot drop. I edge my feet across the two-foot-wide path until I reach safety. We climb over rock and cliffs, gaining confidence in every single step, as the oxygen pulses through my blood, making my brain buzz. When it gets high, I focus on the surety of Rico's step, the way his quad muscles flex as he picks the perfect spot to secure his foot.

My fear of heights keeps me from counting the minutes and hours we're together. It forces me to be present, and even when I teeter on the last rung and close my eyes to make the final move, Rico is there.

I hold his hand tight and let the lightness of the ocean air cool my cheeks. From our vantage point at the mountaintop, we can see the entire bay speckled with islands. An old-fashioned wooden schooner tacks starboard, its boom tight to the wind. Mémère could have been up here with the very same view. It's a place lost to time.

"We made it," I whisper.

"We did."

I pull out a water bottle and some trail mix Renée shoved into my bag at the last minute. Rico picks around the raisins, eating only the peanuts and the chocolate chips. He sinks to the warm rock, making room for me next to him. Instead, I move in front of him and nestle myself between his legs and lean against his chest. He talks low. "When I left Mexico, I saw a peregrine falcon. Do you know what 'peregrine' means in Latin?"

"And how would I know?"

"It means 'traveler.'"

"Traveler," I echo, watching the falcons soar across the sky, dipping and diving in the air streams. "How long are the wings?"

Rico holds his hands out wide.

"Three feet!" His voice becomes more animated, turning into a true science nerd in the most adorable way. "And get this!" His lips pull into a crooked smile. "A female can be a third larger than a male, but the male doesn't care."

"I thought about the falcon when I first met you. You were fierce. Too big for me."

"Shamans, medicine men, historians . . . they believe the peregrine represents success, victory, rising above." His voice lowers. "But also the patience to wait, to get the most out of life, out of the opportunities you have."

I stand up to take a picture of us snuggled into a crack in the rock. I capture his eyes gazing off in the distance . . . he's perfect.

We watch together as the birds play in the wind until the sun grows to midday and it's time for Rico's next stop. I. Can't. Wait.

After the hike, we stop for provisions in a little variety store called Lucky Lou's. It's the type of place loaded with about everything a local would need: nightcrawlers for fishing, whoopie pies, dusty canned goods with questionable expiration dates, Moxie (pure Maine magic), and beer. We gather a cart of snacks, salt-and-vinegar potato chips, Vitamin Water, a wilted salad, and a hunk of peanut butter fudge.

Rico goes outside while I wait in line at the checkout.

An old-fashioned television, the boxy kind with rabbit ears, hums in the corner. I don't pay attention until I hear a familiar voice booming through the room. Trace Taylor fills the screen, doing what she does best.

"This is a true Romeo and Juliet story—two kids from totally separate worlds, desperate to be together despite the odds." The camera spans Laurel Hollow. "Don't let this story end like that one . . . "

I grab the last of my money, a twenty, and drop it on the counter and leave.

A text pops in from Renée:

R: *Operation Finale is a go.*

Rico flips from station to station until Journey's "Don't Stop Believing" blares through the sound system. I think of the new lead singer of Journey. How they found him on YouTube and he came to America and changed his life. Rico sings first, kind of quiet. I join him. It's corny, but I don't care. We sing along together, rocking back and forth to the beat of music, as I lead him to Mount Desert Island High School.

"What're we doing here?" Rico throws the car into park.

"Grabbing a textbook for Renée." I yank him toward me, wrapping my arms around his shoulders. A guy in a soccer uniform raps on the window and yells, "Get a room!" A group of guys in uniforms head toward the turf field in the distance. Two teams are already there, warming up for a summer soccer match.

Rico, who has been quiet for the last hour, comes to life when he sees the soccer players. He's a kid at Christmas with an unexpected gift; he's truly awake and alive.

"Did you know there was a game? Sweeeeeeet! The kid in the red did a Zidane!" "A what?"

"A Zidane. It's named after a French player . . . " Rico points to the far corner of the field.

"Look. He stopped. Turned 180 degrees and pulled to the opposite foot. Some talent."

"Okay, super fan! I need to get Renée's book."

"Yeah," he shakes his head absent-mindedly, barely listening, but follows me out of the car. "I'll keep watching . . . "

Justin, Renée's brother, jogs toward us, quads flexing at each step, referee uniform tight across his shoulders. And I can't stop grinning. "Clementine!" He messes up my hair, like every single time I've ever seen him.

"This is my friend, Rico."

Their hands meet in the middle with a quick fist bump. Justin pretends to consider the field. He scratches an armpit. "We need one more player or this game is a no-go. Turns out some kids on the team have mono. Do you play?"

"Yeah, I do."

Justin pretends to inspect the team. "Well, it looks like they're missing a midfielder. Can you play any position?"

"Of course."

Justin flips him a mouth guard. "Safety first."

"Safety first, huh? You carry brand-new mouth guards around in your shorts." Rico shoves the guard in his pocket. He turns to me, all happy. "You did this, didn't you?"

"With help from Renée . . . "

Justin shakes his head in agreement and holds his arms out wide. "What was I gonna do? You don't want to be on Renée's bad side. She tells me 'Find Rico a spot at soccer,' I find Rico a spot at soccer."

A gangly redhead jogs over and tosses Rico a uniform. "I'm Hunter, captain at MDI High School. And those bozos are from Camden." He points to the other team, where a player immediately gives him the finger. Players shake Rico's hand. I see a swagger not so easy to find on the farm. On the soccer field, Rico takes up more space in the world. His shoulders are straighter, wider, and his chest is puffed. A short squat player opens a duffle and drags out a pair of worn, smelly looking cleats.

"Size 10?"

"Perfect," Rico calls, and I notice his voice is louder, more secure. He sits down under the shade of a maple tree and shoves the shoes on his feet. How much of Rico's personality was hidden while he, too, was basically in hiding?

Justin flips a coin. Hunter calls heads. Rico's team gets the ball first. Rico hangs back at first, as if unsure of the play. He engages, springing into action, breaking down the field, and passing neatly to the center. Another player pulls back his foot, and nails the ball into the net. Rico slaps him five. The team unfolds around him, using him to their advantage, like he's always been part of the team.

My phone pings.
Renée: *Go on Facebook Live.*

I click on the live stream to find Trace standing with Felipe in the middle of the farm.

"I'm Trace Taylor, and I'd like to welcome you to a new segment: People Who Make the Blueberries Happen! World, this is Felipe Ortiz."

Felipe picks up the blueberry rake and launches into a full lesson on the benefits of an old-fashioned blueberry rake. He lets Trace try it, and she looks adorable, scrapping into the bush with zero finesse.

Trace and Felipe have natural chemistry, bantering back and forth and playing up to the camera. When they finish, they both shoot the peace sign and say, "And if you'd like to donate to the Rico Santiago Defense Fund, follow the link below."

I click on the link to the GiveFunds.com page and see it already has eight hundred dollars.

On the field, Rico races toward a guy from the opposing team, taps the ball from beneath his foot, and races to catch up with it.

He T-kicks it hard over the defenders, and it lands neatly in the right-hand corner.

Rico's hands go flying into the air in victory. Somebody from his team yells "GOAL!" just as the sun dips lower under the horizon and slips behind the clouds.

With Rico still on the field, it gives me time to pick away at my feelings. I've got everything tossed in the bowl of my soul: happiness and grief, anger and gratitude, hope and fear. I'm so tired. I twist in the bleachers. Rico jogs to the bench and grabs water. In the distance, the sun is sinking. Layers of yellow, orange, and red burn in the distance, a hazy reward for a perfect summer day.

Trace's phone rings. It's Johnny. "How did you get this number?"

"Clem, they have a spot for Rico in New Hampshire. Dover. He'll have his hearing there . . . I've pulled some strings. They'll keep him in a safe spot." I close my eyes, trying to picture what a detention center would look like but only come up with the Hollywood version: cold bunks, overhead lights, slop for food.

My voice is raw and accusatory. "That's the best you could do?"

"He broke the law, and, once you're in the system, there's nothing to be done. A judge decides his fate, and trust me, they don't make it easy. On top of everything else, Seb doesn't have insurance. Your dad is covering his bills for now."

"Oh God."

"You've got to get home."

"No," I sputter. "Just fucking no."

I spend the rest of the game texting, scheming, and sometimes crying. When I'm finally done, one of the MDI girls—one with a wide smile and gentle eyes—marches over to me and plops herself down.

"Hey . . . " I wipe my nose with the back of my hand, embarrassed. She leans over to me. "I never do stuff like this, but you look like you could use a hug."

My chin quivers.

"I . . . I . . . think I could . . . "

"Okay, bring it in, girl." She opens her arms and pulls me in, like Mémère used to.

"You're all right . . . It's going to be all right." And it does make it a little better, it really does.

After the game, I stood from my spot on the bleachers, waiting for Rico to fill the twenty-foot gap between us. I'm surprised when he gathers me in his arms and plucks me off the ground. He's never reached for me without seeming like he had to think about it beforehand, like he was afraid he'd be caught, like he had to ask for permission. "It was perfect! I felt like, like I used to. Maybe, when I'm home, I can play again."

Directly behind us, the teams dispersed. Players stop to slap Rico on the back while Justin picks up a ball and shoves it into a mesh bag, tactfully looking away before making his way in our direction.

Justin scratches the whiskers on his chin. "You know what, I've been thinking of this all 'effing day. If Seb disrespected my sister, I would've belted him."

"I appreciate it, but my mother raised me to know better than to raise my fist at him."

"Probably the right answer . . . "

"Well, being a raker gives me plenty of time to think."

Hunter wanders over dragging a bag of balls and calling to the kids on his team. "Morning! Captain's practice tomorrow at six."

Justin, Rico, and I watch him as he stops short and turns to us.

"Rico, you're not on a team? Somebody as good as you . . . you should be playing."

Rico, Justin, and I stand there for a minute too long, not sure how to respond.

Hunter leans over and inspects Rico. "Crap. Are you the guy the Staties are looking for? *Shiitttt.*"

I pull Rico toward the Jeep. Hunter is taking no social clues from me, and he gets louder and louder. "I'm no fan of building the fucking wall between here and Mexico. You come here for a reason, right? Not for kicks. Seriously, dude, I did a whole paper on this. You're one of the kids sending money home to your family." When Rico doesn't respond, Hunter turns to me. "Am I wrong?"

Justin snickers. "Nope, not wrong."

Rico's eyes dart from person to person like he's not sure exactly what is going to happen to him next. All I want to do is hightail it out of there, so I jingle the keys in the air.

"Wait." Hunter yells to the goalie now sprawled out on the roof of his car. "Connor, call the No-Tell, I need a room."

Rico shifts uncomfortably next to me.

Connor lifts his head from the hood of the car as he dials. "Why? You having a party?"

"No!"

"Just wait a second," Hunter lifts a bony hand toward me. It's a quick call and soon Connor gets off the phone.

"You got it. Room Eight at the No-Tell Motel. Nobody will look for you there." Connor pulls a Mount Desert Island sweat-shirt over his broad shoulders, pops his head through. "Like I said before, I don't believe in building a fucking wall."

"Me either," I whisper. "Me either."

Rico is so jazzed he doesn't stop talking.

"It felt so good to be part of a team again. It's like I was asleep, and now I'm alive. I don't need to go to a motel. I'm ready to face whatever I need to face."

"Oh, we're going to the No-Tell."

He grins wide.

"Okay!"

My palms are sweaty, gripping the steering wheel. I catch a glimpse of my eyes. They look crazy. Too eager. Too something. Not sure it's the look I want on my wedding day, but I'm going with it anyways. I pull into an old stone church surrounded by pines, my next destination.

"I've got an idea."

Rico's eyes don't move from the church.

"Let's get married. You can get residency if we're married. We could stay together. You could go to college here, be a doctor, part of the family." I point to my duffle bag. "I even brought a dress."

"I was raised Catholic."

"Ummm . . . I asked you to get *married*."

"I've already broken the law once. No, twice; I've broken the law now twice. I'm not doing it again. Besides, you're seventeen. We're not getting married."

"But . . . there's this movie. *Green Card*. I watched it. It helped."

"You know what? Being here is helping." He pushes out of the Jeep. "Give me a second, okay . . . " He walks across the stone parking lot, pauses to give a quick sign of the cross before dipping inside.

Faith. Rico has so much of it. I lean my cheek against the door and will the clouds to show me a sign, but they float away.

Pineland View Motel is indeed a no-tell motel: one story high, the kind of place where you have your own door for easy access and a window in case you need to jump out the back. Rico doesn't unbuckle. He leans his head against the seat and turns to me. "I've had one of the best days of my life."

"It's not over."

"It is. I don't want you getting in trouble. Let's go back. Okay? It seriously can't get any better."

"Rico, I'm not letting you go yet." I point to the crooked office sign, hanging limp and crooked from a rusty hook. "I'll grab the key. You make sure those seagulls don't poop on my car." The seagulls caw at me as if offended. I snap my fingers at them. "I'm watching you."

I jog across the cracked pavement into the shoebox-sized office to find a wiry-looking guy in a Grateful Dead T-shirt sitting behind the counter playing *Call of Duty*. Behind him, a cat lounges on a shelf, licking his paw as though it's the most delicious thing on earth. The clerk rolls his eyes. "Mr. Waffles."

"Mr. Waffles?" I repeat stupidly.

"Yep, Mr. Waffles. Harmless, unless you're allergic. Then he's a certified killer." He points to his name tag. "I'm Jackson. Most people aren't allergic to me."

"Room for Taylor," I give Trace's name. "Connor called about it."

Jackson waves me forward and plucks a key off the hook on the wall underneath a digital Mickey Mouse clock stuck at 1:28.

He places the key in front of me, and I pick up the plastic keychain with "8" drawn neatly in black Sharpie. "Fifty-nine dollars."

I pluck Trace's credit card out of my pocket and put it on the counter. Jackson snatches it, twirls his work chair to the other side of the desk, and slides it through the credit card machine.

He stops. "No way, girl. I'm not using a hot card. That's one N-O. I'll lose my job. I ran one last week, and I'm on probation already."

"It's not stolen."

Jackson rolls his eyes. "You expect me to believe you're Trace Taylor? You got backup I.D.? Are you even eighteen?"

Darts push out of my eyes.

"Dude."

I focus on a little box on the counter with packs of gum and mints. I pick up a pack of Juicy Fruit and put it on the counter with a twenty. Jackson gives me a thumbs up, and the money disappears. "See ya later, Juliet."

Bastard. He knew who I was all along.

Once outside, all I can see is the lights of a police cruiser blocking the way between Rico and me. Connor tricked us. Rico slumps in the front seat of the Jeep, a Boston Red Sox hat pulled low over his eyes, pretending to be scrolling through my phone.

I grip the key in my hand, pretending to watch as a seagull destroys a bag of Doritos while planning my path to Rico. The officer gets out of the car. Blue uniform, tight pants, gun, so much like Johnny . . . *dammit.* He pounds on Room Two's door. I sprint to the car and jump in.

"Open up, police!"

The police officer looks our way. I grab Rico's shirt and whisper, "Let's go. We'll sneak in while he's not looking."

"No, I've got to see Rosa again before I go. I can't risk it."

My head snaps between him and the police. "It's not time to go back."

"Maybe it is. Let's go."

It'll ruin everything...

I lean into the dashboard, twist to entwine my hand with his, forcing him to look me in the eye. "There's only thirty feet between us and the room. The police officer isn't even looking."

"He could though."

"He won't."

"Fine."

We walk gingerly across the parking lot. Five feet. Ten feet. Out of the corner of my eye, the police officer turns our way. I twist Rico toward me, so his back is to the officer and kiss him to block his face.

Rico cups my chin with his hand. "If this is it, it's been the best, Clementine."

"It's only fifteen feet from here to the door."

A plop of cold wet seagull shit runs down the side of his chiseled cheekbone. I laugh like a lunatic, loud and hard. "Damn bird!" Rico smears the goo off of me with the palm of his hand.

The officer yells over to us from a hundred feet away: "Hey lovebirds, it must be your lucky day. Seagull poo is considered good luck. It's true. The last time I got hit in the head with bird crap, I won twenty-seven dollars from the Maine State Lottery."

In the periphery of my eye, I see a flash of a red sweatshirt and white sneakers running into the woods. Must be the dude from Room Two. The police officer sees him, grabs his walkie-talkie, and yells, "I've got a runner!"

The dude runs faster.

The officer leaves in hot pursuit.

We race for our room, saluting the smug-looking seagulls before we slam the door tight.

Everyone at the No-Tell has secrets.

What happens here, nobody needs to know.

chapter twenty-one ♡

THE MOOD SHIFTS FROM familiarity to raw shyness. First time alone in a hotel room with Rico. Last time alone with Rico. I can tell he feels it. The stillness.

Still sweaty from soccer, he walks awkwardly, stops near a little cabinet by the window, and opens a binder full of local attractions. I capture a picture of him in my mind: longish black hair tucked behind his ears, the straight lines of his nose, the way his leg muscles flex when he walks, his strong chin. Next, I memorize the details of the room: crisp, white-boarded walls, a bright yellow bureau with a scrape down the front revealing red paint underneath, the nubs on the old-fashioned looking bedspread, like little blueberries on a bush.

"They have a lumberjack show." Rico lifts a brochure. His wide shoulders tilt from right to left before cracking me a smile. "We don't do lumberjacking in Mexico."

"We don't do lumberjacking in Southern California."

Rico plops the sandwiches we'd bought on the way down on the miniature table and pulls the curtains over the window. He unwraps his sandwich, but I pull it from his hand and set it down on the table. He pushes his hair out of his eyes and leans back in the bed. "I'm scared, Clementine. I don't want to leave Rosa.

I don't want my family to go hungry because I can't send them money. I'm not sure what life is going to be like now."

I lean next to him, so we're shoulder to shoulder, all my anger dissolving like a sugar packet into iced tea, and I do what my mother always did when I was upset. She'd say, "*So tell me the good things.*"

He wraps an arm around me, and I rest my forehead into the curve of his neck and watch the gentle rise and fall of his flat belly. "Good things about Mexico? Umm . . . there's so many. For starters: in Mexico, nothing is damp."

"Damp?"

"Yes, everything in Maine is damp. Every morning, I wake up and my camper is damp, my socks, always damp. It kind of freaks me out."

"I'm sorry Camp III isn't nicer. Dad's struggling to keep it all afloat."

"Figured."

"Farming is hard. Tell me more things about going back . . . "

"Mexico is home. Despite its problems and the trouble I had there, it'll be good to be back in my culture with my mother and sisters." He pulls my chin up and our eyes meet. "But I'll be so sorry to be missing time with you."

"Even if we're not together, we can remember. Plus, I'll be in California if I don't end up in London."

"Clementine, I don't blame you for anything. You, like no other, saw me exactly for who I was. You're one of the good ones. And don't blame your father. The picnic at the start of the season? Nobody else does a picnic for us. Nobody."

I know full well we could do better. And I'm going to make sure we do.

"It'll be okay," Rico says softly, as if he needs to believe it himself. Rico reaches for me, a tentative touch, a gentle tug forward. I see a question in his eyes. Yes, we must do this. I step closer, into the magical force field of his energy and feel the entire summer landing on my chest, every single moment from the first time I saw him until now.

My heart burns raw. He's leaving. I'm frantic with it. I lunge toward him, wrapping my hand around the back of his head, holding him to me and pulling him to the bed because this is it. Our last moments. Our only chance.

We watch the clock move from seven to eight-thirty, to nine-fifteen, until Rico finally gets up and goes into the bathroom. I hear the shower running, and when he comes out, he looks like any other student in the world: clean white T-shirt, loose-fitting jeans, flip-flops. His hair is pulled neatly back from his face, the way I like it best.

"You ready?" he asks.

"Yup." I lie, because in truth, I want to stay in the No-Tell Motel forever—with its nubby bedspread, slanting floors, and flickering lightbulb—and hide Rico from the world. We make our way back to the Jeep, load our stuff in the back, and head down east toward home.

The only thing that keeps me going is my last surprise for Rico. My final gift to him.

We drive in silence, the cool Maine air blowing on our skin, the road a dark snake only broken up by the headlights.

"Clementine," he finally says, "I need to apologize to Seb."

I grip the steering wheel. "No, you don't."

"I shouldn't have hurt him, Clementine. It's not who I am. I can't leave without getting it off my chest. It'll . . . it'll eat me up."

"In sixth grade, all we did was play Manhunt in the Common Ground Cemetery. Every single night, running around those poor gravestones." I glance at Rico. "It felt so dangerous to be out in the dark with boys, running around. In L.A., it's all organized pool parties and roller rinks. You never get the feeling of being out in the fresh air, high on oxygen and danger.

"One night, I got lost from the group. I was all alone, freaking out. Seb found me, sobbing down by the river. He wasn't afraid of my waterworks, he let me cry and cry." I swallow hard. "He never told anyone."

"Real nice . . . " Rico says.

"Did you know Seb brought us doughnuts at least once a week? His mom works at a bakery down in Bensonville. He'd make the trip all the way out there for us . . . I used to go there when I was little . . . I loved the Bismarcks—a raised doughnut cut down the center with raspberry jam and cream . . . "

"Those are real good."

"Sure are . . . "

An hour later, we arrive at Seb's trailer. We walk past an old truck propped up on cinder blocks—probably waiting for new tires—and a couple of overflowing garbage cans before heading up the porch. Rico shifts uncomfortably but stands tall. I knock. After what feels like forever but was probably only ten seconds, we hear the padding of heavy feet, and the door pops open. Seb's skinny legs are lost in loose pajama pants, and his eyes are thin from either pain meds or sleep. It's hard to tell. His chest is bare and surprisingly concave compared to Rico's solidness, and I find it all so disarming. I take a step backwards, and Rico takes a step forwards.

"Can we talk?" Rico asks.

Seb crosses his arms over his chest. I catch a peek into the living room. It's tiny but feels even smaller due to the massive leather couch sitting at the back wall. Just like at Laurel Hollow, he's got a bucket in the corner to catch leaks when it rains. I glance into the kitchen to see the recycling bin full of empty macaroni and cheese boxes and not much else. I expect Seb to tell us to get the hell out, but instead, his eyes well with tears as he chokes back a sob, which makes me feel one part embarrassed and two parts sad.

"Dude, I've been sitting here thinking about you and what a dumbass I've been." I notice a long line of stitches reaching up the backside of his scalp. "I've been drinking since my brother . . . " He pushes the door open wider and points to the picture above the crumbling white mantel of his brother in his Marine uniform, all golden buttons and freshly shaved. He swallows hard. "It's gotten out of control. Rosa is a solid girl, and she didn't deserve bullshit from me." He steps closer to Rico and holds out a hand. "I heard all about it. I'm so sorry you're getting booted from the U.S. of A. I'm so sorry, it's my fault. If you'd told me the truth . . . "

A hard lump grows in my throat.

Rico is stiff beside me.

"I've called the police. I'm not pressing charges. I'm trying to make it go away."

"Thank you," I whisper. "Thank you."

Watching them together, hearing their apologies, I find a small piece of hope in all this.

Maybe we can go back. Maybe there is time.

Time has sped up now and the dashboard clock ticks closer to 10:30 p.m. Neither of us touch the radio; we let the oldies station work its random magic. The song ends, another one begins. The Bee Gees fill the vehicle with oozing seventies.

"Stop. It's horrible."

"But I can't. This is our song. 'How Deep Is Your Love.' It's roller-skating music. You know, like couples skate."

The dashboard light illuminates his serious expression. "I fell in love with you right there at the festival. You were, I dunno, larger than life. You can't let all this . . . you can't let it change who you are."

My throat hurts. "I won't . . . I promise."

I take the turn hard toward Mount Blanc, and Rico steadies himself. "After the carnival, when I got to know you, Clementine . . . it's been everything."

My stomach flutters in excitement for my last treat for Rico, the one thing that I had control of. Trace and Renée both texted that everything was in place. I just hope we weren't too late after seeing Seb.

"I'm okay now," Rico says. "I'm ready to face it all."

"I'm not," I lie because I can face what's coming next.

Cars are stopped on Philmont Street, on the outer edge of Mount Blanc. Up ahead, I see the telltale signs of a roadblock. Rico shifts in his seat, pulls his baseball cap further over his eyes, and slumps lower in the seat.

"It's over."

"No, it's not fucking over," I hiss. "They're looking for drunk drivers. That's it."

The car in front of us jerks forward. I raise my foot above the gas pedal, frantically searching for an answer out of this mess. We have about ten cars between us and the police. My stomach clenches. Panic sets in. He can't miss my final plan. He can't. It'll all be for nothing.

I'm surprised when my voice is loud and steady. "If we turn, we'll be caught. If you jump out, you'll be caught. You've gotta hide. It's the only way."

"How?"

"Let me think."

The cars in front of us roll forward some more. I coast behind them. There are four cars between us and the checkpoint. Rico's beautiful mouth is a long thin line. His shoulders are stiff. I grip the steering wheel so tight my knuckles are white, my palms sweaty. Somebody behind leans on their horn.

The driver in the truck in front of us yells, "Chill out!"

I close my eyes. We're only ten miles away from Laurel Hollow. We've got to get back. I'm not giving up now. Rico's backpack sits on the seat; underneath is Roscoe's dog blanket, caked with dirt, which we keep in the car in case he rolls in mud on a hike.

"Get in the back," I hiss, "underneath the blanket. Get low."

The car in front of me inches forward. The radio is playing Calum Scott's "Dancing on My Own," and it's so wrong I almost can't stand it. Rico slips through the opening between us and jimmies his body between the floor and the backseat. I glance in the mirror and remember my blue hair. I grab the Cubs hat and pull it low over my eyes, covering up the best I can.

The song flips to Twenty-One Pilots' "Stressed Out." Flipping fitting. I cover Rico with the blanket and turn up the radio. I'm a girl with not a care in the world, grooving to the perfect beat in the front seat of my car.

"Here we go . . . " I pull up to the checkpoint, frantically looking for Johnny. But he's not here.

I'm relieved when I don't recognize the officer sauntering up to my driver's side. I turn down the radio, show him my dimples, and pull a fake New York accent. "Omigawd. I'm so late. My dad's going to kill me if I don't hit curfew. You looking for drunk drivers? Let me blow in your little machine . . . what's it called? Just make it quick."

I twirl my diamond necklace nervously.

"Destination?"

I take a risk he won't ask for my ID and give him Pearson's address. "I'm staying with the Smiths'. Over on Highland."

He winces like he's dealt with Christine at one point or another. The officer glances into my back seat, flashing his light across the multiple bags.

"I've been visiting friends. They're taking summer classes at UMaine. Were you a Black Bear? I bet you played hockey. You look like a hockey player. Let me guess. Right forward?"

"As a matter of fact, I did play. But defense."

"I knew it." I inch the car further a little. "Where . . . "

"Southern Maine."

"I love Portland!" My smile cuts through the night. "So, can I go? My dad. He's so strict . . . "

"Sure . . . get going."

I slowly drive away, keeping the music low, resisting the urge to press the gas pedal into the floor and drive a hundred miles-per-hour to home.

I pull onto a side street, going all the way down to the end, parking underneath the cocoon of a willow tree. The irony's not lost on me—trees are our safe place—our meeting spot.

We've come so far since the start of summer, and it's still not far enough.

I pull the blanket off Rico. "It's okay. We're safe."

He climbs into the front seat, his forehead sweaty and his hair mussed. I touch his arm. He smooths his hair away from his face, pulling a few of Roscoe's dog hairs from his shirt.

"Damn dog . . . " I say, because what else am I supposed to say?

He laughs, but it's forced. His hands are shaking. I gather them, hardened from *my* blueberry fields and hold them until they've stilled.

"I've got one more thing for you . . . We'll figure the rest out later . . . okay?"

chapter twenty-two

IN THE LAUREL HOLLOW driveway, Rico twists his body and leans into the door. It's as far away from me as he can get. We've crossed the line to the farm, back to Miss Fountaine and the blueberry raker. I lean against the wheel of the car, the images of our last twenty-four hours settling into a small room in my brain where I lock my favorite memories.

"I did something for you."

His hand inches closer to mine.

"It's . . ."

"Boom!" Felipe pounds on the car window. He's dressed in nice pants and a shirt. Rico rolls down the window. "It's time! What you've been waiting for: Rosa's quince? We're doing it buddy. Right here. Toooo-niiight. We're just waiting for you. You guys are late!"

Rico opens his mouth and closes it again. I think I see tears well in his eyes, but he blinks them away; they were there. I'm sure of it.

Felipe smooths his dress shirt. "Sucks being the head of the family, dude. I don't know how you handle it. But cross this one off your list. It's happening. Look at me, I'm looking fine!"

Rico says, "It's all Rosa talked about growing up, the dress she was going to wear, the foods she was going to eat. She lost it all when they came for her, and she never talked about it in the same way . . . "

"Felipe told me."

"You did this?"

"My friends did."

Renée stumbles out of the barn, a pair of high-heeled shoes dangling from her right hand.

She's wearing a skin-tight, green and white striped vintage 1970s wrap dress. It accents her long thin waist and makes her look at least twenty-five. She gasps, "You're here! It's about time!"

Trace follows, swiveling her hips toward me in a tight mermaid dress. "Romeo and Juliet of the blueberry fields . . . " She hugs me tight and whispers, "You okay?"

"Trace, where's my dad? Is he here?"

"Who do you think is paying for this? Your dad. He left berries rotting on the vine to organize this party because, once you were gone, all he cared about was you."

Renée pushes me into the bathroom where a strapless dress hangs on the door. It's exactly the same shade as the ridiculous romper I wore for the commercial—so I know it'll match my eyes perfectly. It slips over my shoulders and settles into my curves. I can tell Trace altered it for me. I plop onto the toilet to think, happy for the confined space to have a moment alone.

Renée raps on the door. "You need help?"

"No, give me a minute."

"Everyone is waiting."

"One minute!"

Renée sticks her head around the corner. "Get off the shitter. We gotta go or you'll miss it. It's getting late!"

Hundreds of paper bags filled with sand and glimmering candles turn the path into a maze of lights, forcing guests to loop their way to the entrance. I'm reminded of an article I read about labyrinths, how they bring you back to center and align you. By the time I make my way to the back door to find Rico waiting for me—so flipping handsome in his suit—I am suddenly dead calm.

"Clementine, you look beautiful."

"I clean up nice." I adjust the tie around his neck. "This . . ." He swallows hard, and I smell the sharp bite of shaving lotion and soap. "Today. Me and you."

"A perfect day."

Rico points to the table where a huge tray of tamales is piled high. There're taco fixings, stewed red beans, a heaping pile of rice. On the other side of the room, a towering cake decorated with marigolds sits next to trays of caramel apples. Lights are strung all over the dance studio, reflecting in the mirrors, making the world feel alive with stars. All of the rakers are there, and Pearson with a couple of his buddies, and Beau, and even Justin. Dad, in a suit, is in the corner, pacing back and forth. We meet eyes, and he waves a hand in the air.

"Who helped?"

"Everyone. Even Pearson's mother."

"Christine?"

"She donated the cake. Even drove to Bangor to pick it up. Pearson helped, too . . . " I peer across the room and notice him pouring vodka into his punch. He sees me watching and lifts his glass to me.

The lights go off. Beside me, Rico clutches my hand tighter, no longer caring. A spotlight cuts across the room and captures

Trace in its center. She flashes her trademark grin, waits for attention, and gets it. The room hushes. "I'd like to introduce our *quinceañera,* Rosa Louisa Santiago, formerly of Salinas, Mexico." Rosa steps into the light, wearing a teal blue satin A-line style dress, a waterfall of curls cascading across her shoulders. Trace must have done her makeup because she has the polished look of Hollywood you never see in Maine.

"She's lovely," I say, voice hoarse.

"Sí," Rico agrees. Felipe comes up beside us and hands me a crown. It's covered in tiny little rhinestones, organized into random flower-shaped bursts, "She wants you to put the crown on."

Rico nods. "It symbolizes the unity of God and the world. Once she is crowned, her relationship to God becomes closer, and she promises to remain loyal to her community and family."

"We've been joking all summer about me being the blueberry princess, and it's a role I gave no thought about . . . and your culture has all of this . . . "

"You were born into it. Rosa has been waiting. She still is. Go!"

Trace points toward me, "And our first part of the ceremony is the traditional crowning. And it will be done by our own Clementine Fountaine."

I step across the floor, and people clap gently. I raise the crown into the air until the clapping grows louder. Rosa beams from the seat and motions for me to come toward her. So I do. I rest the crown on the top of her head. She hands me a hair clip, and I secure it in place.

"I wish I could have done more. "

Her curled lashes flutter. "No. You've done all you can. I know that now." She pulls a six-inch doll from beneath her seat. Amazingly, it looks like Rosa, with long dark hair and deep brown eyes.

"This is for you, so you can remember your childhood, as we both walk away from ours."

I'm stunned, because I no longer feel like a child. Maybe this entire experience has brought me further into adulthood than I even knew.

"I'll cherish it," I say and move slowly across the dance floor.

The light moves back to Trace. "The next step of the ceremony is the surprise gift. This will be presented by our host and my friend, Dev Fountaine."

A shiver of hope runs through me because Rosa and I both want the same surprise gift: for Rico to stay. I will Johnny to come out of the shadows like he did one Christmas, dressed as Santa with surprises for all. But he doesn't.

Instead, Dad shoos away the microphone.

"Well, this is a first for us here at Laurel Hollow, to host a *quince*, and it's been an absolute pleasure."

Rosa fiddles with her hands, not meeting his eye. So Dad goes to her and puts his hand gently on her back.

"And darling, I know you must be thinking of your own father and wishing he were here instead of me. But we can't fix that. I'll tell you all what I'd expect he'd have said today. You, Rosa, are a good girl. You work hard for your family, and I do hope you'll look at the world as a place of opportunities and family."

Rosa is crying openly now as Dad holds up a chain with a round pendant. "This is a medallion my mother wore." He holds it into the air, and it shines under the small lights "Saint Fiacre. He is the patron saint of the garden." He hands Rosa the necklace. "I hope you'll cherish it."

After a quiet moment, dad announces, "It's time for the changing of the shoe!"

Rosa sits on the chair, and Rico steps sheepishly into the spotlight. The entire place is still. Rico pulls off her ballet flats, tosses them to the corner of the room, and places a high heel on each foot, Cinderella-style.

Renée whispers in my ear. "The shoe, it's a symbolic shift. She's officially a woman now." Rico pulls Rosa to him, and they dance like cousins, stiff and polite, until the music shifts from a traditional waltz to "My Girl" by The Temptations. Dad holds out a hand to me. I want to roll back time, but I know I can't.

The music shifts and changes, and next, I'm dancing with Rosa and Renée and Trace and, most importantly, Rico, wishing more than anything that this night would never end.

Most people are in bed. It's late.

Rico and I eat the last of Rosa's cake directly from the pan, tired and happy. All the dancing reminds me how ready I am for auditions in two weeks. My rhythm is intact, my steps sure. My dance studio: it represents so much of this summer, from being stuffed full of blueberry crates to this moment where it's sparkling clean, full of light and people enjoying each other.

Rico grabs my fork and cuts another chunk of cake. A small piece sticks to his lower lip.

I brush it away.

The room stills.

Calaca walks toward us, followed by a bunch of rakers from Bluette's. Nothing about this feels like a social call with their serious faces and mouths clamped shut. It feels like the start of beating I saw once in East L.A.

Rico feels it, too. He says, "Go in the house, Clem. Now."

"I'm not going anywhere."

Calaca is in front of us in a second, taking up space that I don't want to give him. I'm fixated on his Adam's apple, bobbing up and down his throat. His energy is off, almost as if anger is boiling in his veins, radiating angry heat.

Rico leans back in his chair.

"Here to play some soccer? Clem, did you know we were on the same team in school?"

Calaca scans the room, and I notice the lights from the ceiling reflected in his eyes.

"Looks like I missed the party."

"Yeah, kind of a last-minute thing," I say. "Didn't get a chance to put the invitations in the mail."

Calaca scratches his chin. "Funny, information moves so quick in today's world. I could have known about it in a second, just like I know about the video. The one with you beating the crap out of that kid . . . Seb, was it? With the Romeo and Juliet bullshit on television. You're not the poster boy for migrants. You don't speak for all of us."

"Obviously . . . " Rico takes another bite of cake, chews slowly like he's not worried at all, but I can tell he is by the slight quiver in his jaw. "The video was a mistake; me and Seb have worked through it all."

Calaca taps his fingers on the side of his thighs. "You don't know the deal, do you? You're on Antonio's list. There's a bounty next to your name."

"Wait," I interrupt. "What?"

Rico's forehead crinkles then relaxes. He didn't know but pretends to. "Trust me, I know. We're both here in Maine. With him tucked back at home with all his money . . . "

"Do you know how much he's offering to find out where you are . . . "

"Enlighten me."

Calaca shakes his phone at us. "Five thousand dollars. Almost one hundred thousand pesos."

"Wait. You sold us out?" I push him hard.

Calaca looks at me, his wiry muscles flexing. "What would you know about *us* . . . "

"If you want to tell Antonio where I am, tell him. Just leave Clem out of it," Rico says.

"No!" I yell, pushing forward. "What is it you want? Money? I've got some saved up. Let me run into the house to grab it. Calaca . . . wait . . . what is your real name?"

"His real name is Carlos."

"Carlos . . . " I force my voice to sound calm. "Tell me how much money you want."

He wipes his nose with the back of his hand and looks away.

"So, what's your number?"

"I need two thousand dollars."

Two thousand dollars is the price to save Rico. Two thousand. A number I've heard a lot this summer . . .

Calaca's shoulders tremble. I realize we don't have a clue what other people are walking through in their lives. Out of habit, my hand reaches for my throat. I carefully take my necklace off, feeling first the ruby and then the three diamonds: Mom, me, and Amelie. I crumple it up, push it into Calaca's hand.

"There's a pawnshop off Route Fifteen, a guy named Lenny; go to him. He'll give you the money."

"Clem, no . . . " Trace is suddenly behind me. "I can help . . . "

I shake her off, ignoring Rico's eyes pleading me to stop.

"I need to help him myself."

Calaca inspects the gold, looking closely at each small diamond. "Are these real?"

I bite my cheek until salty blood flows. "Yes."

"And you'll do this for me, for my family . . . "

"If you keep quiet about Rico, I'll do just about anything."

"Don't . . . " Rico hisses in my ear.

"It's a thing . . . an object. It was something dear that helped me remember. But people are more important. You're more important."

So. Much. More. Important.

Calaca holds the necklace thoughtfully, cupping it like the precious object it is.

"I wish it all didn't need to be this way."

"Yo también!" Rico agrees, "Me too."

It's three in the morning, Trace snores softly next to me while I watch moonbeams creep across my ceiling. I study them, trying to hold them back, like when Rico and I moved the clouds.

I dig my fingernails into my palms, trying to push back my tsunami of nerves. I need my mom. I need someone who might be able to help. It's only midnight there; she might be up. She answers in one ring. My vocal cords feel like they are filling with sand.

"He's undocumented."

Her voice is low. "I saw the GiveFunds.com page. I donated a thousand dollars."

"Mom, if they take him . . . when they take him. I'm not sure when it will be, a month, two? Can you pick him up? Can you help him get a job far from where he grew up?"

"Clementine, leaving the United States isn't a death sentence . . . "

I consider her words, "I hope not."

"Love you, darling."

"Love you, too."

The next morning, I wake slowly at first, my face pressed against Mémère's twenty-year-old sheets. The room glows with perfect long light. It must be eight, or even nine. Trace's arm is flung over her head—like Ophelia floating in the bog, unaware of danger. I pull the covers up and roll over as a quick flash of memory flames, lapping first at my frontal lobe before burning into my whole soul. I'm off the bed, my feet twisting in the yellow coverlet as it falls to the floor and gets caught on the bedpost. I try to make my way to the window. I might be sick, right here on the floor, as all of the magic of last night drains from my body, leaving me only with festering regret.

"Trace! Get up!" She sits upright in bed, eyes now as wide as mine. Out the window, immigration police drink coffee with my dad, like they're old friends shooting the shit, not monsters taking Rico from me. "I should have made him run. We could have driven to a state where we could get married . . . like Montana . . . or Mississippi."

Johnny stands alone in the center of the driveway. He spies me in the window. If only I'd listened, maybe Rico wouldn't be going back and we wouldn't be in this mess. Johnny motions toward the police cruiser where, in the backseat, I see Rico's profile. Even today, he's holding his shoulders straight and proud. Trace joins me at the window, patting me like you would a scared dog, light and quick.

"Go," she whispers.

Out the back door, the smell of warm berries and the late summer smell of decaying plants tickle my nose, making me once again hate August for its dream-ending persistence. Dad tips coffee to his mouth, screwing his eyes together in recognition, but I keep moving. I'm a cat, running from the lilac bush to the side of the barn and to the back of the police cruiser where Rico's encased inside.

I've come full circle.

"Johnny!" I shout. "You can't do this. You're like a father to me. One of my best friends." I push him aside and rush for the car door. I'm a wild animal.

"Don't you come close to me!" I yell at Johnny.

Legs shaking, I dip lower. I open the door slightly, jimmying myself into the small space. Rico's eyes meet mine. I force a smile. It fades when I see his cuffed hands.

My eyes well; tears spill onto my cheeks. His shoulder rolls forward, dipping lower toward me. "Stop. It's been the best summer of my life. The seasons change. They would have changed anyway. This makes it more—"

Johnny pounds on the window, making me jump. I bury my head in Rico's lap and hold on. "I'm so sorry. This isn't the end. We can email. We can call."

Dad pats my arm, pulling me gently away from the car. *"Mon chou…"*

"Dad! Make it stop! This is your farm. You have power."

"I don't have power over this, Clem."

Rico calls my name softly, but my begging doesn't stop. "Johnny? I'll do anything . . . "

Johnny stands firm. "Clementine . . . I don't want this either. It's the law."

"Right . . . " I spit. "The law, where bad people get to stay, and good people sometimes need to go."

The uniformed immigration officer steps forward, hands on hips. "I'm Officer Ron Manning, U.S. Border Patrol. I'll be transporting Rico Marquez to Bangor, Maine, for extradition to Dover, New Hampshire."

Roscoe rounds the corner, spies Johnny, and lets out a yowl of delight, his tail whipping back and forth in complete adoration. He's the only happy being on the entire farm.

Rico whispers, "Good boy, Roscoe."

Johnny barks. "Ronny, let the boy say a proper goodbye. He's not going anywhere."

"It's on you if he does." Officer Manning yanks the door open, unhooks the cuffs.

Rico's a brave warrior. The only sign of emotion is in the hard line of his jaw. The rakers await, twenty feet from my unraveling, understanding exactly what I'm going through. Rico moves down the line of people who love him, leans into Rosa, and says something, making her smile, and, before I know it, he shakes hands with my dad and kisses me one last time.

He's gone.

My heart breaks.

Later, I get on my hands and knees. I crawl along the mud-room floor, searching under the heating ducts for my forgotten plastic heart. When I find it behind one of Johnny's gum wrappers, I shove it deep into the sole of my Birkenstock. Right where it belongs.

chapter twenty-three ♡

WEEDS HAVE OVERTAKEN MÉMÈRE'S cutting garden.
I dig my toes into the grass and pinch a green blade, pulling it
from the earth.

My time from when Rico left to this moment is a blur. Trace
and Renée tried to make me feel better, but I wasn't much of a
friend—more like a psychopath who sits in the darkness of her
room listening to the Bee Gees obsessively on Spotify: "Too Much
Heaven," "Islands in The Stream," and my fave, "Love You Inside
and Out." For three days, all I would eat was slabs of lemon
meringue pie Renée brought me from The Muffin and miniature
cups of green tea from Mémère's favorite *demitasse* cups.

I attack the crabgrass, but there's too much of it. I get frustrated and go in search of Mémère's miniature rake and twist it
into the border of the garden, making the line between it and the
grass defined and neat.

I miss Trace.

Trace and Felipe kept their Facebook Live series going, man-
aging to raise over sixteen thousand dollars for Rico while increasing
hits on the Laurel Hollow Organics website by seventeen percent.
She's now officially dating Beau Routhier, the local she met at
the bonfire.

Her romance might have started the moment mine ended, but I'm happy for her. She's back in L.A. now, but she's going to meet up with Beau in Boston for a first showing of *Salem's Tooth*.

When she left, the paparazzi left. On to better things.

The pile of weeds next to me gets bigger. I wipe sweat from my forehead and look around the quiet barrens. The blueberries have been picked clean; the rakers have moved on. Even Roscoe senses the change of energy. He doesn't even bother to lift his head when Dad walks from the barn to the back door.

All of Maine packs up for the change of the seasons.

It's five days until I'm supposed to be in New York.

I grab a handful of nightshade and pull hard. "Wild Thing," my ringtone for Pearson, makes me jump. I remember laughing when he'd put it on there. Him telling me it's a Red Sox thing. That if I saw Dustin Pedroia play, I'd understand. Pearson's face appears on the screen, a reminder of a lost dream, a reminder of the start of summer, when everything was different.

I answer, but, before I can even say hello, he rolls into Pearson mode. "Meet me at Squimmies, okay?"

"Life goes on, huh?"

"Yeah, Clem. It's gotta."

I surprise myself. "Fine. One o'clock?"

"Perfect."

I turn back to the cutting garden, seeing, for the first time, the nightshade looping its way through the sedum, choking it tight. The miracle of it all is its roots growing so close to the surface as if the land beneath isn't important. It needs to find a place to be.

I pull the weed, wondering what's currently under Rico's feet. I wonder if he's scared.

How I can go on without him here, I don't know.

Squimmies Seafood Shack is one of those take-out joints where the fattest-looking seagulls known to man watch your every move, looking to grab your lunch as soon as you turn away.

Pearson's burly frame is hunched over his phone on a far picnic table, and I'm hungrier than I've been in a long time. I march across the dirt driveway, practically snapping my fingers at him, like suddenly, he's my assistant and I'm his boss. He sees me, shoos a fly away from his perfect ear.

"You paying?" I ask.

Pearson looks casual in board shorts and a polo shirt with paint on the sleeve. He mumbles something about ordering whatever I want. So, I do. Up the rickety ramp to the takeout window, where a bored-looking college student impatiently taps a pen on the counter. Like Rico, that day in the library.

"Steamers, a lobster roll, onion rings, and strawberry shortcake for dessert." The girl looks at me kind of funny but writes it on a pad of paper. "Plus, I'll have a lemonade with extra ice."

"You guys splittin'?" she asks.

"Nope," Pearson and I say together.

"I'll have a grilled chicken sandwich."

"Always the athlete."

"I like what I like, what can I say? Plus lacrosse season is coming; it's always coming. Just like your dance audition is . . ." He pulls out a wad of cash and pays the bill. He adds a generous tip to the prominent tip jar with stickers of college names: Endicott, Syracuse, and the University of Maine at Farmington. The tip entirely changes the server's attitude, and we see her very first real smile. She hands us a little ticket. "Lucky thirty-two."

"Lucky thirty-two!" Pearson echoes, holding it up in the air.

I follow him to the weathered picnic table nearest the shore. I sit down, careful not to impale myself on the weathered wood. He scratches a shaggy chin. His hair keeps landing in his right eye. He pushes it away, and it falls again to the exact same spot. He's brought a manila folder with a pen clipped over its edge. Would things have turned out differently if he hadn't held me back when Seb and Rico fought. He won't even look my way, reminding me suddenly of a sketchy rescue dog.

I hear our number over the antiquated sound system. "Number 32, pick up at window."

Pearson comes back balancing two trays. My belly rumbles. I grab ketchup from a little tray in the center of the table, flick the top open with my thumb, and give it a harsh squeeze.

"I'm waiting. Can't you see I'm waiting?" I fling a clam neck into the shell bowl and go in for another. Pearson doesn't touch his food. I push the onion rings his way. "You're making me nervous."

Pearson stares off in the distance, his eyebrows screwed together, not listening to a word I'm saying. Pearson grabs a crusty-looking salt shaker and pours a stream over the onion rings.

"What is it?"

"I know I messed up by sharing the video; hell, by not stopping the fight."

I'm not so sure I even know why I'm so mad at him. It's easier to be mad at Pearson than it is to be mad at Seb, or even my dad, or Rico.

Pearson struggles not knowing where to start. "Do you even know how I feel about you?"

"What did you say?"

"I said, *do you even know how I feel about you*?"

"The flowers? They were real?"

Frozen in my spot, I'm oddly fixated on the congealing cup of butter in front of me. I push it away. All of this is about me.

"I was jealous, I'm not going to lie."

"I know . . . " I squish an onion ring flat and take a delicate bite. "Do you understand what it means to be privileged, Pearson? It means you don't have to worry about the safety of your family. Or if your little sisters are getting enough food . . . Pearson, Rico's family . . . he was the breadwinner. His father is dead."

Pearson cracks his fingers. Dark circles smudge the spot underneath his eyes.

"Dad's firm will take Rico's immigration case. It won't be easy, but we're gonna try to help. I didn't ever think about what it might be like for Rico and Rosa." He pushes the chicken away. "There's one more thing that's bothering me. Think back to the start of summer, what was important to you."

"What do you mean?"

"Your audition is this weekend."

I rip a clam out of its shell, swish it in warm clam water, dip it in butter. "I'm not going. I can't go."

"Tell me why?"

"I dunno, it seems not important anymore."

Pearson grabs a stray steamer shell and tosses it into the bowl, looks me directly in the eye and says, "What would Rico say?"

His words hit me.

"Excuse me?"

"What would Rico say about you quitting? He never quit. Never. Came here, did his best, tried to keep up in school. Set his goals. What would he think of you quitting, Clem?"

"I . . . it's been . . . I . . . "

"The fact you don't have an answer to the question concerns me. Have you learned nothing about us working together this summer? You bought a ticket, right?"

"Yes."

"You get your ass to NYC, and you at least try. Don't live with regret."

"You know, if things had been different this summer . . ."

He pushes his thick hair away from his face and cracks a bright smile. "There's always next summer. Hope springs eternal . . ."

Four more days. In the dance studio, I flip on the lights and corner fans. I walk in front of the mirror to see how I've changed. The blue streak in my hair has faded, but my muscles are long and lean. I push up onto my toes, warming up my body, and pull my arm across my chest. I flip the music on, moving my body through the positions.

I do it over.

And over.

And over again.

There's a picture book called *Blueberries for Sal* by Robert McCloskey. Mom and Mémère used to read it to me when I was a little kid. In it, little Sal's mother always says, *"Don't eat the berries, we're saving them for winter."* In turn, there's young baby bear, whose mother says, *"Eat, get ready for winter."* Both baby bear and Sal get mixed-up and wander away from their parents, and it's only the *kuplink, kuplank, kurplunk* of Sal dropping the blueberries into the metal bucket alerting all to the problem at hand.

I feel like Sal, not sure which blueberry path is right, which is wrong. But one thing I know for sure: Mama Bear and Sal's mother love their babies, like Rico loved Rosa and his mother to the point of endangering himself. Like I love my dad.

I head over to the window and sit in the chair overlooking the now-harvested fields. I pick up my phone and dial my mother's number to make sure she'll be there to work on filling my empty bucket.

My body moves over and over, day after day, until there isn't a movement not committed to muscle memory.

Two more days. Dad drags his suitcase into the room, his weird mix of farm clothes and country club wear replaced by a sleek-looking tan sportcoat and a light blue oxford. He's lost weight in the last couple of weeks, and I notice his belt has moved a rung.

"California, here we come."

"I'm going to New York, Dad. I'm doing the audition. I need to know if I can make it."

"I saw the credit card bill a long time ago."

"You didn't say anything."

"What should I have said?"

We face off, Fountaine on Fountaine, but there's not much fight left in me. "You should have said, 'Clem, what's your dream?' The trouble with all the dreaming is that we have different visions, Dad. Yours is this farm. And, maybe someday, it'll be my dream. But right now, it's dance. It's New York. When I'm done, I don't know, Dad. My brain, it's pretty messed up. Maybe I'll go to NYU with Trace. Maybe I'll study film, maybe law. I don't know. But I do know there's a big ass world out there, and I've got to experience it. Beyond these walls."

He rolls his fingers through his hair, seeming to settle into his sportcoat.

"Aunt Vivi will meet you at the airport. You've got this." A grin takes over Dad's face. "I heard this morning, everyone has the fungus. The crop price has been boosted by two dollars a pound."

Dad flicks off the light over the stove. *"Après la pluie, le beau temps."* He switches to English. "After the rain comes sunshine."

chapter twenty-four ♡

AUNT VIVI DRIVES THROUGH New York City like a mad-woman: her bright red fingernails alternating between flipping an occasional cabbie the bird, gingerly holding her vanilla latte like it's the most important thing in the world, and tapping the steering wheel of her Mini Cooper. Her black hair is pulled back from her face in a tight ponytail, her smooth skin is eternally tan like my dad's, but her whole being's infinitely more sophisticated. She's a sleek cat but with sharp edges.

Down the Avenue of the Americas, she gives me a long string of advice for the Summerset School of Dance. "Now, when you get in there, don't size up your competition. Truly, the person you're competing against is you. You've done the work. You've got the skills. This is between you and the judges. That's it, not some bullshit little waif from Madame Oulette's trying to intimidate you with her evil eyes and sharp elbows."

"Noted."

"I'm not kidding, Clem. This city could eat you alive. Look at what I'm dealing with here." She yells out the window. "We've got places to be, buddy!"

What can I say, she's a Fountaine.

"Aunt Vivi, did you know Mémère was in love with a blue-berry raker?"

"Why do you think she tried so hard? The raker village. The rec hall. The yearly picnic. The rakers were family to her. She loved them."

I swallow the lump that likes to live in the back of my throat, thinking back to last week. When the roofers finally came to fix the house. Surprisingly, Seb was on the crew. I watched him work all day. He's not perfect, but the dude knows how to work. When he was done, I brought him a soda, and we'd walked to Camp III. We're in the process of cleaning up. Dad's already hauled out all the old campers and bulldozed the site. Next year, he's bringing in a fleet of those adorable little homes on wheels after the whole place has been wired for electricity and water. Mémère would have loved them.

"Clem! Clem! We're here."

The car is stopped in traffic, and people are already beeping their horns at us.

Aunt Vivi smiles hard, and, in the smile, I see Mémère, too. "Go kill it, girl!"

I walk alone into the cavernous building and follow the other dancers, tall lanky girls in sweats and leotards, up the ornate stairs to the *Summerset School of Dance*. My hands are sweaty, my stomach clenched. But, after living through Rico leaving, well, it's nothing. One girl gives me a soft, "Good luck."

Look, Aunt Vivi, no bitches! I throw myself in check. *If this were six months ago, would I be harder? Judging these girls up and down maybe, throwing around my shoulders and trying to take up more space?*

Now, I smile back. "Good luck."

I follow the herd to the changing room, stowing my bag in a locker. My phone beeps and beeps and beeps. I fumble with it, to shut it down, but not before reading my messages.

Pearson: *You've got this, Clem!*
Mom: *Sending you positive energy and good vibes. You know I'd be there if I could.*
Johnny: *I'm here with Rico in Dover. He's safe. He sends his best.*

My heart, once again, is warm butterscotch pudding.

I go to the warm-up room, stretch my legs, twist my arms above my head. A calmness overtakes me. He's safe.

When they call my name, I almost feel Rico coming out of the shadows, like he did that day in the studio. I dance with him watching, I dance with the magic he introduced me to flowing through my veins. *The Little Engine That Could. I think I can.* I dance with the peregrine falcon. I dance with the intention of someone who can move clouds. I dance like I did at Rosa's quince, trying to make time stand still.

When the music stops and I'm still, the judges nod, writing furiously.

I'm not truly sure what happened, whether I was good or bad. And I'm not totally sure if I care. It's done. It's time for fate to decide.

Out on the street, with the bustle of New York all around me, I reach for my phone to call my mother. This is her time, too. All those dance recitals, the hours spent practicing, when she watched instead of doing anything for herself. I think of my sister, the loss my mom endured. The promise of something so precious, then lost; she must've felt like she lost me, too, in the process.

I'm frantic for her. I hit her number.

"Mom, I did it. It's done! I did okay. I might have done better than okay . . . "

"I've spoken to your dad. The week before Christmas, would you come visit?"

"Yes, Mom. Yes. I'd love it."

Aunt Vivi comes squealing to a stop in front of me. "Get in, darling, before we get run over."

"Is that your aunt? Tell her to slow the hell down."

"Can't stop. Won't stop," I say while dipping into the car.

Mom laughs and hangs up the call.

Apple Season ♡
October

TRACE AND I FLY back to Maine to button up the farmhouse for the winter because Dad has a gig at the Blueberry Farmers of America convention in Vegas. Trace stands at the window wearing a Carhartt knit hat, hands on skinny hips, feet tucked into Timberland work boots. The diva could be a poster child for Maine if they'd let her. I saw her the other day pounding down the hallways to Physics in a similar get-up. The next day, work boots were all the rage with all the wannabes at St. Andrews.

"It's even better in the fall," Trace says, mostly to herself, peering out at the blueberry fields, now looking almost like a box of Crayola crayons had melted there, morphing the bushes into shades of red, pink, dark purple, and yellow. "Summer is nice, but this . . . "

"I know, it's special."

A flock of Canada geese descend on the field by Camp II, their black and white heads frantically pecking at the ground for bugs or whatever else they can find. Renée honks from the driveway. We rush out to greet her. I'm surprised to see she looks hipster chic in skintight jeans with embroidered flowers up the thigh.

"Did you make those?" Trace asks.

"I did!" Renée giggles. "I'm starting to think fashion design. NYU?"

"I'll be there," Trace says. "Enrolling fall of 2017. Film!"

"When do you find out about London?"

"Today." I say. "But I'm not waiting or anything. A watched email app never beeps."

"Truth," they say in unison. Weird twins.

Down the long dirt road, we drive to Alligraw's Organic Apple Farm, past the PICK YOUR OWN sign. Families pour out of minivans before having to make the decision about what size to pick—a half peck, a peck, or a bushel—and meandering toward the fields with plastic bags hanging over forearms. A toddler face-plants in the tall grass, popping up immediately and holding an apple triumphantly in the air. His family laughs at him—or with him—it doesn't matter.

I listen to Trace and Renée banter, liking when my worlds come together and feeling even more complete at the familiar sight of José Luis's and Felipe's vehicles parked over by the edge of the orchard. I take in the crop hanging ripe and heavy on the trees: Dev Fountaine's daughter until the end.

I haul the huge picnic basket from the backseat, packed to the rim with ham and cheese sandwiches and bags of Lay's potato chips: salt and vinegar, barbecue, regular. Renée brought thick brownies, cut and wrapped in wax paper, and a couple of pounds of plump red grapes. Trace grabs a bag full of the cold Cokes and water we'd picked up at Mount Blanc Market. Renée points up a well-worn path.

"I bet they're up there. Picking the Cortlands. Best for pie. Trust me, I know these things from my magical career at The Muffin."

"I do love pie," Trace says, best southern accent fully in play. "Ya'll should see me at the pie eatin' contest dawn in 'Bama. Where I eat, and eat, until I'm full as a tick."

"You're a freak," I laugh.

"Clementine!" Felipe waves to me from the top of a tree. He practically jumps down the ladder, and, before I know it, he's hugging me tight. The music pours from his headphones, as always. José Luis stands a few feet away, and, for the first time, he doesn't have the questioning look in his eyes.

"Have you heard from Rico?" Trace asks.

"Not yet."

"Soon . . . Johnny says soon." I say.

"Why are you here?" José Luis looks at Trace, questioning.

"To keep a promise."

Trace ducks under a gnarled apple tree to meet Rosa. I know Trace's telling that her mother saw the pictures from the fire and the possibilities in her future if she'd only sign with the great Cher Taylor. Trace gets her selfie arm into position, and they both grin wide for the camera.

Renée flips a black and white checked blanket high into the sky, shaking out the folds, settling it neatly over the bumpy grass. She lays wrapped sandwiches on a platter like logs in a woodpile, before pushing her sunglasses to the top of her head and considering me with such an intensity I back away.

My email beeps. I open it.

Dear Clementine,

I'm happy to inform you that you have been accepted into the Summerset School of Dance semester abroad program in London 2017. More details will be forthcoming.

Sincerely,

Sonia Mathers, VP, Summerset School of Dance

I close my eyes and think of the first time I saw Rico standing three feet from me, his eyes intent on the carnival game. A damselfly buzzes through my imagination, so I send it off to Mexico to be with him. I open my eyes to see the first star flickering in the distance, a single spot on the horizon. I thank the star for him, the mover of clouds, and the maker of magic . . . the person who changed my life, and for that, I'm grateful.

Lime Season ♡
December

I FLY FROM LAX to Maya Riviera, giving me more than four hours and twenty-minutes to adjust my attitude and latitude for Christmas break. I wait in the customs line with a family from Toledo carting wild twin toddlers directly in front of me and a French woman behind me, spending her time making dramatic sighs. I hold my passport tight until it's my turn.

"*El siguiente!* Next!" A border agent whose name tag says George yells. He's a mini Johnny LaMonde, all formal and ready for business in a tight uniform and big old badge front and center. I hand him my passport. He pulls it open, looking first at me, then my picture, and at me again. A nervous flutter swims through my belly. I try to look innocent, even though I haven't done anything wrong.

"What is the purpose of your trip?"

"Holiday," I respond.

"How many days?"

My backpack shifts heavy on my shoulder. "Seven glorious days with my mother."

He gives me an appreciative shake of his head.

"Do you have any perishable fruit?"

"No!" I laugh at the very thought of it. "I don't. No rhubarb, no strawberries, no blueberries, and no apples."

He leans forward and taps his temple with a pointer finger. "A weird answer."

"Sorry, I deal with a lot of fruit."

"You know what, I don't even want to ask." He stamps my passport with a satisfying smack, and I jump from the sheer force of it. George gives me his first real grin, and it's sparkly.

His voice is even lighter, "Lime season is almost over. You don't want to miss it."

"Good to know! *Feliz Navidad!*"

"Merry Christmas, fruit girl!"

George waves me away and calls to the next person in line. I follow the parade of people through a long hallway arriving at the airport terminal, all decked out for the holiday. Red, green, and white flags zigzag across the ceiling, and a tree of lights sits dead center of the atrium. A towering team of basketball players from Ohio State passes me by, dwarfing me in the process. To the right of me, a little girl spies what looks to be her grandmother waiting by the news stand and sprints ahead of her parents to get there first. Watching them puts a smile on my face.

I turn the corner to the airport exit.

My smile fades as fast as it came.

My name's written on a huge piece of paper, in bold looping cursive: *Miss Clementine Fountaine.* Mom sent a driver to pick me up, versus being here herself. What is this? First, my dad, now my mom. Always too busy to schlepp it to the airport or bus station.

"I'm her," I say, fiddling with the handle of my suitcase. "Clementine Fountaine."

The sign drops a little bit, showing a hint of short dark hair. "Well, let's go."

That voice!

I snatch the sign away only to be met by those amazing dark eyes enthralling me from the first second I saw them. I fling myself into Rico's arms. Now more than ever, there are truly no borders between us.

Those with dreams make things happen.

Through trouble.

Through everything.

Acknowledgments

The Space Between You and Me was built on the growing seasons, so was this book. So many growing seasons.

To Marilyn R. Atlas, of Marilyn R. Atlas Management, you were the greatest champion of this project. I appreciate the Friday night check-ins, the endless enthusiasm, and the pure joy that knowing you has given me. I'm so glad we met that day in Boston. To Elizabeth Lopez, V.P. of Literary Development at Marilyn R. Atlas Management, thank you for your story insight, taking those frantic calls, and *gulp,* the extensive editing. I truly appreciate everything you've both done for me.

Special thanks to my literary agent, Lane Heymont, President of The Tobias Agency, I will forever appreciate your direct and honest approach to publishing and being a fabulous advocate as we moved through this complicated journey. Appreciate you.

I always say, the publishing world is about the people you meet along the way. To the Cape Crusaders: Lynda Mullaly Hunt, Janet Costa Bates, Jenny Bagdigian, Laurie Murphy, Carlyn Beccia, and Brook Gideon . . . what a journey! To our very special and dear friend, Liz Goulet Dubois, who we lost in 2022, your creativity inspires. I'm a better person and writer for knowing you all. Thank you for the round-table critiques and teaching me to toast the accomplishments. I adore you all.

To Sarah Claytor for those full manuscript reads, glasses of wine, and being the best international writing travel companion. I won't forget walking the streets of Florence, Italy chatting about this project. Jennifer Reck for those Friday goal-setting breakfasts that helped with way more than writing. To Peg Lane (Scott True, thank you for bringing her to us! Well done!), appreciate those reads and check-ins.

BFAK, Anna Conathan, my favorite hilarious cheerleading book coach. How lucky I was that you moved directly into the house next door, to be at my beck and call with all bookish story things (and everything else!). Thank you for peeling me off the floor on the dark story days and racing over to celebrate the wins.

Cameron Rosenblum, we started this long journey together and it has twisted into so many exciting directions and adventures. Who would have thunk from those early days sitting solo in the corner of all the writing action? We've done so many cool things since. Thank you.

Jessica Sinsheimer, how amazing that I get to work with one of the coolest people in publishing daily. To the entire Manuscript Academy team, you make every day better.

My parents, John and Brenda True, who no matter what made sure I had money for the Scholastic Book Fair (the most glorious time of the year!), kept me in paper and pens, and made sure I always had everything I ever needed. Much love.

To my not-so-little birds, Jack and Rachel Kingsley, appreciate the time you both gave me to write (you were both so easily bribed by promises of future LEGO and American Girl gift cards, hope you enjoy your shopping! Sorry it took so darn long!). It's the best to be your mom! To my husband, Eric Kingsley, the morning coffee bringer, the kid wrangler, and the true supporter—all my love and thanks.

About the Author

Julie True Kingsley, is the co-founder of The Manuscript Academy, an online writing community that focuses on education on the road to publication, and co-host of *The Manuscript Academy* podcast. She has also taught from preschool to grad school and everything in-between.

A life-long Mainer, Julie enjoys all aspects of the state whether it be body surfing at Higgins Beach, noshing on BBQ in Monson, or zipping down the carriage trails in Acadia. She lives at Willard Beach in South Portland with her husband, Eric, and their rescue dog, Lulu. She is the mother of two adventurers, Jack and Rachel, who keep her on the edge of her seat as they learn to climb their own mountains.